OUT OF THE SAND CREEK MASSACRE

To my dear friend, Jo Ann, happiness always,

Nellie O. Jackson

OUT OF THE SAND CREEK MASSACRE

Nellie O. Jackson

Copyright © 1999 by Nellie O. Jackson.

Library of Congress Number:		99-91288
ISBN #:	Hardcover	0-7388-0740-0
	Softcover	0-7388-0741-9

All rights reserved. No part of this book may be reproduced or transmitted in any form or by any means, electronic or mechanical, including photocopying, recording, or by any information storage and retrieval system, without permission in writing from the copyright owner.

This is a work of fiction. Names, characters, places and incidents either are the product of the author's imagination or are used fictitiously, and any resemblance to any actual persons, living or dead, events, or locales is entirely coincidental.

This book was printed in the United States of America.

To order additional copies of this book, contact:
Xlibris Corporation
1-888-7-XLIBRIS
www.Xlibris.com
Orders@Xlibris.com

CONTENTS

Introduction
    THE SAND CREEK MASSACRE 9

Chapter One
    The Crow Powwow 11
Chapter Two
    Little Dove's Wedding Dress 55
Chapter Three
    On the Mountaintop 73
Chapter Four
    Home in St. Louis 107
Chapter Five
    Home in the Big Sky State 134
Chapter Six
    Crossing Over the Shining River 159
Chapter Seven
    Love, Was, Is, Always Will Be 185
Chapter Eight
    The Wedding of Big Bear and Little Dove 195

*This book is dedicated to the Cheyenne and Arapaho Indians
whose ancestors lost their lives
in the Sand Creek Massacre in 1864.*

INTRODUCTION

THE SAND CREEK MASSACRE

In 1864 the Cheyenne and Arapaho Indians were moved from the Dakota Territory to Sand Creek, Colorado. Little Dove was a Cheyenne medicine woman, daughter of Black Kettle, who was the chief of the encampment and principal peacemaker.

Big Bear, a Crow warrior, wandered into the Cheyenne village in the Dakota Territory before the move to Sand Creek. He fell in love with Little Dove and planned their wedding. In the winter Big Bear promised Little Dove he would return when Mother Earth would be covered with fallen leaves. He returned in despair to find his promised bride and her people were missing from the Dakota Territory.

After searching, Big Bear retraced the trail Little Dove had left for him to follow. The horrible devastation of the Cheyenne and Arapaho camp resulting from the Sand Creek Massacre caused Big Bear to search for Little Dove. He found her body and the dress she was to be married in. Little Dove had been killed trying to save her father. Big Bear carried the bodies of Little Dove and Black Kettle to Montana, burying them in the mountains, in the Crow burial grounds.

Big Bear stayed in the mountains the rest of the winter with his grieving pain. There Little Dove's spirit returned speaking to him with great care in her voice, "Grieve no more for me, Big Bear, for I am with you, now and always. Our hearts were drawn together by the Great Spirit of eternal peace. Our mission is to bring peace to the heart of man. All the days you have left on Mother

Earth, speak no more of war. The white man will run rampant in this land and cause many to die. But the day will come when the quiet ones will inherit the earth, for out of us will come a new Mother Earth, giving man a new heart, never remembering this time again, only love and beauty of the Great Spirit. Then again we will live in this land we love, free; no more will man destroy the beauty of all.

All must pass through their spiritual birth; some will desire to return and live again for the spiritual life of our people. Our lives have not ended; they have just begun. All that we have missed now, will be added to us. The purest love will be ours, because we love the spirit of truth. This spirit will come in all the earth to try man's heart. All who love the truth, their hearts will be changed." The spirits of Big Bear and Little Dove would live again to finish their life circle and purpose on earth.

Big Bear and Little Dove's love was an eternal love of the spirit, recorded in the Book Of Life, a love that would never die and that would manifest itself in the reunion of their spirits in the late twentieth century. This book is the joyous story of that reunion and the love that results, not just between them, but for friends, children and captive spirits longing to be free.

CHAPTER ONE

The Crow Powwow

Montana is a sprawling land sparsely populated. Her rugged beauty is seen in the Rocky Mountains, grassy plains with rolling hills spotted with cattle and underlying natural resources. Its frontier atmosphere creates a mood of the Old West traditions of cowboys and Indians. The huge state's rivers are a fisherman's paradise. Montana is a land of opportunity, not only cattle and agriculture; oil fields brought prosperity to rural areas and in Billings, which became headquarters for the state's petroleum industry.

To define the Montana spirit, neighbors are to be trusted, but it is the ability to take care of oneself and his loved ones that makes a true Montanan. It is also their ability to survive the winter and cope with their losses, to weather the change of seasons, to see the beauty of the land and her people.

Montana is called the Big Sky State, Carol Fletcher thought as she continued her drive toward Billings. The sky was endless, covering the earth as a globe, only the landscape with natural beauty hindering nothing from eyesight. This was so different from St. Louis, with no man-made structures blocking a view of the horizon with the mountains in the background. Once in a while there would be facilities to meet the traveler's needs.

The road sign read BILLINGS CITY LIMIT. Carol turned her truck off the interstate highway heading into the city. There she had reservations for five days of the Crow powwow. This being her first time in Montana, on assignment for magazine photography, she drank in every attraction of interest. Turning off on 27th Avenue, she followed it to 6th Avenue to 16th Street, west. There she pulled into the Best Western Motel, entering the office at 4:00 p.m. to check in.

The lady behind the counter was elderly and kind: "We have your room ready for you, Miss Fletcher, just sign the register. Room number 2, to the right just past the restaurant. If there is anything you need, please don't hesitate to call us. Just dial 9 for an outside line and 1 for the office. Please park your truck in front of your door," the desk clerk added, smiling as she handed Carol the key to the room.

"Thank you. How long does the restaurant stay open at night, and when does it open in the morning?" Carol asked, slowly placing her key in the pocket of her jeans.

"I'm proud to say our restaurant is open 24 hours a day during the Crow powwow, we have so many guests coming and going at all hours. We have excellent food, hope you enjoy your stay," she answered Carol's question.

Carol slung her purse over her shoulder, and headed out the glass doors to her truck parked in front of the office. She had to back up and go around the office past the restaurant to number 2. She slid in the seat, started the motor, putting the gear shift into reverse. Just as the truck was in motion she saw a white truck passing behind her, and *bang*, she hit the bumper of the truck. She quickly stopped the motor, jumping out of the truck. Her bumper was bent in just enough to tell, but the white Ford truck's bumper was bent in enough that it would have to go to the shop.

Out came a tall Indian man in his early forties. "Are you hurt?" he asked. "I was trying to get out of your way, but it looks as though I didn't make it. My name is Jim Nelson; most people call me Big Bear. Don't look so worried, I'll fix this truck; yours is not so bad. Where were you going?" he asked, staring into the blue eyes of the woman who seemed lost for words.

"I was backing up to go around to my room. My name is Carol Fletcher, here for the Crow powwow. I'm sorry and my insurance will pay for your bumper being fixed. All you have to do is file a claim on my insurance." She wanted to assure him she was covered by insurance.

"That's not necessary. I have a friend who can straighten this bumper. I'm concerned that you may be hurt; you will be sore tomorrow. You may have to miss the first day of the powwow, Miss Fletcher. I hope not, for I'm going to look forward to seeing you, bent bumper and all." He laughed, showing his perfect white teeth. "I'm staying here for the next five days, if you want to get in touch with me," Carol said. Thinking she had said enough, she went to get in her truck. Carol watched him as he pulled around in front of the office, going into the building. There was something about this accident that made her think it was no accident. Maybe she was supposed to meet this man for some strange reason. She was extra careful as she backed out her truck, slowly moving around the building to number 2.

She unloaded her camera equipment and luggage into the open, airy room. A hot shower is what she needed to relax her body after the jolt in the accident. She twisted her long blonde hair up on top of her head, stripping off her clothes, turning on the water and waiting for the right temperature. The warm water soothed her muscles and neck. She thought he could be right about her being sore tomorrow, but sore or not, she had to be at that powwow for the opening day.

She stepped out of the shower, when the phone rang. Carol pulled a towel around her body and answered the phone. "Hello, yes, this is Carol Fletcher. Hi. Yes, I'm just finishing up a hot shower, coming over to eat in just a few minutes. Let me slip into some clothes and I will be over; yes, I agree, a glass of wine will do me good. I will be over in fifteen minutes." Carol thought that was strange for him to call her so soon. Maybe he was staying at the motel. The thoughts continued to run through her mind as she pulled on clean jeans with a denim shirt. Her makeup was light with a little eye-liner. Her brown suede boots were next. Letting down her long blonde hair, she looked at herself in the mirror. She felt a little nervous meeting this man, Jim Nelson. The apprehension left a restlessness in her spirit, as though something was not finished between them, as though they had known one another before. Carol couldn't put her finger on her feelings as she walked to the restaurant.

She walked past the entrance to the bar, surveying her surroundings, focusing on the interior of rustic wood and rock, huge wooden beams hewed into the native rocks, casting a certain Southwestern charm. In the south corner of the large restaurant was a rock fireplace to hold logs for the cold winters. Sitting next to the fireplace was Jim Nelson, dressed in his western clothes down to his shining black boots. Carol noticed more about him than before at the accident. His hair was long in the back, coming down to his shoulders, cut neat on the sides, the top laying back, seeming to be tinted a deep blue it was so black. The light through the window touched his face, showing years of work and seasons outside with the weather.

He stood as she approached the wooden table set for four. Water glasses were next to two settings. He pulled out the chair for her; after she sat, he took his seat next to her. "Would you like to have that glass of wine now?"

"I think that would be a good idea, are you having one?" she asked, watching his reactions. He had the deepest dark eyes she had ever seen. They were piercing.

"If that is what you want, Miss Fletcher, I'll have one with you. Please call me Big Bear; that is what I'm known by around here," he said smiling, showing his pearly teeth.

"That is fine with me, if you will call me Carol." Now the introductions were over. She looked at the white western shirt with flowers stitched into the fabric he had on.

The conversation turned to her again. Why was she in Billings and how long would she be here? His questions were endless although he said very little about himself. Carol was careful to ask no personal questions of him, such as if he was married. He had no wedding band on, but this meant nothing in farming country where men worked with machinery. Big Bear kept staring into her blue eyes, searching her soul and her intentions.

The waitress came over, asking for their order. "We will have a glass of red wine first, then two large green salads with baked potatoes."

"Thank you, Mr. Nelson," the waitress smiled sweetly at Big Bear as she picked up the menus.

"I thought everybody called you Big Bear around here; maybe she is new," Carol responded as the waitress twisted her back end in her tight jeans. She smiled at Big Bear, waiting for him to get out of this one.

"That is right; we have hired a lot of new waitresses for the powwow. Obviously, she hasn't learned my name yet, does this bother you?" he asked, picking up Carol's hand, looking at her wedding ring finger.

Just as Carol was about to speak, the waitress returned with the wine, setting it down carefully on the table, keeping the same sweet smile on her face. She was part Indian, with long black hair and dark skin. Big Bear politely said, "Thank you."

"Now, where were we? I see you're wearing no wedding band. That must mean you are unattached, maybe a boyfriend, or soul mate that is not free," he said, teasing, yet curious about her availability.

Carol could feel his humor; he was toying with her like a sly fox until he gained the information he was seeking. She wanted to be truthful, but discreet in her answers. She made it a habit to never tell strangers about her private life. After all, she did travel alone and stay alone at night, and she just met this charming man who must have charmed a lot of women, judging by the way they looked at him and catered to his needs.

She sipped her wine, watching him as he watched her out of the corner of his eye. What was he thinking? He became silent, just staring at her. She begin to feel uncomfortable.

The waitress broke the silence by placing the food on the table with salad dressing, asking, "Is there anything else I can get you?"

"Not at this time; I will let you know, thank you," Big Bear said taking charge of the situation.

He must be used to taking control, Carol thought as she nibbled the salad with Ranch dressing over a small part of it, mashing her potato down and putting a small amount of butter on it.

He watched her, saying, "I bet you are one of those women who watch their weight. You have to the way you fit into those jeans."

Carol blushed, thinking what he must be thinking of her in her tight fitting jeans. She could feel the heat come up in her face, and he laughed at her. What was the use of acting as though she didn't like the comment, for she felt like a beautiful woman in his company and enjoyed it.

"You are blushing like a teenager and it looks good on you. I know this is not the first time some man has complimented you on your body. It is pleasing to look at. I'm not trying to be fresh or forward. You're a beautiful young woman and I would like to dance with you. What do you say we move to the bar and dance floor?" His voice carried in her ear words she longed to hear, but she couldn't trust him or any man.

"Hey, I'm here talking to you; would you like to dance after we finish here? Last chance," he added, laughing at his own joke.

The waitress returned with the dinner check, asking once again, if there was anything they needed, smiling enticingly at Big Bear.

Big Bear counted through his money until he come up with the right amount, leaving a tip on the table. He pulled out Carol's chair, taking her arm and leading her to the entrance of the bar. There at the solid wood bar with stools to match, he said, "Please send two glasses of red wine to the back room." The lady bartender poured the wine as they listened to Willie Nelson sing "Always On My Mind."

The floor was a polished wood, not yet covered by the feet of dancers. Big Bear stepped out on the floor with ease, taking Carol in his arms, turning smoothly to the rhythm of the music. They glided across the wooden floor. Chills ran up and down Carol's spine as she felt his strong arms around her. "I bless the day I found you," Willie Nelson sang, "Let it be me."

They talked little on the dance floor, holding to the moment of life, wanting to dance the whole night. As they turned on the dance floor the bartender came to the door calling Big Bear to the telephone.

"Will you please excuse me, I'll be right back," he said, leading her to a table and seating her.

Carol listened to the couples in the back of the room. Laughing, making jokes with the two girls setting at the table with them. The dance room had a bandstand with a set of drums on the platform. Carol sat, sizing up the situation as well as the room. She needed to get to her room and prepare for tomorrow's shoot at daybreak. The early morning light was the best time for taking pictures of the Montana sky and the background of the mountains. Her mind was off somewhere with her camera when Big Bear entered the room.

Merle Haggard was singing, "Looking For A Place To Fall Apart." Carol watched Big Bear coming across the room. He just held out his hand for Carol to move into his arms, as they turned on the dance floor. Carol lost her breath in the moment of excitement. She forgot the song, moving with the rhythm of the music. She felt life coming into her heart, being suspended in space where nothing could touch her. Only lovers could go where she had been, only those who loved with their spirit.

The music ended. Big Bear led her back to the table, wanting to ask her out to his ranch, yet afraid she would say no to his invitation. She was cautious and unwilling to let him in, although he knew she liked him.

Carol sipped the last of her wine, pushing the glass back, preparing to leave the table. It was getting late, and tomorrow was a work day. "I have to go and prepare for tomorrow. I have enjoyed meeting you and thank you for the dinner and the wine, but how did you know I was a vegetarian?"

"If you have time sometime, I will tell you how I know a lot about you," he said grinning, showing his white teeth. "I would like for you to accompany me out to my ranch and be my guest at the powwow. I have a fifth-wheel trailer I take to stay in. The arrangements would be easier than coming to Billings every night. What can I say to persuade you and let you know my intentions are completely honorable? There are people I would like for you to meet." His power of persuasion was great, but Carol refused the invitation.

"I'm sorry; I can't accept your offer. I have too much preparation for tomorrow. I hope you understand." This was her final word; she couldn't go.

"Will you consider bringing your clothes and belongings with you tomorrow, and stay the rest of the time with me and my family at the powwow? They would love having you. Just think about it and I will see you at the powwow." Big Bear walked out of the building with her to her room.

He held her hand to his lips, kissing it tenderly and saying, "Good night." Carol watched out the window as he drove off in the white Ford truck. In one way she was mad with herself for not taking him up on his offer; in another way, she was proud she never gave in to the flesh. She wanted something more than a physical relationship, something to last forever in flesh and spirit. She had been cautious for five years since her divorce; she would stay cautious until she met the right one. But how would she know the right one? Carol pulled her thoughts together concerning her job and the reason why she was in Billings, Montana. Checking out her photography equipment, and closing her camera case, she felt the presence of someone in the room.

Standing in the corner of the room was a small, aged Indian woman. She just stood patiently, watching Carol prepare her things for tomorrow. Finally, Carol recognized the spirit visitation and asked why she had come to her. "Little Dove can't trust own heart, whose heart can she trust? Fear drain life out of Little Dove and she can't even see Big Bear holds her in his heart. Why don't Little Dove go to powwow with love in her heart instead of fear? Fear will cause Little Dove to be alone after all these years of searching for Big Bear. Little Dove now go with me to the mountaintop."

Carol closed her eyes and she could see herself standing on a mountaintop in a beautiful doeskin dress with dried flowers in her hair, standing next to Big Bear, with him in his Native American clothes. His bronze skin shone in the moonlight, giving to her all his love. Carol felt warm water running down her cheeks with such love as she had never felt before. What was happening to her?

Carol lay (for how long she didn't know) across the motel bed in a state of trance, not wanting to move or see the little Indian woman again. Why was she calling her Little Dove? A thousand questions ran through Carol's mind about the visitation and the visitor. After midnight, she finally closed off her mind and went to sleep, making no decision about staying at the powwow with Big Bear.

The morning sun was peeking through the opening of the curtain in the motel room. Carol sat up, looking at the sun rays and pulled the bed covers over her head. It was too late to worry about the early morning light, she would take it as it came. She tried going back to sleep, but was unsuccessful. She couldn't get the words of the Indian woman out of her mind, "Little Dove can't trust own heart, whose heart can she trust? Why don't Little Dove go to powwow with love in her heart instead of fear?" Over and over the words rang in Carol's ear, maybe the old woman was right; she had lived her life in fear instead of love. She would try and change this attitude regarding her heart, but it wasn't going to be easy.

At eight o'clock she was taking a shower and brushing her teeth and hair, getting ready for the day, when the knock came at the door. "Just a minute, please," she said, quickly pulling on her jeans and a blue plaid western shirt. Tucking the shirt tail into her jeans, she went to the door. When Carol opened the door, there stood Big Bear, smiling as wide as the morning sun.

"Good morning, I was afraid I would miss you, will you have time to have some breakfast with me before going to the powwow? If so, I will wait for you in the restaurant," he offered, waiting for her answer.

"Yes, I have something to ask you. I had a visitor in my room last night, and I want to know something about this visitation," Carol said, pushing her hair out of her face. "I'll be there in about ten minutes."

"I'll be waiting," Big Bear smiled even wider when she said she would be there.

Carol rushed to finish dressing and put some makeup on, although Big Bear seem to be unaffected by outward appearances, yet it was her habit to always look her best. She had finished putting on her eye-liner when she suddenly felt foolish about talking to a stranger about what happened to her in the spirit. She had to talk to someone. Would he think her to be a woman with big fantasies; regardless of what he thinks, she had to talk to someone.

Carol locked the door to the motel room and walked around to the front of the restaurant. Parked in the parking lot was Big Bear's Ford truck with a long fifth-wheel trailer hitched to the back. Carol noticed the bumper still bent out of place. She felt bad that she was the one responsible for the bumper. The thoughts kept coming to her mind as she crossed the crowded dining room, going back to the same table where they had met the night before. Big Bear rose, pulling out her chair, waiting for her to be seated.

He seemed slimmer and handsomer this morning as she looked at his bronze skin and deep dark eyes. They always seemed to be laughing at something, maybe it was her; maybe he thought she was a foolish woman. After all, she couldn't even back up a truck without hitting something. The country music was going and the place was busy with waitresses coming and going with coffeepots. This was a big day for the Indian people and those who love the Indian way of life. Carol wished her spirit could be as free and happy as some seemed to be. Her thoughts were interrupted by Big Bear.

"Sorry to intrude on your world, but what kind of coffee do you want? I drink decaf; I'm high-strung enough without caffeine. What is bothering you? You seem to have something on your mind. Don't tell me you have had an encounter with an Indian spirit; you know this happens when you get mixed up with these Indians. Their spirit is free to come and go as the wind," he said, smiling at Carol, meaning his words to be a joke.

"Why do you say that? Have you had encounters with Indian spirits before? What did they say, and why do they come to certain people and not to all people?" Question after question came out of Carol's mouth; she wanted some answers.

"Wait a minute; you did have an encounter with an Indian Spirit. This subject is not going to be covered in a few minutes; are you willing to go with me to the powwow and meet some of my family who can answer some of your questions? Do you want to tell me about your encounter? I'm a good listener, especially to a pretty lady." He sipped his coffee, never taking his eyes off of her.

"Well, I have to tell someone who has more insight into these matters than I do. A small, wrinkled looking Indian woman came to my room last night. She had on a long dress with a shawl covering her head and shoulders. Peace surrounded her, as time seemed to stand still with her in the midst of all things. Her words were of love and wisdom and to the point; they cut to the core of my heart. I had never seen myself in the light she revealed to me. She called me Little Dove. I think she came to the wrong person, maybe she got me mixed up with somebody else, or something; I don't know. She called me Little Dove and said I was to trust my heart, and she said I couldn't even see that you hold me in your heart. I was to come with love in my heart instead of fear." Carol wiped the tears from her eyes as she thought of the words spoken to her.

Big Bear was silent, wanting to say the right thing, not knowing what to say. It seemed that the spirit had said it for him. He would have to tell Carol the legend of Big Bear and Little Dove. "Carol, you have more love for the Indians than you know, first by being able to see the woman who came to you; you are a visionary, one able to see into visions. This is nothing to be afraid of; it is a gift, a gift for you to use in the right way to help others. I'm going to tell you the Cheyenne legend of Little Dove and Big Bear. It goes this way: a young maiden who was a medicine woman, loved her people; she was willing to die for her father. They were killed at the Sand Creek Massacre in 1864, the fall of the year she was to marry her lover, Big Bear, of the Crow nation. He found the camp of the Cheyenne and Arapaho right after the massacre, for they had been moved from the Dakotas, where Big Bear first met Little Dove. While Big Bear was trying to find Little Dove and her people, the massacre happened. When he found her body, he also found the wedding dress she was to be married in. Instead, she was buried in her wedding dress beside Black Kettle, her father, in Montana, in the Crow burial grounds.

Big Bear roamed the mountains until Little Dove's spirit returned, telling him many things to come, and about the Indian people; also, about that day when Mother Earth would cry out to be delivered from man's anger and greed. Big Bear and Little Dove will return and teach their people of this day and how to prepare for it. The Indians believe that out of these two, with their love so great for Mother Earth and her people, a new Mother Earth will be created for the Indians to live free in this land of plenty, with beautiful streams filled with fish, and all the animals the Great Spirit put here to beautify the Indian land." Big Bear wiped the water from his eyes.

Carol couldn't speak for a moment; it was so enchanting. She could see the gleam of tears in his eyes. He was so strong in his feelings for this legend of Little Dove and Big Bear. Why didn't she sense his love for his people before? Maybe fear had pushed love out of her heart and she could no longer feel deeply. Is he Big Bear of the legend? Is she Little Dove? She couldn't ask.

Big Bear waited for Carol to say something; he motioned for the waitress to come over. He ordered eggs, over easy, with hash brown potatoes, whole wheat toast, and more coffee.

Carol waited until after the waitress had left the table before speaking: "Do you think I'm Little Dove? If so, why? Has a spirit come to you, telling you something I need to know?" Her curiosity was getting the best of her. She wanted him to talk to her, but Big Bear was quiet and distant.

"Carol, there are things I would like to tell you, but you're in no state of mind to accept these spiritual facts at this time; maybe later, after you have been around the Native Americans for a while. These things take time to adjust to. They are not of the natural man, but of the spirit. There is a lot to learn about spirit; all will come out when it is time. Now about the powwow, will you go with me? You will have your own bed and privacy. The best way to learn Indian ways is to live with them." His eyes were fixed on her as he spoke.

The eggs were overcooked, the potatoes were too greasy and the coffee was cold. Carol looked around for the waitress; usually she was watching Big Bear, waiting for his call. Now she was nowhere in sight. Carol pushed back the breakfast and the coffee. "Against my better judgement, I will go to the powwow with you on the basis of friendship and nothing else. These are the terms: I'll drive my truck out, in case I have to come back to the motel."

Big Bear had a smirk on his face: "You sure must have known some loose characters. You will be treated with the utmost respect for the lady you are. Now, let's pay this bill and get out of here; it's almost noon and every body's going to be wondering what happened to me." He laid some money down on the table, paying the breakfast check.

The restaurant was almost empty and the salad bar was being set up for lunch. The lady at the cash register spoke softly to Big Bear as if she knew him well. "Was everything okay, Mr. Nelson?"

"Just fine, just fine," he answered with reluctance in his voice. Carol hoped he wasn't going to say anything about the eggs and cold coffee. She excused herself to go to the ladies room. She sat there thinking, What am I getting myself into, staying in a closed up trailer with an Indian man. Or any man. She decided to call her parents back in St. Louis before leaving for the powwow. Washing her hands, then going out the door, she passed their waitress in the doorway. They exchanged glances and went on their way.

Big Bear waited outside the door leaning against his truck. As Carol approached he said, "You see what some pretty girl done to my truck, but she going to pay."

"I bet she will, one way or another," Carol answered in the same joking manner. She wanted to loosen up and be as free as he was. Maybe fear was holding her captive. "I'll gather up my things and meet you out at the grounds."

"I'll be parked with the trailers up close to the front row, don't worry; I'll find you." He reached out his hand to her, taking hers in his, kissing it politely.

She smiled at him, turned and walked slowly to her room, watching him pull away with his long trailer. He made her feel like such a woman, inside and out. When she had started seeking spiritual truth in place of fleshly pleasures, her husband began to have his affairs. At first this devastated her, then she saw the spirit was bringing a separation for her spiritual growth. She accepted the situation, realizing that it was good for both of them. In her spirit she had been taught to give thanks and gratitude to God in all things. This she had done, yet there was that fear of another man wanting only a fleshly life with no desire for spiritual truths. All these past life thoughts crowded into her mind as she picked up the phone to place a call to St. Louis.

"Hello, Mother, yes the trip was good. Yes, Billings is a big town, around one hundred thousand people, a busy place with a lot of people here for the powwow. You can see a lot of beautiful horses and cowboys. I'm looking forward to the all-Indian rodeo and the many different dances. Mother, I have to go; give Dad a kiss and I will call again in a few days. Take care; I love you. Bye." She hung up the phone, thinking of her place of security. She had lived at home for five years after her divorce, what time she was home off the road from her job as a freelance photographer. During the past two years, most of her work has been for one magazine in St. Louis. Their assignment of the Crow powwow and others had put her in Montana, the Big Sky State.

The annual Crow Fair Celebration, powwow, and All-Indian Rodeo was in the middle of August. The days were warm, with the nights quite cool. Carol had thought two sweaters with a western jacket would be enough warm clothing, now she didn't know about sitting out late at night. The Crow Fair Celebration started August 14, running through August 18, ending on Monday night. There was a lot of effort put into making one of these powwows run smoothly. Powwows were booming in popularity, but just a few years ago, most took place only on reservations. Now some are held on fairgrounds, college campuses, and in convention centers. The growing popularity of powwows may be evidence of what many call a resurrection of Indian identity. Others say it's because of the return of the Bird Tribes, or it could be the big prize money one can win in the dance contests. Powwows are largely free of alcohol and drugs. The Indians say this is their happy time, more than a salute to the past, but a celebration.

Carol was on Hwy. 90 going east toward Hardin Road; the land is wide and open, Montana is dramatically big country. It is a land of canyons and badlands, fossils and timbered hills, treeless plains, and rivers that sustain life in a near-desert climate. Southeastern Montana is good grass country, and, therefore, cattle and cowboy country. It is also Indian country, specifically, Crow and Northern Cheyenne territory.

The Crow Agency is located on Interstate 90 south of Hardin. Carol turned her truck into the fairgrounds. Taking the lane to the trailer hook-ups, driving down the row slowly, Carol saw Big Bear outside working on hooking up the water. She pulled her truck up next to his; she proceeded around the trailer to face him. He looked up at her from making the connection of the water. "I see you made it; the door is unlocked, just set your belongings in the trailer. Make yourself at home, you're going to get an Indian view of a powwow," he assured her, taking the electric line, going to the electrical box to make the connection.

Carol finally gathered the courage to say, "There is one question I would like to ask you. Indians used to always seem so sad, with no hope. Now they smile and laugh, having fun. Take you, for instance. Is there something going on the rest of us don't know about? It is good to see Native Americans full of life and joy," she added, still talking as he went inside the trailer.

Stopping in the doorway, looking straight into her blue eyes, he responded to her question. "This is a celebration of the Indian spirit and our families, friends like you coming together. We dance, sing, gamble and make new friends, have horse races, do all the things we enjoy. Does that answer your question, Little Dove?" His eyes were sparkling as he called her Little Dove.

She followed him inside the trailer, wanting to ask why he called her Little Dove. Instead, he changed the subject before she could get over the shock. Big Bear open up the cabinets filled with supplies. "We have plenty of food in the refrigerator, supplies in the cabinets. Toiletries are in the bathroom; Songbird shopped before we left for the powwow. Also, there will be countless food stands by tonight."

Surely, he had a lot on his mind, and Carol was beginning to feel she was in his way. Lighting the gas stove, he looked at her sitting at the table. "I don't want you to feel as though you are in my way; if you do, we will leave this place, going somewhere we can be alone," he said, finishing lighting the stove and blowing out the match. "There will always be another powwow. I'm lighting the hot water heater; we run the bath water out on the ground. We use the portable toilets on the grounds as much as possible. That helps keep the odor out of the trailer."

Carol could hear him working with the hot water heater. She unloaded her luggage and camera case. Sitting at the small trailer table, she checked to see if her 35-millimeter camera was loaded with 400-speed film, thinking she would walk around taking pictures of the powwow setup and the picturesque setting as the participants came in. Hearing Big Bear's truck door open, Carol reached for her luggage to get a lighter shirt. Just as she pulled the shirt over her head, the door opened.

Big Bear looked at her with her hair all messed up, saying, "Come on, go with me; I can't leave you here, get your camera. You can take pictures of those beautiful horses. I can't leave you, so hurry up."

By the time the last word was out of his mouth, she had slung the camera case over her shoulder, and was out the door, almost jumping on top of him. "Is that fast enough for you?" she teased.

Laughing at her, he pulled her to him. He hugged her tightly, showing his perfect white teeth. "Now I'm going to get plenty of hugging," he vowed, sweeping her up in his arms, carrying her to his truck.

With the surprise action of Big Bear she hung onto her camera. He grinned at her saying, "You better look out, the Indian blood is coming out of me."

Carol settled herself in the seat wondering what would happen next with this man. He certainly was a compulsive person, always so free to go with his feelings. She cast her eye to the tepees set up; there must have been at least a thousand for people coming in. Some had started setting up tents, tepees and campers. There were hundreds of pickups, tents, and campers; with Crow boys racing bareback on horses through the camp. Over 150 portable toilets were set up for the use of the public. Big Bear and Carol crossed the grounds, then went down by the Little Bighorn River, turning toward the arena where the rodeo would be held Saturday. A corral had been built to hold the horses, with hay to feed them. The portable pens were set up for the rodeo; it seemed everything was ready. Coming to a stop, Big Bear asked if she would like to meet his ranch foreman and his wife, Big Eagle and Songbird. And I want to show you my pride and joy, my Appaloosa horses."

Carol placed her camera into position for shooting pictures when a large Indian man and a short, stout, middle-aged woman came toward them. The Indian man had the bridle in his hand leading a horse, a captivating creature with the white blanket and spots across her hind quarters, with white stocking feet. She was just stunning, well-kept and proud to be noticed. Her nature was gentle and loving, her large brown eyes looked straight at Carol, as though renewing an old acquaintance. Carol immediately felt the love was mutual.

She lifted her camera up and begin snapping pictures of the

horse, then the corral and those working with the horses. Big Eagle posed for her with the beautiful horse; by this time, Big Bear had gone to the corral, bringing another prize-winning Appaloosa horse. "This is Quickfire, and the one Big Eagle has is Babe; one day these two will produce a prize-winning colt." Songbird begin rubbing the neck of Quickfire, while Carol continued taking pictures of the horses and the people who raised them.

Afterward, she set her camera down and apologized for being rude for taking pictures first before talking to them, but she couldn't pass up the opportunity to photograph such beautiful horses and their owners. She shook Big Eagle's hand, then Songbird's. Songbird looked deep into her eyes wondering why she had come at this time. Carol turned her head to keep from staring back at her. The informal introduction was made by Big Bear. "This is Carol Fletcher, from St. Louis to do photography on the powwow for a magazine. This is Big Eagle, my right hand; and Songbird, my cook, so you know why I'm so skinny," he added, teasing as always.

"Big Bear not skinny off Songbird cooking, he don't eat, too busy teaching school and ranching and raising horses. Songbird good cook, ask Big Eagle." Songbird kept her eyes on Carol as she spoke, wondering if Carol doubted her. "First trip to Montana for Carol, like Montana?"

Carol waited for a minute before answering: "The country is vast and the spirit of the people is wise and giving. The longer I stay, I know I will like it, although it is different from St. Louis. Montana is a photographer's paradise, especially with these horses; I've always loved horses, but living in the city, I've never had one." She rubbed the neck of Babe, pouring her affection into the horse.

"Can you ride?" Big Bear popped the question she knew she would have to answer sooner or later, for this was horse country. "If you can't, this is a good time to learn; let's saddle Quickfire and Babe and take a ride down by the river. You know Montana has some of the longest and greatest rivers in the United States." Now he sounded like a school teacher or Billings Chamber of Commerce member.

Carol quickly took him up on his offer: "Yes, I would like that; I've always wanted to learn how to ride a horse. I saw some boys riding down the trail by the river."

The Crow Indians were expert horsemen; in relay racing, they would jump from horse to horse bareback. This daring feat fascinated Carol.

"You better watch those boys; they are full of Indian blood and life," Big Bear cautioned her. Big Bear and Big Eagle were busy saddling the horses as Carol continued taking pictures. Big Bear handed her the bridle from Babe. He mounted Quickfire, waiting for Carol to place the camera around her neck. She placed her foot in the left stirrup, pulling herself up into the saddle. She continued talking to Babe; to her surprise, she was not afraid of the horse. Big Bear moved the horses ahead with caution. Carol could feel the excitement of being on such a magnificent creature. She stayed with the movements of the horse.

"You are doing fine; just go with the horse, loosen up and enjoy the ride. Babe knows you are green; she'll take care of you." He started the pace at a slow trot up the path of the Little Bighorn River. There they met Indian boys in the river with their horses; six young boys, ages fifteen to seventeen, maybe. Carol stopped her horse and began to snap pictures of them. They seemed to enjoy the idea of someone taking their picture, so they put on a show for her, running their horses fast, then standing up on the back of them. With the background of the river, Carol was getting some spectacular shots.

All at once one of the boys raced up beside Carol, letting out an Indian war whoop; Babe launched forward up the trail at a gallop, opening up into a fast run. Carol was too frightened to do anything but hold on. With her camera slung around her neck, she tried to hold on to her camera and to her life.

She could see Big Bear coming up behind her yelling, "Pull back on the reins, pull back on the reins."

The words he was saying registered in her head. Carol pulled back hard on the reins, and Babe began to slow. Carol gently worked with the horse until she got her stopped. Then she wanted to cry, because she had never been so afraid in all her life. Now that Babe was stopped, Carol wanted to get down and walk back to the truck, but she had to show these Indians she was no greenhorn, although she was. She sat panting as Big Bear watched her.

"Are you okay? You took that like a real trooper. Now you can say you're broken in to riding. The rest will be easy. That was Andy; he is always wanting attention." Big Bear finished his sentence as the Indian boy came riding up the trail.

He pulled his horse up next to Carol. She looked straight into his eyes, waiting to see what he had to say. "I'm sorry I frightened your horse, but you stayed on good. You're a natural rider. We were just having fun. I'll race you now that you can ride." He was laughing at her for being such a greenhorn.

Carol could have said a few things that weren't so nice, but she kept her cool, just thinking I'll be ready next time. "No, I don't think that is necessary, I've had enough riding for today, maybe another time." She watched the reaction on his face when she said "No"; she could tell he didn't like being told no. He had an ego problem and it showed.

Big Bear stepped in, helping Carol down off her horse: "We'll take it from here, Andy, just be careful next time when riding up on people. There are going to be a lot of people out here in the next few days. I'm sure some can't ride as well as you can." Big Bear turned to Carol, helping her back on her horse.

"Okay, teach, if you say so," Andy agreed, riding off to catch up with the rest of the boys. Off a ways he let out another war whoop.

Carol was prepared for his action by holding back on the reins and it seemed as though Babe was ready for him this time. Babe held steady with Carol's firm hand. Big Bear stayed beside her; he started talking about Andy.

"I'm glad you meet Andy. He is a troubled young man. I've had him in math class; he's brilliant, but he has problems with drugs and alcohol. He always has to excel in everything; when he can't live up to his expectations, he gets high on drugs until he lands in detox." Big Bear spoke with deep concern in his voice. Carol could feel his concern for the boy. "That is sad," she said.

"Yes, they are young men with their whole life ahead of them. What they do now will determine their future. I hope, in some way, I can help some of them. Let's enjoy the rest of our ride," he said, picking up the gallop.

Carol truly enjoyed the rest of the uneventful ride. Coming up to the corral, Big Bear waved at someone driving up in a pickup. They started to unsaddle the horses. A tall Indian man walked over where they were unsaddling the horses. "Carol, this is my brother, Two Feathers. He lives here on the reservation, poking cows. Two Feathers, this is Carol, a photographer, here covering the powwow. How is Mom?"

"Pleased to meet you, Miss Carol, I hope it is Miss. You sure change things around here. Where did you meet this brother of mine? I know he was looking for you," Two Feathers said, flirting with her.

"Oh, we bumped into each other at the Best Western Motel in Billings," she answered with her eyes as well with words. She liked Two Feathers, she could tell he was a hard-working person with a fun personality.

"Brother, you'll have to tell me all about this. Maybe we can get together one night after all the noise," he suggested, pushing the corral gate closed. Then he helped his brother carry the saddles to the truck.

The collie lay in the way. Big Bear told the dog to move over, laying the saddles and blankets in the bed of the truck.

"Thank goodness we had enough rain to settle the dust around here," Two Feathers said. Big Bear really didn't want to answer his brother. Then Two Feathers saw the bumper of the truck: "What horse did you hit?"

"Just a filly," Big Bear answered, looking at Carol, but saying no more on the subject. "We're going to get something to eat; you want to come with us?"

"Nope, Mom and Yellowbird are fixing something. Are you dancing tonight?"

"Haven't thought too much about it," he answered, starting the truck's engine moving away from his brother.

"I know something is up, if you're not dancing," Two Feathers commented, his words fading as the truck crossed the field.

Carol asked, "Do you dance and have one of those fancy costumes with feathers?"

"Yes, I usually dance, but this year I can pass it up to be with you. Is that okay with you?" he asked, grinning as he looked straight into her eyes.

Words were hard for her to find when he looked at her that way. "I would rather stay at the trailer, listening to music with you." He must have read her mind, for she was thinking the same thing.

"Well, I don't think we can do that when you have so many friends here who are glad to see you," she said, looking back into his eyes.

Crossing over the grounds, they saw Songbird and Big Eagle talking to some people outside of a tepee. "That's Songbird's family," Big Bear said, waving at them.

Music was playing, country songs over the public address system at the arena. The platform was finished and some were already playing drums on stage.

"Hey, we need Big Bear up here. Where is Big Bear? Has anyone seen Big Bear? We need him immediately," someone announced, calling over his wireless mike.

Big Bear laughed as he parked the truck. "Immediately, life or death," he mimicked. He then commanded the collie under the trailer, and out she went. "I better go see what he wants or he will be over here. I'll be right back," he promised.

"I'll find us something to eat while you're gone," Carol replied as she stepped up the steps into the trailer. She first put her clothes away in the closet, placing some of her things in the bathroom. The trailer was well equipped, with everything needed to live comfortably. Up the stairs from the kitchen she could see two twin beds made up neatly with Indian blankets. The kitchen had a microwave oven, a gas range, a double sink, all any one could ask for. The refrigerator was large for a trailer, Carol thought as she looked inside, hunting for something to eat.

Carol found potatoes and green salad in a bowl in the refrigerator. She prepared a meal of vegetables and baked potatoes. As she was making iced tea, he opened the door.

At first he was quiet, then he began to talk. "They want me to sing tonight. I told them I wasn't singing; let some of the young people take over the singing. But some they counted on haven't showed up, and by popular demand, I have to sing. Only three songs and no more," he said, smiling at her. "I bet that is a surprise to you, me a singer."

Carol listened intently about this singing, "Nothing surprises me any more. I know music is in your spirit; you love it. I'm looking forward to this."

"After hearing me, you may take off and I'll never see you again," he said touching her hand softly.

"I hardly think so. When does all of this take place?"

"They get started about 6:00 p.m. with young groups, playing the drums and some rock bands. I'll sing around eight o'clock, just before they start the dances."

Carol sat quietly, finishing her meal and thinking about after the powwow.

"What do you have planned after the powwow?" he asked, reading her mind again.

"I'm planning to go to South Dakota for the Rosebud Fair, then back home to St. Louis. My deadline for turning in the film is September the eighth. I need to be there the twenty-third of August," she admitted, finishing her salad.

"What would happen if you cancel the shoot in South Dakota?"

"I don't know, I never canceled a shoot before. I could call and find out if it is possible. You have something planned?" she asked, now that he had her interest.

"I have to report back to school the twenty-fifth of August. If you have to be in the Dakotas on the twenty-third, that leaves us little time. The decision is yours," he said, clearing the dishes from the table.

"I will have to get a lot of good pictures here to make up for those I would lose," she said, rising to help with the dishes.

"No, you sit and talk to me. I'll do the dishes; you cooked."

"Cooked, there was no cooking to that meal," she answered, laughing at him. "I'll finish the job; go ahead, do whatever you have to do."

"Trying to get rid of me already? I'll go and see if I can help with the rest of the setting up. I won't be long," he said, putting on his white Stetson.

He reached over, kissing her on the cheek. Carol placed her hand on her face as he went out the door. He was so handsome, yet so gentle and so kind. Something was happening in her heart; she liked everything about him. She wished she could get out of going to South Dakota. She wouldn't go, if only . . . a voice said, "Pray." Carol sat down. Was she hearing voices? The voice had said to pray. So she prayed, asking the spirit to persuade the editor to cancel the shoot in South Dakota. After she obeyed the voice, she took a long shower, washing her hair, using the blow dryer and curling iron. Carol wanted to look beautiful, the way she felt. She looked at the clock, 5:00 p.m. She lay down on one of the twin beds, falling sleep. She was awakened by the same feeling someone was in the room. She sat up, looking around; there, standing next to the sink, was the same little dried-up Indian woman.

Carol had goose bumps all up and down her body; she surprised herself by asking, "What have you come for, I'm trying to adjust to what you told me before. What else can I do?" Carol began to sob softly as if her heart would break.

"Little Dove can be happy, if she lose fears of past, Walking Elk come to help. Live for the moment you have with Big Bear."

Carol cleared her eyes. When she looked up, the woman was gone. Carol considered her words. To get over the past is to get over my fear, why should Big Bear pay for something he had nothing to do with? Would he have enough patience with her to work these things out? She heard him coming in the trailer. She wiped her eyes and continued to lie with her eyes closed. He climbed the steps to the twin bed, sitting next to her.

"You have everyone upset trying to figure us out. I told them not to worry; we're just friends, but they know better. Maybe it's the way I look at you, or the way you look at me. Or maybe the spirits have told them," he said, walking back down the steps.

Carol raised herself up on the bed, looking at him and saying, "You are the most disciplined person I have ever met."

"After twenty years I have learned to be. When the spirit is your life, you teach your mind to stay at peace in your spirit; besides, I hadn't met the right one," he explained while heating a cup of water for coffee.

"Well, that is good, but I don't know if I'm that disciplined. I have been waiting for five years, but as you say, I hadn't met the right one, either." She moved off the bed pulling on her jeans. She wasn't ashamed of her state of undress. She walked down the steps, going into the bathroom. Soon she came out with her western shirt on, prepared for the evening.

"You better take a shower; it will be time to go soon. I'm going to take my camera and walk around taking some pictures before the place gets too crowded." Carol thought she had to get out of there now or she wouldn't be responsible for making a fool out of herself.

She pulled on her brown suede boots, grabbed her camera case and went out the door. She could still see his grinning face; she did find him irresistible, the most complete man she had ever met, but she had to deal with her problems. Carol set her camera to take pictures by flash, for the sun was going behind the trees. She got closeups of the band playing and the group that was singing. She kept her flash going; the time was 7:00 p.m. and the shadows were crossing their path. Carol thought of spirits of the past. What was Walking Elk trying to tell her? Each time the spirit appeared, Carol felt a little stronger within herself to overcome her fear. Had the spirits of Big Bear and Little Dove, a Crow warrior, and a Cheyenne medicine woman, returned to live again in her and Big Bear? She didn't know why; she pondered all of it in her heart, however.

Elk and deerskin drums reverberated from the high-powered sound system. Dancers were dressed in tanned buckskin, beadwork that takes months to complete, eagle feathers that require federal permits. Big numbers were safety-pinned to their costumes, to identify them for competition in dances representing spiritual ceremonies, preparation for war, healing rituals, or celebrations of triumph, also categories of men's fancy dance and women's jingle dress.

Lights flooded the arena. People were gathering with chairs to sit in and blankets on the ground for the kids. Dogs and children were everywhere. The night air brought cool breezes blowing across the plains.

Big Bear set two chairs down as Carol came around taking pictures of dancers waiting for the dance ceremonies to start. Carol noticed his clothes, neat and fitting every part of his body, jeans, blue western shirt, white Stetson hat and black shiny boots. She could smell his aftershave lotion; he smelled good. Carol knew he must have broken many hearts. Maybe hers would be just another heart broken by him.

Carol placed her camera case under her chair. Big Bear, looking around, said, "I see my mother over there. I better go and speak to her. I'll be right back."

Carol reloaded her camera, checking the flash. She didn't want to miss photographing the colorful costumes. Living close to Mother Earth, Indian people loved color. Many wore beautiful, handsome costumes of vibrant colors.

Big Bear returned with a little, dried-up, wrinkled woman, saying, "Carol, this is my mother, Walking Elk. She wants to meet your spirit."

Carol couldn't believe her eyes, she rose to her feet too astonished to speak at first. She quickly gathered her thoughts: "I'm glad to meet you, Walking Elk, in person. I know your wisdom is gathered from years. It is my pleasure to meet you."

Walking Elk turned misty. Turning her head, the old woman tried to keep them from seeing her tears.

"I'll go back to Two Feathers now. Glad you make my son happy. Hope you will stay," she said, walking away in the dim light.

Carol's heart was pounding and a little sad, but honored to meet someone like Walking Elk. Carol could see the wisdom of years in Walking Elk's eyes, but why did she cry? Were they tears of sadness or joy? Indians were often hard to read.

Wondering, Carol asked Big Bear, "Did I say something to upset her?"

"No, you honored her and she never expected that from a white woman," he replied.

Carol knew there was more to the tears of Walking Elk than just the words she spoke. It was the quest of their spirits meeting in physical life, looking to each other for love and understanding. She knew Walking Elk's love was there to help her understand what was happening in her life, to help her fulfill her dreams of finding a spiritual partner and true husband. Carol kept all this to herself, saying nothing to Big Bear about Walking Elk being the one coming to her at the motel.

On stage, the speakers were broadcasting the message, "Big Bear, we need you and your guitar up here."

Bending over, he kissed Carol lightly on the cheek before he thought of what he was doing. By now the place was almost full. Carol kept noticing an Indian woman looking at her; middle-aged, a little stout, with long black hair. She seemed to keep an eye on Carol. The spirit spoke, "She is Big Bear's ex-wife."

Big Bear took the stage with the crowd going wild. Carol thought of George Strait: tall, with black hair, so handsome in his western clothes. The audience stood on their feet, clapping, whistling, beating drums.

With his electronic music giving backup, he stepped up to the mike. "I want to send this out to my friend from St. Louis, here to do photography of the powwow. Here goes with, "Beyond A Shadow Of Doubt."

Carol felt the vibrations of his voice; without looking, she would have sworn it was George Strait singing. Removing her camera from its case, Carol took pictures one way, then from another angle. The flash continued to go off. His grinning face loved the camera. Carol thought, This is not the first time he has done this.

The next song was, "I Miss You, And You're Not Even Gone." His voice was plain and clear. Carol thought, His life was the same; what you see is what you get.

Then he sang Merle Haggard's "It's All Over Now, But The Crying." Carol took her chair, thinking This crowd can't be satisfied with just three songs.

"Sing, 'You're Always On My Mind,'" the crowd was yelling, "Come on, sing 'You're Always On My Mind.'"

"For my friend from St. Louis, 'You're Always On My Mind,' and that is no lie," he announced, laughing as he started the song. "Maybe I didn't tell you quite as often as I should have—if I made you feel second best—You were always on my mind. Maybe I didn't hold you—I'm so happy your mine. Your always on my mind. Little things I should have said and done, I just never took the time, to tell you—I hope your sweet love hasn't died. You're always on my mind, you're always on my mind. Give me one more chance to keep you satisfied, you're always on my mind, little things I should have said and done, you're always on my mind."

The crowd shouted, "Sing it again," so Big Bear sang it again to her. The Indian woman kept staring at her. What is her problem? Carol thought.

Leaving to loud applause, Big Bear made his way to the seat next to Carol. No sooner was he seated, the Indian woman came over, wrapping her arms around his neck.

"I was so glad you sang our song. Did you know that was our song? We used to dance all night to that song. How much in love we were. Tell her, Big Bear, tell her how much you loved me," she said, looking at Carol.

Big Bear gently removed her arms from his neck, leading her back to the man she was sitting with. Sitting her in the chair, he said something to her, but Carol couldn't hear what they were talking about. Walking Elk came over to them, motioning Big Bear to go.

He returned to Carol without a word. The colorful dances started, and he explained to her what each dance stood for. After an hour or so of Carol taking pictures, Big Bear asked her if photography was completed for the night.

He carried her camera case, as they walked back to the trailer. Closing the door, they closed the world out. Then they looked at each other.

"You know who I was singing to, tonight?"

"Yes."

"In the bottom of the refrigerator is a bottle of wine; let's take it out and have a glass to celebrate," he suggested, grinning in his loving way.

He never said a word about the woman, and Carol never asked. She already knew what had taken place.

Taking glasses out, he locked the door. "I've had enough for tonight; I just want to shut out all except us, just you and I on our spiritual journey," he said, pouring a half-glass for each of them.

"What do you think of these Indians? Some of them get crazy, as you can see," he said, grinning at her.

"We all have our moments," she answered, making excuses for the jealous woman.

"Some have too many moments, over, and over, even after three husbands," he said, holding his glass up to her.

Carol could see he had little tolerance for the woman, so she wasn't about to add fuel to the fire. Gladly changing the subject, she made a comment, "You said we would have a glass of wine to celebrate. What are we celebrating?"

He sat quietly staring at her. "You know how long I have waited for you? Not just twenty years, since eighteen hundred—," then he stopped.

"Go on; what were you saying about eighteen hundred? Don't leave me with no place to go," she pleaded, trying to put the pieces together.

"Carol, there are things I can't talk about now; we have to go to the mountaintop before I can say what I want to say, or before I can think of you the way I want to think. There are times we have to abstain from earthly pleasures while seeking the spirit. I hope you understand what I'm saying. God, I hope you do, for I want you so bad. But this can't be just a physical thing to pass the time away. True love is eternal, and this is what I have to have. Nothing else will do. I've waited too long."

Carol felt her pain and his. Life was in the spirit, not in the flesh. How she wanted to be loved and to love, but she couldn't.

Big Bear continued to open up to her, "I never had truth or spirit in my first, and only, wife. Married right out of college, started to teach, worked to build a ranch out of the land my father left me for some reason that I couldn't understand, but now I do. My wife couldn't settle down, always drinking, fighting, until she lost our baby. That's when I divorced her, never regretting a day of it, knowing I had done the best for myself and for her. Since then I have worked two jobs, waiting for the day I would find that one the spirit promised me. I am glad I have waited. I would not settle for another one who was not spiritually matched with me. For a life with two has to be in the spirit or it will not work." His words were firm, delivered with the strength of his feelings and experience.

"I know this to be true," Carol answered. "When I started seeking spiritual truth in place of fleshly pleasures, my husband began to have his affairs. At first this devastated me, then I saw the spirit was bringing a separation for my spiritual growth. I accepted that it was for my own good, that it was good for both of us." She held his attention as she confessed these truths.

"Don't worry about anything; give thanks in all things, and it will work out for both of us. I know that I had to be at that Best Western Motel yesterday. I had to meet you with a big bang! There you were, so pretty in your blue jeans and eyes so blue I could swim in them and lose my soul forever. What else could have brought us together except the spirit? When there is a perfect match, the spirit does this," he said finishing his wine, pushing his glass back on the table. He went into the bathroom, closing the door. Carol felt all kinds of emotions. Taking a flashlight, she stepped out the door. At first she thought he would follow her. Then, after a while, she knew he had gone to bed.

The arena was dark now, the lights were out and most of the people were in bed. The dogs barked as she passed them, going to the river. She needed to go somewhere alone to listen to that inner voice that always gave her peace. The water offered her solitude and she made her way down to the surface. She sat pitching rocks in the water, sending waves across the water. She thought That is the way of our lives; whatever we do, it sends waves across our spiritual path. What kind of waves was she sending now? She didn't know about Big Bear, he seemed real enough. He certainly wasn't seeking only a physical affair. She could hear the voice again, "Pray and ask the spirit." As she started to pray, alone on the riverbank, she felt the presence of someone. Looking behind herself, she saw Walking Elk.

"What Little Dove doing out here alone? What can she not understand? Tell Walking Elk. She will tell Little Dove the truth. Your spirit loves Big Bear; Walking Elk sees in eyes. Why worry about other things? They pass away; only true love given by the spirit lives on. You are lucky one; the spirits have blessed you to love one so true. Generations have come and gone, yet he has waited for you. Don't be foolish, little one, and let it pass, for it only comes once. Big Bear loves Little Dove with all his heart. He is man of spirit, discipline flesh to spirit. For he is called to Indian people. Why fight who you are? Skin don't make Indian; it's your heart. Your heart is Indian; come, let Walking Elk answer Little Dove questions. She has right to know spirit way placed before her."

Carol was deeply moved and she sobbed quietly in her hands. Walking Elk came down the embankment to where Carol was setting. Walking Elk took her face out of her hands, looking into her red eyes. "Tell Walking Elk, what Little Dove seek in her life?"

Carol felt so small, so humbled talking with one with so much wisdom. "I can't understand why you call me Little Dove when I am Carol Fletcher from St. Louis. I know my spiritual life unfolds out of me to give me the desires of my heart. Big Bear and I come from two different worlds, two different cultures. I seek my spiritual partner in life so we can make our lives count, with the purpose to help mankind. Is this wrong to desire to live for others? Walking Elk, I don't know if Big Bear is the right one or not. I can't get past this fear." She placed her face again in her hands.

"Indian call person name by spirit; Little Dove is spirit name. Little Dove chose to live again in Carol's heart, the spirit of love for Indian people. Carol see she has Little Dove spirit before leave. Carol have own personality, but Little Dove's spirit. Little Dove's desires is deeper than Carol's, for her spirit is total love for her people. Maybe this is Carol's fear, afraid she will have to give more than Carol wants to give. May cost her, her culture and thoughts of what she thought was her life."

Carol could hear Walking Elk talking, but the words weren't going to her ears; they went directly to her heart. She could feel a love she had never known for a people. She could feel their shame of not being accepted for who and what God created them to be, the tremendous suffering of losing their land and being moved from one place to another. She could feel all their pain down through the generations. Her spirit spoke, "We're one, one people, one God, just different expressions." Carol cried harder, her heart broken and love taking the place of fear.

Her pain muffled the words as she tried to speak, "I'm so unworthy for such love to live in my heart. Walking Elk, why me? I have never done anything special in my life. Why me?" She started sobbing again.

"Walking Elk not one to say. Only Great Spirit knows answer. Love is the greatest of all gifts. Little Dove have greatest gift to give to others. Come, let Walking Elk walk you back to camp," she said taking Carol's hand.

Carol wanted to ask more questions, but she kept quiet. What more could she say to one so wise? When they arrived at Walking Elk's trailer, she kissed Carol on the cheek, then went in the trailer. Carol proceeded to Big Bear's trailer. Upon entering, she noticed a small light had been left on over the sink. She sat down, removed her boots and quietly climbed the steps up to the twin bed. Then she realized the light was still on, so down she went to turn off the light. She could see Big Bear asleep on the other bed; she reclined her body on the other twin bed in her clothes and fell into a deep sleep.

Thursday morning, Carol pulled the trailer curtains back to see the morning light breaking. Climbing out of bed, she headed for the bathroom, brushed her teeth and hair, pulled her hair up in a ponytail. Then she reached for her camera and boots, ready to go out the door, when Big Bear moved, sitting up in the bed saying, "You are the sneakiest person, last night, now this morning."

"I thought you were asleep, and I was trying not to wake you." Carol set down her camera and boots. "I'll be back soon, I want the quietness of the camp of morning in my day shots."

"I'll have breakfast ready when you return," he promised, lying back down.

Carol walked a long way from the camp. Climbing a hill, she looked down upon the powwow. The light was just right for photography. Few were stirring around the tepees, only dogs chasing each other. Finishing up the roll of film, she started back to the camp. While walking through the camp, she saw an Indian woman coming toward her. At first, she thought it was Songbird, then she knew it was the jealous woman who was at the show last night.

Catching up with Carol, she asked, "What you doing here with Big Bear?"

"We are friends, and that is our business," Carol responded to her question.

"Friends? Friends don't look at each other the way you do," she replied. "Big Bear will never love anyone but me, so you better go back where you came from," she said, with bitterness filling her words.

Carol gave her no answer; she just kept walking. A man came out shouting at her, "Gladys, come in here and get some breakfast. Nobody wants to hear your foolishness; get in here, now."

Carol never looked back; she kept her eyes fixed on the trailer, going straight for the door, which was open. The wind was blowing out of the west and it was a beautiful day, and that was the way it was going to stay. Stepping in the door, Carol could hear Songbird and Big Eagle talking to Big Bear. They saw her coming and they became quiet. What were they talking about that they didn't want her to hear? What was the difference? Nothing was going to spoil her day.

"How was everything?" Big Bear asked.

"Oh, fine, everything is fine," she replied.

"We waited breakfast for you; the potatoes are ready, just have to fry eggs," Songbird said as she moved to the stove. "Sit, Songbird get coffee and food."

Big Bear and Big Eagle talked about ranching and hay fields. Songbird was quiet. Carol only listened, thinking of the night before and the things Walking Elk had said to her. Little Dove was a spirit of love for the Indian people that lived in her heart, yet she was still Carol, with her own personality. She could see how this was possible, for the spirit was able to live over and over in many forms. She wanted to talk more with Walking Elk about these spiritual things. Carol knew something had happened in her heart and the way she viewed the Native Americans. Before they were just another people with their culture and their problems, now she could feel their pain and struggle to maintain their identity.

The men continued to talk, but after another hour of talk, Carol interrupted with the question: "Where is the nearest phone? I need to call my editor."

"I'm sorry, Carol, I should have asked if you needed to use a phone," Big Bear said, offering to help.

Songbird and Big Eagle got up to leave. Carol motioned for them to sit down, saying "I can go alone; you stay with Big Bear."

"We have to go and meet some of our friends; we'll be back again," Big Eagle said, being pleasant as usual.

Big Bear picked up his white Stetson, placing it on his head saying, "I want to know why you never told me you needed to use the phone."

"Well, it's no big deal, I would just like to call and see if I can get out of the Rosebud Fair, if that shoot can be canceled." She looked in his eyes, finding joy.

Only a few miles away, they pulled up to the public phone. Taking out her calling card, Carol dialed the number. Placing her hand over the phone, she said to Big Bear, "I hope she is there."

"Hello, is Mrs. Shell in, please?"

"Who is calling, please?"

"Carol Fletcher, from photography."

"Hi, Carol, how are things going? Yes, she is in. I'll put you through, just a minute."

"Hi, Carol, what's up? Having a good shoot? I hope so," she said, always businesslike.

"Yes, Mary, everything is going well, good weather and all the makings of a good trip. I'm calling about this trip to the Dakotas, to Rosebud. What are the chances of canceling Rosebud if I get enough material here?" she asked.

"Do you think you will have enough good material for the article without covering another powwow?"

"Yes, this is the largest powwow in Montana, and I will have five days covering it."

"What is the matter? Getting tired of Indians? Well, I'll make you a deal. If you will write the article going with the pictures, I'll let you off the hook. Before you start telling me you're not a writer, just write the damn article and let me be the judge. We can always polish it. What do you say?" she asked, pushing the issue in her business voice.

Carol thought for a moment; she knew she had to write the article or go to Rosebud. "You have a deal, but what is my pay for writing the article?"

"Same as any freelance writer, you know that; have the pictures and article on my desk by September 8, no later. See you when you get back, bye," she ordered, hanging up.

After hanging up the phone, Carol couldn't believe she had agreed to write the article on the powwow, but who would know it better than she or could put their feelings into it the way she could? "It's perfect," her spirit spoke.

Big Bear looked at her: "You got the Rosebud shoot canceled?"

"Yes, but I still can't believe it; she has never done something like this before. Something is working for me, what I don't know, but I like it."

Riding back to camp she smiled at him, sliding over closer to him. "I'm glad you found your place over here," he said, taking her hand.

Meanwhile, the crowd was gathering at the arena, the drums were beating out the rhythmic steps of the dances. This afternoon was for the small dances, working up to juniors, and older age groups. All Indian nations seemed to be there, the Cherokee nation from Oklahoma, Cheyenne and Blackfeet from Montana, and many more, all coming in their bright colors for the ceremonies.

Carol had to have a bath and clean clothes. She told Big Bear she would meet him back at the arena in a hour. She washed her long blonde hair, blow drying it and pulling it back in a French braid. She chose a western shirt, careful to match her jeans and boots. After applying her makeup, she slung her camera case over her shoulder and headed for the powwow, following the sound of the drums.

A young Shoshone woman was singing in her native tongue. Her voice was loving and luring; you could tell she was singing to her lover, in her Indian spirit. Carol took her place beside Big Bear; he looked at her and whispered, "You sure are pretty."

Big Bear was looking in her eyes as the sun passed under the treetops on the second day of the powwow. He gazed into her blue eyes, deeply searching her soul. She met his gaze as the lights came on. The lady continued to sing, as another band prepared to come on next.

"We're going to ask Big Bear to come up and pick and sing a song or two for us. Come on up, Big Bear, and thrill these young ladies with your voice. Give him a hand as he comes on," the emcee urged the crowd.

Still holding his gaze on Carol, Big Bear said, "I have no choice; I'll be back soon," he promised.

"I'm singing this for Carol Fletcher, 'Together Again,'" he announced.

His smooth voice rang in her heart: "Together again my tears have stopped falling, the long night is now past tense, the long lonely night is now past tense, the key to my heart you hold in your hand, and nothing else matters, now we're together again. Together again. Praise God, you're back in my arms, back where you belong, nothing else matters now, we're together again, the love we once knew is living again. Praise God, you're back in my arms where you belong, we're together, together again."

He finished the song, handing the guitar back to the young man, saying "You said one; that is one, I'll be back tomorrow night, good night."

With the spectators yelling Carol knew it was hard for him to walk off of the stage, but for some reason he didn't care to entertain people tonight. After breaking the news of not going to the Rosebud Fair, he had been on a cloud walking above what was going on down here. She, too, was caught up in the enthusiasm.

"The song was beautiful, thank you," she commented as he took his seat.

"It was my pleasure to sing it to you," he said, bending over to kiss her. The kiss took Carol by surprise; she blushed as people watched her.

They sat in full consciousness of each other, longing to touch, yet unable to indulge in their freedom. Carol released herself by taking her camera and doing her job, taking pictures of the fancy dances, all of the participants in their colorful costumes.

The night was going as planned until thunder clapped loudly, sending a streak of lightning across the wide Montana sky. The sky lit up and the people hurried out to their shelters. Dancers stopped dancing and the electric power was cut off. Rain drops started to fall in the darkness. Carol quickly put her camera in its case, as Big Bear ran for the truck, putting the saddles and blankets in the front seat. The rain was coming down harder.

"This won't last long; at least I hope not, for the sake of the races tomorrow. I'm letting Andy ride Quickfire and Billy, my nephew, ride Babe, your horse, with your permission," he told her as he pulled off his shirt.

"Of course, but I didn't know that was my horse."

"The horse is a wedding present," he said, smiling at her.

"A wedding present? We're not married yet."

"Yes, we are; when an Indian puts his horse at a woman's tepee, and she doesn't run him off, or accepts his horse, then she is his woman. Will you accept my horse?" he asked, anticipating her answer.

"Ill have to think about that proposition. I'm going into Billings tonight, no use just letting that room sit there empty. I'll be back early in the morning." She could feel his disappointment.

She picked up her carrying case with the things she had packed in it earlier, along with her camera case. Big Bear just sat watching her without saying a word. Carol thought at least he could say something.

She slowly drove out of the camp with rain coming down just enough to prevent her from seeing through her windshield. She was out on Hwy. 90, heading west with the radio playing country music. The program was for listeners to call in and request songs for their sweethearts, wives or loved ones. Carol listened as women and men called in, requesting songs of love. George Strait would sing his love songs and she would think of Big Bear, seeing him so handsome in his western clothes and white Stetson. She started to cry, why she didn't know. Then she heard his voice over the radio, saying he wanted to request a song for Carol Fletcher, "You're Always On My Mind" by Willie Nelson. "She has always been with me; I hope she is listening," he added. The tears flowed down her cheeks, as Carol listened to the song. She knew she had to get past this fear in her heart and love again.

Carol came into the motel parking lot; going to room 2, she saw that someone was in her parking spot. She moved over two places, noticing the white van with California plates. She took her carrying bag and camera case, then she unlocked the door. The room was clean and seemingly waiting for her. She immediately thought of calling home.

Carol removed her calling card from her purse and dialed the number in St. Louis. "Hello," came her brother's voice loud and clear.

"Carol, where are you? Sis, it's good to hear from you," he said anxious to talk to her.

"I've been busy and I'm staying out in the wide open spaces. I'm fine; don't worry about me. How are Mom and Dad?"

"They are fine, but I'm back home; Sue Ann and I are getting a divorce. I woke up one morning and out of the blue, she wanted a divorce. So I moved out, giving her the house."

"Well, Tony, it's for the best; you haven't been happy for a long time. That's just the reason I can't see myself getting mixed up in another physical relationship." She wanted to tell Tony the whole story, but she knew he had his own problems to deal with right now.

"Carol, you can't let one bad marriage make you bitter toward all men, if you don't try, how will you know what is for you? What's the matter? I'll bet you've met someone and you're getting cold feet. Loosen up and live a little bit; you've been in mourning long enough." He laughed at his own joke.

Carol was sobbing as her brother spoke. "Sis, tell me what's going on; I don't want to catch a plane and come out there, but I will."

"No, Tony, it's me; I can't get past this fear, but I have to. Yes, I have met a wonderful man, a real man: handsome, caring and everything a woman could want in a man. Tony, he is a Native American." She wiped her eyes and waited for what she had said to sink in.

"So what? What does his skin have to do with his heart? Maybe it's not his heart, but yours. Carol, you are thirty-two years old and it's time for you to quit running, if you ever plan to remarry," he said, trying to convince her by being logical.

"I know how old I am, and I know what you are saying is true.

I'm going to give Big Bear a chance and see just what we have in common." She felt better when she said she was going to give him a chance.

"How do you like the powwow?"

"It's exciting to see and learn about the Indian culture. Tony, tell Mom I will call later. Take care of your self; I love you." She hung up the phone.

There she sat thinking of what Tony had said: How would she know if she didn't try? She would try and get past this fear of loving again, with Walking Elk's help. Carol went into the bathroom and took a quick shower, putting on her oversized T-shirt, then going to bed. She was soon sound asleep.

Carol awakened upon hearing a noise outside the motel. She sat up, looking at the clock—three a.m. Without turning on a light she went to the window, looking out and being careful no one could see her. The parking lot lights were shining brightly so she could see three Indian boys trying to break into the van parked in front of her door. A lump came up in her throat, and fear took over her heart. If only Big Bear were here, but she had to do something. She took the phone off the hook and dialed 911. A voice came over the line: "Can I help you?"

"Yes, my name is Carol Fletcher; I'm staying at the Best Western Motel in room two. There are three boys trying to break into a van parked outside my front door. Please hurry."

"Just stay on the line for a few minutes, Miss Fletcher. You say there are three of them. Did you see them?"

"Yes, I could see them because of the parking lot lights; it sounded like a door slamming. I think they must have the door open. Wait, I see blue lights flashing. The police are out there, thank you." Carol hung up the phone, slipping on her jeans. Just as she pulled on her jeans a knock came on the door. She looked out the peephole, seeing an officer standing there. She opened the door slightly, leaving the burglar latch in place. "Miss Fletcher, I'm Officer Brown; you're the one that called in the burglary. We have everything under control. We thank you for the call. Good night."

Carol closed the door and thought of going back to bed. She pulled off her jeans and lay back down on the bed. It was now 3:45 a.m. She lay there thinking that could have been her truck. She knew Walking Elk was taking care of her. By now, Carol was restless so she decided to get up, dress and go to the restaurant for some coffee. Then she would drive back out to the reservation, getting there before Big Bear got up.

Carol moved her truck cautiously around to the front of the restaurant, going in to have a cup of coffee. She sat in the restaurant drinking coffee when the police officer came in, looking at her. He walked over to her: "Miss Fletcher, can I buy you a cup of coffee? Thanks to you, we caught the ones that have been doing a lot of burglaries around town. If you should need any help while in town please call me," he said, handing Carol a business card.

"Thank you, officer, I'm just glad you were so close or they may have gotten away. You know, that was my parking place, but the van driver took it." She watched his reaction as she told her story.

"Well, I would say some Indian spirit is looking out for you," he said, smiling at her.

"Yes, I believe you're right, and I have to go and see one of them. She rose, leaving a dollar on the table.

"Miss Fletcher, let me walk you to your truck," he insisted.

"I'll be fine, thank you," she assured him.

Carol was alert as she walked in the parking lot to her truck. She could see the policeman standing in the door of the restaurant watching her. She proceeded out on Hwy. 90, going to the reservation. Turning on the radio she heard the weather was going to be sunny with winds out of the northeast.

The lights were on in the trailer when she parked her truck beside Big Bear's. Why is he up so early? Carol wondered. Questions begin to run through her head. Hearing the truck, Big Bear came to the door, opening it for her to bring her things back in. She stepped in the door and into his arms.

He hugged her to him with her still holding the camera case.

She lowered the camera case, returning his hug. "I'm glad you're back; you saved me a trip after you. I was preparing to go into town and bring you back without a truck, so you couldn't run away again." He held on to her, looking into her eyes. "Don't tell me you were planning on leaving without giving me the courtesy of a good-bye."

"No, I would never leave without telling you. I had to have some space for one night, and make a phone call. I called home, found out my brother and his wife are getting a divorce. Sometimes divorce is good; I hope this is one of those times," she said, sitting down at the table as Big Bear poured her a cup of coffee. "I heard your song on the radio, thank you; you're always on my mind, too."

He smiled at her, showing his perfect teeth: "I think you and I have been so cautious too long, trying to protect our image of what we thought we wanted. Why don't we loosen up and enjoy each other for now and let happen what will happen? I know there will be a lot of tension released. If we can't trust our spirit to lead us down the right path, then what good is it? I want to love you, dance with you, and feel complete, having fun with you. If it only lasts a day, tomorrow will take care of itself. But I know our spirits were meant to meet for a purpose in Mother Earth, and we will fulfill that purpose." He took Carol's hand, kissing it.

Big Bear said everything she wanted to say, much better than she could have said it. "I have made up my mind the same way; you and I have met for a reason other than a mere affair, for neither one of us was looking for that. There is a deep love in our hearts and we are afraid of releasing that love, but we have to; love is no good unless you share it." She watched his dark eyes dancing as she spoke her heart to him. His profile was strong and caring in the dim light. "Big Bear, will you let me love you?"

He was shocked at her words, but he answered, "Carol, will you let me love you? Yes, I will be the happiest Indian alive to know you love me." They reached across the trailer table, embracing each other.

"Hey, this is crazy." He got up, taking her hand he helped her out of the seat. He put his arms around her, pulling her close to his bear chest, gazing into her eyes and stroking her hair. He warmly kissed her lips and she returned his kiss, releasing her fear. "I have wanted to do that every since you bumped my bumper," he said, laughing and kissing her neck. She gave herself fully to his loving actions, and they held tightly to each other.

Carol didn't want to break the spell of love, but she wanted to tell him what had happened at the motel. "Let's sit down; I have something to tell you, what happened at the motel. About three a.m. I heard a noise outside the door of my room. I looked out the curtain and I saw three Indian boys trying to break into a van parked in my parking place. When I came to my parking space someone else was parked there, so I parked two spaces down. If I had parked there my truck could have been broken into. I called 911 and the police came and caught them. That is the reason why I was back here so early; I couldn't sleep. I went over to the restaurant, had coffee, and happened to meet the policeman that answered the call. All I could think of was you, and seeing you; I'm glad to be back here."

The light of morning was escaping into the trailer windows, as Big Bear looked into her eyes: "You have some Indian spirit watching over you, protecting you until you can find your place in Mother Earth, and with me. I know those boys; they have been in trouble at school. I knew it was just a matter of time before they would be caught. I will call the police station, to see if I can be of help to them. If they are Indian, I go to the jail as a counselor to Indian juveniles, being responsible for some the court releases in my custody. When I retire from teaching I plan to take some on at the ranch, working with them for a year or longer. I have this year of teaching, then I will retire from part of my job. I want to keep teaching agriculture at the reservation, because doing this, I'm helping my people. I'm talking too much; what do you want out of your life?"

Just as Carol thought of an answer to Big Bear's question, there came a knock on the door. The knock got louder before Big Bear could get to the door. Big Bear's brother, Two Feathers, stood at the door staring inside. "Come on in, brother, Carol and I are having some coffee."

"No, I have to get back. Mom wants you and Carol over for breakfast; now, not later; I'm hungry. Get your shirt and boots on and come over."

"All right, we will be over in a few minutes," he said, hoping that would get rid of his brother so he could finish his conversation with Carol.

Carol had sat quietly, thinking about the question she was asked before the knock on the door. "What do I want out of life? That is a difficult question to answer off the top of your head without much thought. I'm in a position now in my life to find out what I want. First, I think I want a spiritual partner in life, one I can relate spiritual experiences to and we both can grow by these experiences, do you understand what I'm talking about?" Maybe she was talking too much, also. She waited for his response.

"I know life is a learning process, but there comes a time when we have to quit learning and be what we have learned. Experiences are good and much needed when growing, but how long before we are grown and able to walk in the fullest of our knowledge? We will have to continue this discussion later, now they are waiting for us," he said. Big Bear pulled on his boots and shirt, then he took her hand and they exited the trailer.

CHAPTER TWO

Little Dove's Wedding Dress

The encampment had come alive with people moving around and dogs barking at strangers. Two Feathers' long trailer was three trailers down from Big Bears'. Carol kept her eye on the Indian children running around and having fun. She wanted children, lots of them, but her ex-husband was too busy making money and involved in his career for children. The aroma of food greeted them as they approached the open door. Keeping the door open was a habit with the Indian people. Carol wondered aloud why.

"Indians keep their doors open because they like open air and plenty of room," Big Bear said, helping her up the steps.

Walking Elk greeting her son with a hug, then she greeted Carol with a hug. "Sit, food ready," she ordered as she poured black coffee, serving up fried potatoes with corn. There were also fried eggs, bacon, and Indian corn bread.

The brothers talked about horse races, the women about dressmaking and how to sew doeskin dresses with all the glass beads on them. Yellow Bird showed Carol the dress she had made. The dress was greatly admired by Carol, then she saw the moccasins to match. What a talent to be able to make something so beautiful, she thought.

Walking Elk said nothing. She sat quietly as they ate, but Carol could see the love she had for her sons. When the dishes were done, there was talk of leaving. Walking Elk hurried to a closet, bringing out a big box, laying the box on Carol's lap.

"For you," she said, then she backed off.

Carol slowly opened the box. Inside was the most stunning doeskin dress she had ever seen. The bead work was exquisite. Tears filled Carol's eyes. Around the neck of the dress, white beads made little doves with red and turquoise beads worked in the design. There were moccasins to match, with a headband. Carol was too choked up to talk. She managed to say, "For me? I can't accept such a lovely gift." Her astonishment was evident. The dress was a work of art that only the older women really knew how to do.

"Little Dove don't like dress?"

"Oh, yes, I love the dress, moccasins and the headband. But it's too much for me." Tears were streaming down her face.

The old woman's eyes were filled with tears as well all the others who sat around the table. "When Big Bear's divorce was over, a beautiful Indian maiden appeared to Walking Elk in the middle of the night, saying for Walking Elk to make a wedding dress and moccasins, too. Put it away, only take out on full moon, for dress have mystical powers to draw Big Bear and Little Dove together. The spirit said one coming to Big Bear would have hair like corn silk and eyes like blue sapphires. When Walking Elk saw Carol, she saw Little Dove, one my son wait for. Now Walking Elk is happy. Beware when wearing dress, it has mystical powers to draw men to Little Dove," she said laughing, slapping her hand on her knee.

Everybody in that trailer was spellbound by the compelling story of Walking Elk. None knew what to say to such a woman. Carol asked to be excused. She took the precious box and went out the door. She had to be alone. What was happening to her life? She thought she had crossed all her bridges; only a few days ago she was a woman with a career, living with her parents. Now, she was somebody else, someone she didn't know. In the trailer she put the dress away carefully in the closet. First Carol pulled the sheets off the beds. Then she cleaned the kitchen, and put clean sheets on the beds. Carol vacuumed the floors with a small Dirt Devil. She emptied the garbage in one bag, starting for the dumpster. Carol saw Big Bear coming toward her. "I'll take that," he said.

Carol handed him the garbage. She returned to the trailer, cleaning the lens of her camera, loading it with high-speed film for the horse races. She was thinking of the dress and what a gift of love it was. She owed Walking Elk an apology for running out before thanking her for such a gift. She loved the dress and the woman who had given it to her. The Indian way was so different from hers; they gave so freely, asking for nothing in return. She liked that way, but she had a long way to go to be like them.

Carol was finishing loading her camera when Big Bear came in the door, opening it wide for the morning air to come in. "I'm going down to the corral, check out the horses. Do you want to come along?" he asked, sitting down beside her on the small seat.

"Yes, I'll come; I'm finished here."

"The place looks good, thank you, but Songbird does the cleaning; that's not your job," he spoke plainly. "You're my princess," he declared, kissing her neck.

"Even a princess has to clean up her mess," she said, laughing at him.

"If you want to clean, that is fine with me, but I pay Songbird to clean. She would be upset to know you took her job," he said, grinning, flashing his perfect teeth.

Big Bear took out a can of dog food from under the cabinet, opening it for the collie. Well, that was another adjustment Carol would have to make, somebody waiting on her. Carol was sure, however, that she could find plenty to do.

The collie wanted to go with Big Bear but, at his command, she ran back under the trailer.

Indian boys filled the corral, getting their horses watered and fed, ready for the up coming races. They were having ten races with ten riders each, starting with the youngest, fourteen years and older. Then the winner from each group would race Saturday morning, running a three-mile race.

The first race started at eleven a.m. with the fourteen- and fifteen-year-old boys. Billy sat proudly on Babe's back, ten boys ready for the starting gun. Get ready, set, and the starter's pistol cracked. Leaping forward, the horses were off. Babe immediately pulled in front. Holding her back, Billy wanted to save her energy for the last mile. He was an expert rider and horseman, as were all Indian boys. On the turn leading to the home stretch, Billy let her run, and Babe ran away from her competition with no problems.

Billy collected his winnings, then he walked Babe around to cool her down. The horse was hot and breathing hard. Big Bear and Carol checked her out; she was doing fine considering the race she had just run. Big Bear told Billy, "Keep walking her until she cools down, then take her to the river, for a little water, not much." Billy gladly followed orders.

Next, the sixteen through eighteen-year-old riders were ready to ride. Andy was talking to Quickfire, patting his neck, lying low on his bare back. Andy and Quickfire shot out front when the gun went off. They stayed out front the entire race, with Andy even holding back Quickfire so as not to waste his energy. Andy let out an Indian war whoop as he crossed the finish line. Jumping off the back of Quickfire, he ran up to Big Bear hugging him, saying, "Hey, teach, I'll work for you the rest of my life for this horse."

Big Bear patted him on the head, saying, "We'll see. Get the horse cooled down, and give him a little water; take it easy with him."

The next group was ready for their turn. Carol was getting a lot of good shots of the bareback riders. She thought the ones of Billy and Andy would be especially good, for she had focused on them in the races. The races continued until all ten were over. The final race of winning mounts on Saturday morning was eagerly anticipated by all.

Everyone was hungry and hot after the races, scatting to find food. Big Bear picked up Carol's camera case, heading for the truck. "Let's get something to eat; are you hungry?" he asked.

"I could eat something," she said getting into the truck, then watching Big Bear slowly moving the vehicle through the crowd.

Opening the trailer door, he latched it back so the wind couldn't blow it closed. "How about peanut butter sandwiches and green salad?" Big Bear asked, taking things out of the refrigerator.

Anything will do," she said, helping him with the salad.

"What is your favorite song?" he asked her out of the blue.

"I haven't thought too much about it," she answered him, wondering why was he asking her about songs. "If I had one, I guess it would be Michael Bolton's song, "Love Is So Beautiful." I bet you have never heard it," she said, looking deep into his eyes.

"Hey, don't do that; I'm trying to be serious," he said, looking back at her.

"Me, too," she said, laughing at his seriousness.

Big Bear stopped making sandwiches, went to a drawer, and pulled out some tapes. "I think I have some of his tapes here or in the truck. Yes, here it is, that is a beautiful song. You want to sing it with me tonight?"

Carol thought, This man must have lost his mind? I can't sing. Speaking her thoughts, she said, "Have you lost your mind? I can't sing. I'm no singer," she repeated, irritation in her voice.

He put the cassette into a tape player. Michael Bolton began singing, "When A Man Loves A Woman." Big Bear put his arms around her, beginning to dance. In the small trailer they kept bumping into the table. He kissed her on the mouth, then kissed her again.

"Don't say, "can't;" that is a copout. If you try, then you will know. Will you try for me? I want you up on the stage with me, just for one song. I don't know "Love Is So Beautiful," but I will learn it for you, if you will learn to sing it for me," he said, kissing her lips lightly.

"I don't know any song well enough to get up in front of people. With all these good singers here, no thank you." That was her reply, and it was firm.

"I thought of doing George Strait, but now I think Jim Reeves is best. You could learn "Have I Told You Lately I Love You?" It's an easy song to learn to sing. You only have to come in on parts. Will you try it?"

Carol could see this was important to him, so she gave in to his request. "Okay, but you have to help me. I don't know what you're getting me into."

"It will be good; don't be nervous, hold on to me. I'll take you through it. Let's eat first, wash the dishes up and I will get out the tapes. Then we'll get started."

After lunching and clearing the table, he set his tape player on the table. Music began to flow and he wanted to dance, saying, "We better forget the dancing and learn this song." She watched him with admiration as he got his guitar.

He started the song, with her humming along with him, learning the melody. The words were easy to pick up, and soon she had it memorized.

After several times he said, "Let's go through it again."

His smooth voice covered her mistakes, until she felt comfortable with it. "Don't worry, our voices will blend well using the mikes. You're good. Who said you can't sing? The Great Spirit put a voice in every person to sing. Let's go over it once again, until you are feeling the song."

After a few more times, she had it. Carol could see how pleased he was with her. He asked her, "Can I ask you to do something else for me?"

"Sure you can; what is it?" she asked, loving his polite way.

"Will you please wear your doeskin wedding dress tonight? This is a special night for me. I'll be wearing my Crow buckskins, dancing in the Celebration of Triumph Dance. It's the last dance; we will be up late, can you handle it?" he asked, smoothing her hair down around her face.

"I'll give it my best shot," she said while thinking, What a strong face, a face of character and love. She had never felt so loved.

The wedding dress seemed to glow with love as she looked at it. Carol wiped back the tears. Big Bear watched her as she slowly pulled the dress over her head. It was a perfect fit. He, too, had tears in his eyes. "You are so beautiful or, I should say, a picture of all life is, love and peace, you look so serene," Big Bear said, seeing it all in her eyes.

Big Bear put on his handsome Crow outfit, brushing his long black hair back until it shined. He placed his feather headdress on.

Waiting for Carol, he started playing and singing, "Beyond A Shadow Of A Doubt." Carol came out of the bathroom with her hair in a French braid hanging down her back, wearing a little eye makeup, and blush on her cheeks. She was a picture of loveliness.

"You are truly my Little Dove, my life, my love," he exclaimed, holding her hand as they went out the door.

The sun had passed beneath the earth waiting for another day. The night lights were on and it seem to Big Bear and Carol as if they were far, far away, dancing in the stars, moving with each reverberation of love and music. Carol held on tightly to his hand as they took their seats. Big Bear placed her camera under the chair; all eyes were on them.

The last band was playing. Afterward they called Big Bear up to the platform. He took the stage with guitar and accompaniment tapes. He opened by singing Jim Reeves' song "Beyond A Shadow Of A Doubt," then onto "Waltzing On The Top Of The World." The crowd went wild, giving out their war whoops. During "I'm Gonna Change Everything," his sweet, smooth voice vibrated in her heart. Carol forgot that she had to go to the stage and sing.

"I have a special treat for everyone; my love, Carol Fletcher, is coming up to sing with me. While she is coming, I want you to take your wife's, sweetheart's or mother's hand and tell them you love them. Love is what it's all about, so tell her you love her. Now, give Miss Carol a hand."

The applause died down as he started the music, "Have I told you lately that I love you? Could I tell you once again somehow? Have I told you with all my heart and soul I adore you? Well, darling, I'm telling you now, my world would end today if I should lose you, I'm no good without you anyhow. This heart would break in two if you should refuse me. Well, darling, I'm telling you now." Their voices blended in perfect harmony. "Have I told you lately how I miss you when the stars are shining in the sky? Have I told you why the nights are so lonely when you're not with me? This heart of mine would break in two if you should refuse me. I'm no good without you. Have I told you lately I love you? Well, darling, I'm telling you now."

Flashing camera lights were going off in their faces. Carol felt as if she could sing all night. "More, more," the crowd roared. They sang the first verse over, bowing off the stage, holding hands. People pushed at them, taking pictures. Big Bear held them back as they made their way back to their seats.

Waiting for them was Two Feathers, who said, "Mom wants a picture of you two, so hug together, place your arms around each other." They did just that, with their spirit taking a flight to another night, long ago, when he had held her tightly. "Good job, little brother, good job," he told Big Bear proudly.

Standing, holding onto each other, Big Bear and Carol watched Two Feathers lose himself in the crowd. They stood suspended in time, but the drums brought them back to earthly time, seeing the fancy dance starting. It was the women's Jingle Dress Dance. All was done in such beauty.

Then the Triumph Celebration Dance started, and Carol began clicking her camera, zooming in on Big Bear. No wonder he liked to dance, she thought, he was so loose-limbed.

There was something about the way Big Bear danced that night that sent chills up and down her spine. The Triumph Celebration Dance was danced in the spirit of overcoming all odds. Truly, it was a triumph for Big Bear. Carol thought of all these things as she lay in Big Bear's trailer as the morning light rose in the big sky. The morning had come too soon, she thought. Sliding out of bed, Carol started making coffee, turning on the radio. Music floated in the air, the aroma of coffee bringing Big Bear out of bed.

Carol stepped in the shower to wash her long hair, thinking about the full day ahead of them. First, there would be the final horse race, then the rodeo. Drying her hair with a towel, then wrapping it around her hair, she looked at the clock 8:10 a.m.

"I have to be down at the rodeo arena at ten for the horse race, but we'll have plenty of time for coffee, cereal and fruit," he said, pouring himself some coffee.

Carol slipped into her blue jeans and denim shirt, realizing she had just one more clean change of clothes. "You better have potatoes and eggs, it's going to be a long day," she said, smiling at him with the towel wrapped around her wet hair.

"Cereal and fruit will be fine for me; the less I have in my stomach when I ride those bucking broncos, the better it is," he admitted, pulling at her towel.

"Is it dangerous, riding those wild horses?"

"If it is your first time, but this is not my first time; I have been doing this since I was born. My pa taught me as soon as I was big enough to get on a horse. Our life was breaking horses and doing cattle roundups and branding. That's how Pa made the money to buy the ranch where I live. But he always wanted a better life for Two Feathers and me. That is the reason, or one of the reasons, I went to college. Pa was so proud to say his son was a college graduate. He died the year after I started to teach," Big Bear said, tears filling his eyes.

Carol set the milk, cereal and fruit on the table, placing bowls with spoons. "If I had known I was going to meet you, I would have canceled this whole powwow, going to someplace to be alone with you," he added.

"What about my photography?"

"Oh, well, you wouldn't need that either, just you and me is all we need right now. Live this moment for itself, think about tomorrow when it's time. This only comes once in a lifetime, so make all of the moment you can," he counseled, winking his dark eye at her.

Winking back, she said, "Just look at what we would have missed." The dishes done, the kitchen cleaned, he pulled on his chaps, then spurs were strapped on his boots. Then he placed the white Stetson on his black hair, looking like a cowboy out of the movies. He had a stern face, ready to face the day ahead. Carol blow dried her hair, pulling it back in a ponytail that reached her shoulders. Big Bear smelled her hair, kissing her neck.

He asked, "You ready to go?," looking at the clock.

""Yes, but don't you think we should feed the dog?"

"Yes, I had forgotten her," he admitted, reaching for a can of dog food under the cabinet. "Dogs around horses make them nervous; it's best she stays here."

People were gathering, full of excitement, waiting for the final race to get started. Carol thought of Andy and Billy competing in this race, wondering what would happen. The competition was stiff; there were a lot of good horses. The gun went off with Quickfire jumping ahead, with Billy close by. Making the turn from the river, Babe just couldn't keep up the pace, falling into second place behind a fast palomino. The palomino was giving Andy a run for the finish. Andy made the finish line by a neck ahead of the palomino rider, then Billy, letting out their war whoops as they flashed across the finish line. Collecting their prize money, they were proud of themselves, and everybody, including Carol and Big Bear, were proud of them.

"Get the horses rubbed down, and cool them, boys; get them ready for the rodeo," he said. Leaving instructions for them to follow, he headed for the rodeo arena.

It was an all-Indian rodeo; that is, all participants were Native Americans, a proud people. Carol thought, I'm proud to be part of the powwow.

She was thankful for having met Big Bear's people and witnessed the spectacular colors, horses, and the men and women that rode them.

Riding and roping—most rodeo events fall into these two categories. Bull riding, bareback bronc riding and saddle bronc riding are included in riding events. Events in roping include steer wrestling and calf roping. The meanest or toughest broncs or bulls makes the ride more difficult, but possibly yield the higher score. Ropers are dependent upon the speed and behavior of the calf or steer they are trying to rope or tackle.

Big Bear and Two Feathers started off the rodeo, riding in on the beautiful Appaloosa horses, carrying the United States flag and the state of Montana flag. Then, behind them came all the Indian nations represented by their chiefs, or one standing in for him with full headdress, riding around the arena. All the people stood, showing respect for the present and past great leaders. Finishing up the parade, bareback riders jumped from one horse to another, sometimes three rides on one horse. Carol looked on in amazement, wondering how long they had to practice before getting it perfect.

Calf roping today is the most competitive of all rodeo events, and some winners make big money. A calf roper chases a 200-to-350-pound calf on his well-trained cow horse, roping it and then quickly throwing it on its side. A quick wrap of the pigskin string around three ankles is followed by a half hitch knot. The calf is allowed to try to break free. If it can't within six seconds, the time stands and the rider holds up his hands when finished.

Trained horses work with the riders who rope calves, knowing exactly what to do when the calf comes out of the chute. Two Feathers held his horse ready. Out of the chute came the calf; in the fastest time, Two Feathers had the calf tied and his hands up in the air. He easily won the calf-roping contest. Carol kept her camera working at each event. As she was getting ready to shoot, there was always a young Indian girl trying to get in front of her camera. The girl would move aside when asked, but she liked her picture being taken.

The next event was saddle bronc riding, broncs or wild horses that have not been "broken" for saddle riding. The broncs are saddled up in the chutes and the rider climbs on, grabbing a thick hemp rope in one hand and sinking his boots into the stirrups. When the gate opens, the bronc goes wild trying to throw the rider off. The motion of back and forth of a good saddle bronc rider makes it appear that he is atop a rocking chair. The ride only lasts eight seconds; when the horn sounds, a pickup man rides alongside the bronc and the rider slides onto the other horse.

Bareback riding is similar, with less equipment, no stirrups and no reins. A small leather rigging held on by a leather strap around the horse is topped with a suitcase-like handle. A second wool-lined strap goes around the flank of the horse to act as an irritant so that it bucks more. The cowboy holds on with one hand and bounces back and forth in a rocking motion. Eight seconds later it's over; if he stays on that long, then a pickup man comes into the rescue the rider.

The next event was bareback-bronc riding with Big Bear coming out first on Hellfire. "Ladies and gents, riding Hellfire is Big Bear of the Crow Nation; give him a big hand."

Out of the chute bolted the horse with fire in his nostrils, straight up, slamming down on all four hooves, then up again with his hind legs in the air. Carol was too busy taking shots of the ride and keeping the Indian girl out of the way to think what damage this violent bucking must do to the rider's body.

Big Bear, incredibly, rode to the time limit. Immediately, a rider came by, picking him up off the dangerous horse's back. The horse continued to buck even as he ran off. Others tried their hand at bronc riding, but none measured up to the skill and excitement generated by Big Bear and Hellfire. Now the young Indian girl had taken her seat beside Carol at the rodeo. Carol looked around for the child's parents. It seemed all Native Americans looked out for one another's children. The girl was still sitting there when Big Bear returned to sit beside Carol.

"Who do we have here, a little friend you have found?" he asked, hugging the girl, then placing her on his lap.

"That was a great ride; your body will pay for it tomorrow," Carol told him, looking at his handsome face.

"No, I don't think so; maybe some, but I have done this every day for a whole summer, working my way through college. Riding broncs and singing is how I made it. Are you two pretty girls thirsty? I am. Let's get a drink and sandwich," he said, the idea sounding good to them.

At the sandwich stand Yellow Bird and Billy were waiting to get their drinks. "Hey, Uncle Big Bear, that was some ride; I thought sure he was going to put your butt on the ground, right out of the chute." His mother handed him his drink. "Who is the little girl?"

"I think she belongs to some of Songbird's people. She is mine right now. We have to get something to eat and drink, but I don't have any money, left my billfold locked in the truck," he admitted, looking at Carol.

His embarrassment was obvious. "I guess I can bail you out," Carol teased him, pulling a twenty-dollar bill out of her jeans. "If it costs more, you can wash dishes. Just kidding," she said, laughing at the fix he was in.

Setting the sandwiches down on the table, he said, "I'll get you for that; it's just a matter of time," he replied, laughing at her.

Silently they ate the egg salad sandwiches and drank cola. He looked deeply into her blue eyes; returning to the stars, they became lost in each other. Carol thought, One of these days all of this is going to express itself in the fullness of our relationship. If the time is short or long, it will be worthwhile.

Big Bear must have been reading her mind. God, she hoped not. "I can't wait to get you back to the ranch. Then we can have time to ourselves. I have somewhere to take you. I know you will love this place, at least I hope you will."

"Will you be there?" she asked.

"Yes, I will be right there beside you," he said, winking at her.

"I'm going to the truck, pull these chaps and spurs off and get my billfold, so I can pay my debt. I'll see you back at the seats. The rodeo is winding down." He left Carol and the Indian girl at the sandwich stand.

Bull riding, and the work of the rodeo clowns, the most dangerous event in the rodeo, was taking place. Carol had her camera working as these bulls put their riders on the ground, then turned on them to get even. When the chute opened all hell would break loose with that 2,000-pound bull spinning, kicking, jumping, running into the fence, anything to get his rider off. There was just a piece of thick rope wrapped around the bull's chest with the free end wrapped rightly around the bull rider's hand.

The eight seconds seems a lifetime, if he is lucky enough to stay on until the time limit. Next is the attempt to get out of the way of a mad bull. This is where the rodeo clowns come in, dressed in their baggy pants and bright colors, creating a diversion for the bull rider to free himself from the charging bull and exit the arena. This part of the rodeo the children love, watching the clowns climb into padded barrels that the bulls butt with their horns. The clowns weave across the arena, confusing the bull as to which way to go. Rodeo clowns play a large part in entertaining between events.

Carol watched the Indian girl as she clapped her hands and laughed at the rodeo clowns. All the children loved clowns.

The last event was finishing up when Big Bear returned. "I found out who this little girl belongs to—Songbird's niece," he said, placing her again on his lap.

Carol asked him, "Do you think I could get a lot of Indian children to pose for a picture after the rodeo?"

"Sure, I'll call Songbird over here; she will help gather the children for you," he offered.

The spectators were now clearing the arena, going their separate ways. Songbird came over with a large group of children, ranging from ages two to ten. Just the right age. Carol directed them to stand according to size, small children in the front, taller ones in the rear. Small faces with dark eyes stared at her camera, innocent and sensitive. Working with Songbird, Carol soon had her pictures; priceless photos they would be. It seemed as though Carol's mission was fulfilled. The emptiness must be filled with love, she thought as she loved each one with her camera.

Big Bear watched her as she brushed the tears away, putting her camera in its case. Kids ran up, hugging her. "They will get next to you," Big Bear observed.

How did he know? "Yes, I'm a pushover for kids."

"Well, that makes two of us. I've spent my life trying to help them, and I have, but I'm supposed to do more, and I know you are to be a part of this purpose." He took her hand and they stood together under the big Montana sky.

"If you have enough pictures, we'll leave in the morning, before things get too busy around here. People will be leaving to get back to work. Is that okay with you?" he asked her.

"Yes, I have enough pictures and memories to last a long time." She held his hand as they moved out over the rough roads.

"Then we will pull out early, eat breakfast in Billings, and do some shopping. I need to buy some supplies for a worker living up at a camp." That sounded funny to Carol, but she asked no questions. "I'll tell Big Eagle tonight we are going home in the morning. He'll take care of the horses. I'll find someone to drive your truck out to the ranch, so you can ride with me."

That sounded good to her; he had all the bases covered. She needed clean clothes, and to get her mind on the article she had to write. While the events of the powwow were fresh was the best time to get it on paper.

Carol couldn't get her mind off the children though; she was thirty-two and had never been pregnant, although she had tried, without success, to have a child. She wanted children, lots of them, even with the problems of raising children today. She wanted them despite all the problems; it was still worth all the giving. Tears would fill her blue eyes as she thought of Big Bear and how different he was from Bill. If she had met him earlier, things sure would have been different.

No, I'm not going to dwell on the past, she thought, for all things work out for the good. That is why she was in Montana, being with Big Bear, because of the things she had been through.

Taking a shower was the next thing to do. They both felt dirty from the dust of the animals and activities of the rodeo. Big Bear took his shower first. While he was showering, Carol fixed a green salad for them. She sat at the table as he came out of the shower, looking at her hard. "What is the matter? What is eating at you? Is it me?" he asking, smiling, showing his white teeth.

"Yes, it's you, you good-looking man, I can't keep my eyes off you," she said, smiling back at him. "I can't get those children off my mind, either. I wish I had ten little ones running around; does that shock you?"

"Not at all; if you didn't love children, you couldn't have been drawn to me. Why ten? Make it twenty or thirty," he said, kissing her hand.

"Now wait a minute, there are only two of us," she replied.

"No, there are a lot more feeling the same way we do about Indian children. The Crow Tribal Council is studying some changes to be made about their programs for children, and the child welfare programs. There must be better ways to reach these children at a young age. Drugs and alcohol are taking too many of them. Even one is too many." He looked away to keep Carol from seeing the tears in his eyes. "I'm sorry, I didn't intend to get into this."

Carol's presumptions of Big Bear went out of her mind, she was glad she had found him. She appreciated who he was and what he was about. Children were his life, and he wanted to share that life with someone. They reluctantly got ready for the evening at the powwow, knowing they would rather stay in the trailer sharing this love.

This was a big night; final contests were being held on some of the fancy dances. Also, it was an important night for bands, who poured out their emotions in their music and the dancing. "Calling Big Bear, up front with your guitar, please; we need you, man, give us a hand." He kissed her lips.

Then walking slowly up on the stage, he announced, "To all the young lovers here tonight, I'm sending this out to you, 'Together Again.'" Big Bear's heartfelt words found a lodging place in Carol's heart.

"Together again, my tears have stopped falling, the long, lonely night is now past tense, the key to my heart you hold in your hand and nothing else matters now. We're together again, together again, praise God, you're back in my arms, back where you belong. The love that we knew is living again, and nothing else matters, girl. You're back in my arms where you belong. We're together again and nothing else matters."

The crowd went wild. Big Bear sang the second verse again as a brief encore for the appreciative audience. Coming off the stage, he went over to his mother's chair, bringing her back with him to sit with Carol and him the rest of the evening. The remainder of the evening they spent in celebration, Big Bear and family, with all the beauty of the Indian spirit. If only people could see by the spirit, they would understand these people: hearts of gold, holding on to the values of the past, yet wise enough to know changes were coming in the younger generation. Maybe the Indians would save mankind by doing the impossible first. It certainly can't be done through education alone; there has to be something to fill that void in the lives of people of all races, this void in their spirit. Their spirit had to be reached by loving and helping them to grow in their spiritual experiences of their lives. The Native Americans could understand this and could be the first to step out, teaching the spiritual life in the schools as well as math, English, and history. What better teachers were there than Big Bear and Walking Elk? The lessons to be learned in Mother Earth now couldn't come out of books, but from the spirit. Carol thought of all these things as she watched the children.

They ended the evening with the family over for coffee, and a lot of laughing. The joy of the family filled Big Bear's trailer as they crowded in, some at the table, some on the floor, some sitting on the steps leading to the beds. Carol looked at them thinking, The world would think these earth people had nothing, when they truly had everything of value: good earth, friends, love for one another. What else could one ask for?

Big Bear talked to Big Eagle about the hay they were having cut Monday. No matter how much fun they were having, his mind eventually returned to business.

"Little Dove like powwow?" Walking Elk asked Carol.

"An experience I will never forget," Carol answered.

"Little Dove be back next year? Maybe sing again with Big Bear, huh?" she asked laughing.

"You never know what you may do around here, maybe the rodeo next year," she joked, laughing with Walking Elk.

Walking Elk slapped her knee in glee, saying, "You never know what Little Dove do."

After midnight, the conversation ran out and everybody got ready to go home. "We will be gone when you rise in the morning," Big Bear let them know.

When the family members had left, he surprised Carol, closing the door, taking her in his arms and lifting her to the bed. She said, "Wait, let me pull my boots off!"

"No time, girl, I want to love you now," he insisted, laying her gently on the bed, kissing her on the mouth.

"You are the life of my world, my morning star; all of my soul and spirit loves Little Dove. I love you, my family loves you, my friends love you. The whole world loves you. This love will never grow old or dull. Every time I look at you I see life," he said, kissing her over and over.

Carol responded to his passionate kisses, saying, "Please take off my boots." Big Bear removed her boots, jeans and shirt, handing her a nightshirt. Removing his boots, jeans and shirt, he came to bed in his jockey shorts. They held each other tightly until the morning light.

Early morning in Montana is a special time, seeing the vast country, feeling so small against the big sky. Big Bear was unhooking the water and electricity after they finished in the bathroom and kitchen. As Big Bear was backing up the truck, hitching the trailer in, Walking Elk came over carrying coffee for them, handing Carol a cup. Carol could see sadness in her eyes.

Carol asked, "Walking Elk, why do you look so sad? We will see you soon."

"Walking Elk feel for Little Dove, for her heart don't want to go. But because of family and job, she feels she has to go. One day, Little Dove will follow her heart," she predicted, hugging Carol.

Big Bear took the coffee in silence, saying nothing about what Walking Elk had said. As the old lady walked away, they started off toward Billings. Carol looked back at the tepees, thinking of all the people who were staying back there. What a beautiful people, she thought.

CHAPTER THREE

On the Mountaintop

Country music was playing in the background of the busy restaurant. Big Bear and Carol took a booth, smiling at each other. "Potatoes and eggs with whole wheat toast, please, with decaf coffee," he ordered for both of them.

"Big Bear, what was your mother trying to tell me back at the camp?" Carol wanted to know.

"My mother is a wise woman and sees deeply into your spirit, seeing your love for me, also your love for your family, and the negative vibrations you're going to shake off. She was trying to warn you, in her way," he was saying when the waitress brought coffee, cream and sugar.

Carol wanted to hear what else Big Bear had to say about his mother. "I have to realize if you don't ask for it, you don't get it. I'm only telling them what I have to, that I will be living in Montana for photography purposes. It's not that I'm ashamed of you or your people, but why put yourself through something when you don't have to? They will try persuasion by mentioning the harsh Montana winters. I'm going to Arizona for the winters. I'm prepared for this," she said, reaching for his hand.

"That is all well and good, but who am I when I call asking for you, some business associate? No, Carol, the truth is the best way; if they don't accept it, at least you will have it out in the open. That way you don't have to backtrack. Clear your path as you go," he said, holding her hand tightly.

Carol was glad the food came in time. Knowing he was right

about telling the truth, she would do just that, get everything out in the open. No use having to go over it later. Carol ate her food in silence, thinking Big Bear was a wise man like his mother.

After paying the bill, they were on their way to shop for groceries. "You're right; it is best to tell them my plans, but I don't know what I'm going to do," she admitted, fear knotting the pit of her stomach.

"What do you mean, you don't know? You're coming back here and live with me as my spiritual partner, in this life as my beautiful wife," he said, firm in his reply. "You don't go until you understand how much I love you, and that you love me."

"Walking Elk will be with me, and I have my wedding dress," she said, smiling at him.

"The wedding dress stays here; you're not taking that dress back to St. Louis, too many men there. You know what Mom said about that dress, and she was right. Did you see how all those men looked at you at the powwow?" he reminded her, kissing her hand.

"All right, the dress can stay. I believe that it is magic," she said.

Finishing the shopping they headed home, listening to George Strait songs on the country music station. Laying her head on his shoulder, she whispered in his ear how much she loved him, resting in her spirit. When they took the turn off the main road to the ranch, she knew in her heart that all was well.

Carol surveyed her surroundings, after passing under a sign with the letters Double B&B Ranch, over the gravel road up to the ranch house. He slowed the truck down, pulling up in a large yard full of dogs. Out in the middle of nowhere sat a log and stone ranch house, a large barn to the left of the house.

Big Bear turned off the motor. "Well, this is home, hope you like it. Stay in the truck until I get rid of these dogs." He gave one command and the dogs headed for the barn. "Now I think it's safe," he said, opening the truck door for her.

Carol grabbed her camera case, following his long strides up the steps onto the porch. He opened the front door to an inviting room. Carol followed him through the house to a bedroom in the back of the house. She placed the camera case down on the bed, looking around. The room was large, with a closet across one end. A door led into the bathroom; Indian rugs covered the wooden floors. Indian blankets were on the bed. Everything was neat and in place. She could feel the eyes of Big Bear on her.

"If you get lonesome in here, my bedroom is in there," he said, smiling at her, showing those perfect teeth. They followed the hallway back into the large room that was a living room with a fireplace made of native rock. The dining room with glass doors opened out to a deck around the house. The house was rustic, but beautiful in its simplicity and elements of Native American culture. Large planks made up the floors, covered with Indian rugs. The kitchen was tiled with modern appliances; in the west corner of the kitchen was a door that led downstairs to a laundry room, then out to the garage. The sink faced the front of the house, making it easy to see anyone coming up the road.

The dining room table was handmade, a large slab of wood—what kind she didn't know—fitting in the room. Chairs of the same wood appeared to be handmade; maybe they were made by school shop students.

After showing her the inside of the house, everyday life resumed as they cleaned the trailer. Carol's truck had been placed under the barn by the boys Big Bear had hired to bring it out to the ranch. Big Bear had to move it to make room for the trailer under the barn. There were clothes to wash out, food to put into the refrigerator. All this couldn't wait for Songbird, so the job was up to them. Carol wanted to wash his clothes with hers. She wanted to do things for him, hoping he would understand that she wanted to care for him, as he wanted to care for her. Big Bear said nothing as she collected the dirty clothes, putting them in the laundry room. Big Bear left to take supplies to a ranch hand—where she didn't know.

That night, she prepared vegetables and fruit they had bought at the market. She enjoyed cooking and doing things for him. Big

Bear helped clear the table, putting the dishes in the dishwasher. He turned on soft music, and they lay on the couch in one another's arms. Words weren't necessary then; just being together was enough. They valued each minute recorded by the ticking clock before she would have to leave.

"Why don't you leave your truck here and fly back? Then you wouldn't have to drive back alone. Then I would be sure you will be coming back," he said, kissing her neck.

"I can't; I have things to bring back, lots of things to go through, cleaning out Mom's basement. Some I will give to charity, some I'll keep," she said, raising herself up to look at him.

"Don't bring anything you had in your first marriage. Let's start over again with us. The old has passed away, including pictures, dishes or anything you had before," he said, seriousness in his dark eyes.

"You're right. Old things are old memories, old spirits. We don't need that. I understand what you are saying. If you're going to change, go all the way. Why bring the garbage with me? You have made my load lighter. All those pictures and dishes, pots and pans, I can give away or let Mom sell in a garage sale. She would like that," Carol said, suddenly feeling free.

Big Bear sensed her newfound freedom. "We all have to let go, sooner or later, of things we thought were our life, because there is no life in them, only dead memories. We can't live on memories; we must live for now, creating a better tomorrow for a lot of children. Now I'm going to bed; if you need anything, call me. The men will be here early to cut the hay if the dew is not too heavy."

Carol repeated Big Bear's words over and over in her mind that night. She wondered what her mother was going to think when Carol began discarding things that were given to her for wedding presents, birthdays, and holidays. He was right; things do have memories, and memories produce feelings of those times. This wasn't going to be easy. She closed off her mind and went to sleep. Tomorrow would bring another joyous day in Montana.

The morning light was bright coming in the window. Carol

could hear the shower running. Rolling over, she looked at the clock—6:10 a.m. Pulling the cover over her head, she thought, If only I could sleep until eight. Opening the bathroom door into her room, Big Bear came over to the bed, sitting on the bed next to her. He kissed her, then he slipped quietly out of the room. Carol lay there quietly until he was out of the room. She thought how her life had changed in the past five days. She had known Big Bear only five days, yet it seemed a lifetime of being together. Smelling coffee, she arose and showered, dressing in her last clean suit of clothes. Today, she had to do laundry. Carol looked around the room, pine paneling made up the walls, with only a clock hanging over the bed.

She walked into the large, open room, finding Big Bear reading some papers. "Thought you wanted to sleep later than six," he said, smiling at her as she poured a cup of coffee.

"I couldn't lie there while smelling your coffee," she replied, smiling back at him.

"What are you reading?"

"Some agricultural reports I'm behind in reading. Why didn't you sleep a little later? I know you're tired from all the powwow activities," he said, reaching for her to come closer.

They talked about the ranch and life on the ranch, while eating their breakfast of cereal and fruit. Soon the morning sun was high in the clear sky. Carol and Big Bear sat on the front porch waiting for the hay crew to come. "Have you ever seen hay cut?" he asked.

"No, only while taking photographs on farms; I'm a city girl, you know." She watched his handsome face as a worker's truck pulled up in front of them.

"This is it. I'll see you later, after I get them started," he said, climbing down the steps to meet the man in the truck.

Carol had plenty to do: clothes to wash, some to be ironed, her suitcase to repack, her camera to clean, film to be organized, then writing the article on the powwow.

Around ten-thirty, Big Bear came back to the house wanting

to know what she was doing. He found her in the laundry room putting clothes in the dryer.

"I hope you found everything you needed. I have to go into Billings for a part that was broken on the hay cutter. Do you want to go with me?" he asked her while watching each step she took.

"No, I don't think so. I have work to do here. I want to get started on the article I have to write. May I use your typewriter?" she asked him, wishing he didn't have to leave.

"Sure, in the office off the living room is a computer, printer and a typewriter. Typing paper is in the desk drawer. Help yourself to whatever you need. I should be back in a few hours," he said, kissing her good-bye.

Engrossed in the article, Carol forgot about time and food. The office was comfortable and neat, with leather furniture, and Indian rugs on the floors. Photos of Big Bear with blue-ribbon-winning bulls hung on the wall, also rodeo pictures. She noticed one picture of him standing with his arms around a young Indian woman. Carol looked closer to see if the woman was someone she knew from the powwow. No, Carol couldn't recognize the woman, but she could see that they were more than friends.

Still working on the article, Carol heard Big Bear come in. He looked in the door where she was working, saying, "Looks like everything is under control. I have some fresh trout for supper. I'm taking this part to the field, then I'll be back," he said, kissing her on her neck.

"I'll be finished here in a few minutes. Did you have lunch?" she asked hurriedly as he went out the door.

Carol finished the first draft of the article, then had a glass of tea and an apple. Looking out the glass doors, she could see the men working in the hay field on the equipment. Big Bear was getting into his truck as the other men moved out into the field. They would work after dark cutting the hay, while the dry weather held.

Thinking of the fish he had brought for supper, Carol turned her thoughts to preparing them with baked potatoes and a salad.

Big Bear came in the door, wiping grease off his hands. "It's a nasty job working on equipment," he said, heading for the bathroom.

"The fish smell good. I'll have to take you fishing Indian-style; you will love that. We use bow and arrows," he said loudly from the bathroom. "It is good to have you here when I come in, but I better not get used to this. You will soon be gone."

The word "gone" brought tears to Carol's eyes. She would soon be gone. Just a few days would seem but a few minutes to her before she had to leave. Big Bear sat down, beginning to read a paper he had brought in from town. Carol set the table, placing iced tea and salad next to each plate. Soon the fish and potatoes were ready. They ate in silence, looking deeply into one another's eyes.

"Do you think you will like Montana ranch life?" he wanted to know.

"Yes, although I would have to have plenty to keep me busy. I would love to learn how to quilt, and other home crafts and stitching doeskin dresses the way Walking Elk does," Carol said, smiling as she thought of Walking Elk.

"Big Eagle and Songbird will be back tomorrow around noon. I'll spend the day with Big Eagle, setting up the crew on getting the hay in the barn. Wednesday, we can have some time for riding the ranch." That made him happy; he would be proud to show her the ranch.

"Do you know when you will be leaving for St. Louis?" he asked.

"The twenty-fifth, the morning you start back to school," she said with difficulty. Her voice sounded far off as she spoke.

"That is soon. We will go to the mountain this Thursday and come back Sunday." He was sad thinking of her leaving, but when he spoke of the mountain, his eyes lit up.

They passed the night listening to country music, with Big Bear working on his computer. Carol looked at the picture on the wall of the young woman and him. He saw her looking at the picture and said, "That was a long time ago, and we couldn't even come close to terms of life." He took the picture down, pitching it in the garbage can. "What is good for you, is good for me."

Carol was shocked at his actions, but agreed that if one was to clean out their past, the other had to do the same. Carol decided to call it a night and left to take a shower. The warm water felt good on her body. After washing her hair, she felt refreshed. She had finished drying her hair and was getting into bed when she heard Big Bear coming in to take a shower.

Carol thought about the day and about the picture he had thrown into the garbage. She knew there must have been other women in his life, some of them special to him. She ran these things through her mind until she decided to go to sleep.

Carol heard the sound of Big Bear's boots going down the hall. Soon the aroma of coffee floated into her room. Pulling the cover over her head, she lay in bed for another hour. He came in with coffee. "I got lonesome without you," he said, handing her a cup of coffee. It was made just right, she thought.

"I'm getting up now, but the bed felt so good this morning. Thank you for the coffee," she said, holding the coffee cup carefully.

Big Bear sat beside her, kissing her. "If you will get up, I will make some whole-wheat pancakes with warm honey."

"You have a deal. That sounds good," she said, returning his kiss. Then she headed for the bathroom. Coming into the hall later, she could smell pancakes. After she took her place at the table, he served her pancakes and warm honey. They were delicious and just what she needed to start her day.

After breakfast conversation of the day, Big Bear went to the hay field, while Carol thought of what to prepare for lunch. Next she had to clean bedrooms and the bathroom.

Carol hesitated before entering Big Bear's room, then she thought he would want her to feel free to roam about the house. That room was part of him and she wanted to know that part. She approached the room decisively wanting to experience all his world. The room was quite spacious with one full-sized bed and one chest of drawers. The same wooden floors were covered with Indian rugs. The walls were pine paneling, the same as the rest of the house, but the walls had a captivating hold upon her. Mounted upon the walls a bow and arrows hung on the wall. Then there were the pictures of great Indian chiefs: Sitting Bull, Red Cloud, Chief Joseph and some she couldn't identify. The room was filled with Indian history, and the Indian way of life. The bed was neatly made, with no clothes laying around. Carol left the room feeling as though she had just participated in a history lesson that passed in a parade across Big Bear's wall. She left the bedroom, going into the bathroom, cleaning the sink and tub, all the time wondering if Big Bear held anger in his heart for what had happened to the Indian people. She would listen and see if there was anything other than love for all people. The more she knew about this amiable man, the more she wanted to know.

Carol returned to the kitchen: what would she fix for the four of them to eat for lunch? A large chicken pot pie, her mother's recipe, a green salad, a homemade blueberry cobbler. That would be made from her mother's recipe, too. She put the chicken on to boil, while preparing salad and sourdough biscuits for the topping of the chicken pot pie.

At 11:05 a.m., Big Eagle and Songbird were coming up the dusty road to the ranch. Parking the horse trailer, they began to unload the horses. They were laughing and talking with Big Bear. They seemed so happy. Songbird collected clothes and other things out of the back of the truck, carrying clothes to the laundry room.

"Songbird smell something good. Little Dove good cook," Songbird said, sniffing as she came in from the basement. "How is Little Dove and Big Bear?"

"We're doing fine, loving every moment of our time together. How was the rest of the powwow, lots of things happening?" Carol asked, wanting to know if she had missed anything.

"All about same: finish dance contests, lot good dancers this year, many young people. Little Dove not go home, stay with Big Bear?" she asked, concern in her voice.

"No, Songbird. I have to go home to close out bank accounts, clean out Mom's basement of my stuff. It's not right to ask her to do this. It's just for two weeks or a little longer," she said, hoping it would be sooner.

"Big Bear be lost without Little Dove, Songbird knows," she said, noticing the table. "Little Dove have everything ready to eat. Little Dove take my job. Songbird go out, find job."

Carol felt bad because she made Songbird feel unwanted. "No, Songbird has her job. Just now I have to keep busy. Don't worry. I will find plenty to do," she said, reassuring Songbird.

The men came in for lunch, sitting around the table. The conversation was about the powwow and hay fields. Carol dished up the blueberry cobbler with cream, and everyone enjoyed the lunch. Big Bear ate little. Carol thought that he didn't eat enough. The men went into the office talking business, while Carol and Songbird cleaned the kitchen.

"Songbird do dishes, Little Dove done cooking," she insisted. Carol thought that would be best; she would take a walk, getting out of the way.

"Okay, Songbird, it's all yours. I'm going to get some exercise."

Walking out on the porch, she decided to walk to the hay field. She wanted to see the hay cutting, and now seemed a good time. Slowly she made her way up behind the house in the direction of the hay field thinking, I should have brought my camera. The last few days she had forgotten about taking photos. She thought now of taking pictures of the ranch, to show her parents where she would live when returning to Montana. Tomorrow, when Big Bear showed her the ranch, she would take pictures of Babe, her beautiful horse, and the green fields with cattle grazing.

Carol came up unexpectedly on the men working in the hayfield. Some were eating and drinking pop, while two tractors were cutting rich alfalfa hay. They spoke casually to one another while she kept walking around the field, staying in the roadway. Carol looked at the endless fields, thinking there must be a lot of work for a place this big.

She came to the end of the road, where a gate opened into another field. She could see the cattle. The cows stood staring at her. She saw an enormous bull, then another huge bull. Carol thought, Don't worry about me intruding on your territory. She could hear a tractor coming up behind her. Turning around from the pasture fence facing the tractor, she saw a young Indian man. He turned off the tractor motor, climbing down to the ground.

Carol noticed the young man was quite handsome and playful. He loved being noticed by her and would have made any excuse to come over to meet her. He was tall and muscular from outdoor work, but fun loving; she could see it in his eyes. He probably liked good times with the ladies on a Saturday night.

"Lady, I wouldn't go in that field; those bulls don't cotton to strangers in their territory, especially at this time," he warned, looking straight into her eyes.

"You don't have to worry about me going into their territory. I'm just looking at those healthy animals," she said, smiling at the stranger.

"Yes, Big Bear has some of the finest cattle in the state of Montana. My name is Billy Joe. This is my crew and equipment," he said proudly, coming closer to Carol.

"I'm Carol Fletcher, staying a few days after the powwow. I'm a photographer. Pleased to meet you, Billy Joe. Well, I better be getting back. Thank you for your concern," she said politely to the young Indian.

He wanted to say something else, but broke off his words, driving off on the tractor. Carol watched this friendly, good-looking man, although she thought he was not as handsome as Big Bear. Carol could see Big Bear's Ford pickup heading in her direction.

Stopping his truck, he jumped out, saying, "This is where you got off to; I have been looking for you." He placed his hat on his head, looking hard at her. "You could have come out with me, if I knew you wanted to come," he said, irritation in his voice. "This is no place for you to be alone."

"What are you talking about? I go everywhere alone, and I've had no problems yet. Big Bear, don't put fear in me. I had to overcome fear when I took this job, traveling alone. I should have told you I was taking a walk, but there is nothing here to harm me," she insisted, irritated.

"I bet you met Billy Joe. If there is a pretty girl around, he will find out who she is. Come on, get in the truck and stay close to me. I want them to know you are my woman, not some stray running loose," he said, kissing her cheek.

Carol listened to him, although not liking his attitude; maybe he just didn't like Billy Joe. She reminded herself that she was a guest at Big Bear's ranch, and he did know the people better than she. Climbing in the truck, she felt he was protecting her. Until she knew this land and its people, she would take his advice.

No more words were spoken. Big Bear drove the truck up to Billy Joe's tractor. He stopped and kissed Carol hard on her lips, then got out of the truck. He walked up to Billy Joe as Carol watched them. It seemed to Carol that Big Bear didn't trust Billy Joe around women. She continued to watch as they talked, once in awhile looking in her direction. She felt as if she were a piece of merchandise, knowing she was too trusting, but instinct had always kept her from harm. Carol could see why a woman would find Billy Joe attractive; he was young, maybe ten years younger than Big Bear. He was obviously out for a good time. She certainly didn't have time for that; if so, she could have found plenty of men like him in St. Louis.

Big Bear opened the truck door with a wide grin on his face. "Now he knows who you are and why you are here. Carol, be careful who you tell your business to," he scolded her out of concern for her.

Carol said not a word. She moved closer to him, holding his hand, thinking, This is not the time to say anything, best to keep quiet. Carol loved him so much, she wouldn't do anything to upset him. She quickly decided to tell him so.

"I love you and I wouldn't do anything that I know would

upset you. I'm sorry," she said, looking at him with deep passion.

"I love you, darling. I don't want anything to happen to you," he said, stopping the truck in the middle of the hayfield, taking her in his arms and kissing her over and over. "I protect what is mine. I know I don't own you, but you're mine in flesh and spirit. I hope you understand. I love you so much."

Carol did understand, putting herself in his place. He was responsible for her, and she was in his home. Yes, she could understand him better every day. Her worry of not having someone to take care of her was over. The thought gave her a feeling of comfort and peace.

They passed Big Eagle returning to the ranch. The two men talked about the hay being ready to bale tomorrow. Big Eagle always listened to Big Bear with great respect. Carol knew Big Eagle to be a man of wisdom from many years of life experience.

Carol went to bed early that night while Big Bear worked at his computer. She wanted time alone to be quiet in her spirit, listening to that voice within her. This added strength to her life, giving direction when she was confused. Carol had never been confused about Big Bear, although it had been her own fear she had to deal with. What would her parents say about her having an Indian boyfriend, and knowing him for only ten days or so? This would kill her dad, as he still considered her his little girl. He would try and talk her out of coming back to Montana, but she knew in her heart she had to come back. Carol wanted to talk to her spirit about these things, so she went to bed early, quietly listening to her spirit, who counseled: "If something is accomplished in life, there is always something to overcome. If love is strong enough, your desire is strong enough, you will overcome all obstacles, regardless of the form they come in. This desire to come to Montana comes from your spirit, your love for Indian children. After you go to the mountaintop with Big Bear, you will understand your purpose, then things will be easier."

Carol knew in her heart she was ready to go to the mountain with Big Bear. Closing her eyes, she fell into a peaceful sleep. At daylight, she was ready to get out of bed to see the beauty of the land and sky at sunrise. She made coffee then sat on the deck, surveying the fields. After sipping a cup of coffee, Carol entered the kitchen to make French toast with peanut butter and honey. She was having a second cup of coffee when Big Bear came in, saying, "You must have slept well; you're up early."

"Yes, I slept well, thinking what a beautiful life this is. All things work for the good of those who wait upon the spirit. We have French toast for breakfast with peanut butter and honey. Are you hungry?" she asked smiling at him.

Big Bear hugged her, kissing her neck and said, "I missed you last night, our hugging and holding each other. We have only a few more days. We have a lot of catching up to do," kissing her again. "I never get enough of you," he added, smiling, showing his perfect teeth.

"I had to have a little time alone, listening to my spirit last night. I have been busy, and I have neglected the most important part of myself. I missed you, too," she said, kissing his lips and hugging him in return.

"Today we'll ride the ranch. It will take about four hours or more, so eat a good breakfast and take some water. We will leave as soon as Big Eagle comes over. Is Songbird coming over today?" he inquired.

"I guess so; she said nothing to me. She was gone when we returned home," Carol replied, wishing she knew Songbird's thoughts about her job. Songbird and Big Eagle came in as Carol and Big Bear were finishing their French toast. They all talked about the day ahead over coffee.

"Big Bear and Little Dove have good ride, Songbird cook, clean. Keep Little Dove away from Billy Joe," she teased, laughing at her own joke.

"Oh, we don't need to touch on that subject this morning," Big Bear answered Songbird. Carol excused herself, going to the bathroom, and coming out with her camera, ready to shoot. "I'm ready to go. It's all yours, Songbird; take care," she said, wanting to go as the light was just right for photographing the big sky.

"I better go. She's pushing this morning," Big Bear said, laughing, reaching for his hat. "Make sure that hay is dry enough before they start baling," he reminded Big Eagle.

They walked hand in hand going to the horse corral, catching Quickfire and Babe. Big Bear slipped the bridle over each horse's head. Carol held them as Big Bear put the saddle blanket on, then the saddle, pulling down the girth, making sure the saddles were secure. Big Bear held Babe as Carol mounted her. Carol took the bridle, her camera around her neck.

They rode first through the hayfield, passing the hay crew, who watched them until they were out of sight. Big Bear opened the gate to the cow pasture. Some of the cows stood watching the two riders, who stayed close to the fence. Big Bear led them slowly through the cow pasture, allowing Carol to stop and take pictures. Then came the pasture with the magnificent Appaloosa horses, splendid in form, Carol thought as she clicked her camera. Babe lifted her head, letting out a neigh at the horses. "If you don't run, they will stay calm," he told her, staying close to the fence and keeping a steady pace.

The vast fields of wheat and barley and oats were amber waves of grain with the purple mountains' majesty in the background, as they towered over the land God had made, then giving it to man as a gift of love, Carol thought as she snapped photos, taking in the beauty before her eyes.

"How many acres are here?" Carol asked, looking over the rolling land.

"In this field, two thousand acres. It's a good ranch. I've put a lot of money and work into this land. It has been my life for twenty years. This is changing; you are my life now," he said, sliding off his horse without using the stirrup.

Carol dismounted her horse, looking around. She had never seen so much land; it was apparently unlimited, like its caretaker, boundless in his love for this land and people.

As Carol cast her gaze across the golden fields, in her spirit, she could see the buffalo roaming the land of the free, Big Bear in his Native American clothes, riding his beautiful Appaloosa horse across the plains: free, free, his spirit was free. She was a part of the land, too, and she was free. Carol's eyes filled with tears as she thought of the Indian people. Her love for them ran so deeply. She couldn't understand this love; only God could have put this love in her heart.

Big Bear watched her reactions, knowing what was happening in her spirit. He touched her and they both were riding their horses across the great plains with hearts that were free: free to love and live as they chose in Mother Earth, with all her blessings.

They rode with the wind in their faces, approaching a chief sitting straight on the back of his black horse, standing in the tall, grassy plains of Montana. In spirit, he waited for his encounters. Big Bear lowered Carol to the grass, laying her back easily, holding her hand.

The chief sat straight as an arrow upon his horse, his face of the wisdom of the ages, with skin like bronze shining in the sunlight, hard, honest eyes. His Indian chief headdress, made of eagle feathers, nearly touched the ground. Carol watched him dismount, taking the blanket off of his horse and placing it on the ground. Then he motioned Carol and Big Bear to sit. They sat face to face, and he open his mouth to speak: "My name is White Eagle. I always was, am, and will always be. I come from the Tribal Council in the spirit. I come in this hour of need, when the buffalo grass is green and the moon is hidden, telling Little Dove things to come. Keep things in her heart, teach others that they may know and believe what was, is, and will be to come.

"First, your winters will become colder, but those wrapped in the warmth of their heart will know all things work for good of all creation. Never judge anything by sight. For this world is illusion of mind; that which is perfect, is created out of spirit. You will find joy of heart unknown to man, spring buds in Mother Earth. she shall come with new life, blooming forth in life of new creation. A new life cycle will start all over, great changes come in spirit and Mother Earth.

"Old ways will pass with old heart of greed and hate. Every man will live in fullest of love. Mother Earth will renew herself with beautiful gardens. My people will return, living on their land in peace, in their customs and culture as free people. The time of the eagle and hawk be full, the circle of life be to all life. Filling circle of knowledge, man will give life to all. Man will understand himself, as all creative life. Creative love will flow from heart of man.

"Little one, listen to Great Spirit of life, write words upon your hearts, so your hearts will be pure. Every man will know his tribe and will go back to his life before time or space, when all were one energy moving in the sky of spirit, forming clouds of water.

"We came to dust the earth with stardust, crowning her with our respect, a woman of beauty, with so much to give. We found comfort in her, hollowing out our hands to hold her magical beauty. Loving her streams, brooks and rivers, we played in her waters, ate of her bounty. We climbed her mountains, swam her lakes, loving every delight she gave freely.

"Now as the snow geese know when to return, my people will return to our land, land of promise to our people. The earth people will return, helping all who desire to live again in the land of beauty and plenty.

"My people need to know what is coming, being prepared in their hearts for a terrible time of trouble. Their hearts must be pure, for this time is time of buffalo and mourning dove. You will go into new creation with pure heart.

"Our land, once again, will be sacred, for the old ones spoke of the day when Mother Earth will cleanse herself, every man inheriting his land.

"The twelve tribes of earth will return to land of beginning, each knowing his own. All Native Americans will return to their land, becoming one giant tree with many branches."

Carol wept. Her heart breaking, she held Big Bear's hand. She continued to listen to White Eagle, "Fear keeps one from greatest, there is no room for fear in Little Dove's heart, only love will take place of fear. Trust love in heart and believe in its greatness. You will feel pain of Mother Earth as she gives birth. People endure pain and sorrow, because of hard hearts. They refuse to change hearts of anger and hate." Carol knew these words White Eagle spoke were true. They touched her heart in deep sorrow, and her spirit grieved.

"Many will leave cities and crowded areas for solitude of earth, few find that solitude in soul, return to old ways. Those of Indian heritage will love Mother Earth, will stand in that day. They will live by spirit.

"The great eagles soaring over this land will call all people to this day. So will Little Dove's voice be heard for my people. the Great Spirit and White Eagle stand with Little Dove; her voice will be heard in spirit world of Indian nations.

"As the flowers of prairie know seasons, you shall know season of change. The birds know when to nest, the buffalo when to calve; change of man's heart will come.

"Little one, have no fear, I will guide you on life path of light you are to walk.

"You will find signs of old, telling of this day. My people will know truth of this day. I will be with you on the mountaintop."

Carol watched through her tears while White Eagle mounted his horse and rode off across the plains, leaving Big Bear and Little Dove in the wheat fields. The sun was low in the sky. Carol opened her eyes to see the sky turning pink. She lay in Big Bear's arms, pondering White Eagle's words in her heart. How many would return to earth to help those with pure hearts in the change that was coming?

Carol sat up, holding on to Big Bear. Had he, too, received the words of White Eagle? Big Bear hugged her. when she could bring herself to speak, she asked, "Did you hear White Eagle's words?"

"I only sat on the blanket with you. He came to your spirit, leaving the message with you. You are the one he came to have this encounter with. If you are ready, we should be getting back; it's going to be dark soon," he said, helping her to her feet.

The sun hid its face behind the trees, leaving the rest of the day in darkness. At a steady trot, they headed for the barn.

Turning on the lights under the barn, Big Bear unsaddled the horses. It was not unusual for Big Bear to have spiritual encounters, but this was her first experience, knowing her spirit was there with White Eagle's spirit. Big Bear and Carol walked hand in hand to the ranch house. Big Bear kept quiet about what had happened out in the wheat field.

Coming in the door of the house, Carol asked, "Don't you want to know what White Eagle had to say?"

"I know you will tell me when you are ready. These words take time to absorb into your conscious mind where meaning is given. Sometimes, there is no meaning at first; we have to take the words just the way they are said. You must write down what White Eagle said," he told her, kissing her lips.

"Big Bear and Little Dove have long ride, food is cold; Songbird will warm up," she said, turning on the stove.

Big Eagle sat reading papers at the table. "All of the hay is cut and two thousand bales in the barn," he announced. "We'll have another two days' work. I hope the weather holds."

Big Bear sat down at the table, listening to Big Eagle. "Can you finish without me?" he asked. "I'm taking Carol to the mountain in the morning. We're taking Babe; we'll be back Sunday," he said, wanting to know if all was under control.

"That is no problem. We have plenty of help and everything is going good. Go do what spirit wants," he reassured Big Bear.

Songbird placed beans, rice and green salad with Indian corn bread on the table in the pots. "Songbird knows one went on spiritual journey. Which one?"

Big Bear was reluctant to answer; he didn't like speaking for someone else. "Carol went into the Indian spirit world, meeting White Eagle from the Tribal Council in the spirit; this is all I know. He spoke only with her.

Carol entered the room while they were eating and talking. She walked over to the counter, pouring herself a cup of coffee.

"Carol, come eat supper, you get used to Indian spirit world," Songbird told her.

"I don't know about that. This is so strange, talking to spirits, having them tell you things. I have to write down what White Eagle told me," Carol said. They understood.

"Can you tell us some of what White Eagle said?" Big Bear asked her, encouraging her to share what she could about her experience.

"Sure." Carol started off telling them what White Eagle had told her; she could hear him again in her spirit. His voice in the wind carried across the plains, placing his vibrations in every awaking heart. She could see his face in the moon as it passed over the great mountains. She was again swept away with him. On her return to space and time, she finished, telling all the things White Eagle had said to her.

They were speechless, with glowing faces, tears streaming down their faces. Carol buried her face in her hands. She felt so unworthy to be honored by the presence of White Eagle, to hear his great love for his people. Wiping tears away, she slowly drank her coffee. The others pushed their plates away. Carol rose, saying, "If you will excuse me, I'm going to bed."

White Eagle's presence was with her and she wanted to be alone. She took a shower, washed her hair, then sat on the bed, blow drying her hair. She could see White Eagle standing in the corner of the room. He told her: "Little Dove, don't be afraid to share my words, for they are truth and life. Truth will stand. These are your friends. They have always been with you, always will. They love you and care for you. Tomorrow, when you go to the mountain, I will be there. Now, my little one, I give you rest." Then he was gone.

She was sleeping when Big Bear came into her room. He sat on the side of the bed, then he gathered her up in his arms, kissing her forehead and stroking her hair. He slept in his clothes, holding her all night in his arms.

Big Bear was up early, backing up the pickup, hooking up the horse trailer. Carol crawled out of bed, pulling on her jeans, denim shirt and boots. She brushed her long blonde hair, pulling it back in a braid. Big Bear had asked her to bring one change of clothes and the Indian wedding dress. She asked no questions, doing what she was told. When she came out into the kitchen, Songbird had coffee with whole-wheat pancakes and honey for her. They ate, packed mixed dried fruits and nuts for the trip. "No camera," Big Bear had said. "This is sacred ground, we're going to."

The sun was peeking over the barn as they left the ranch road, entering the main highway, 90. They headed west toward Bozeman, with country music playing on the radio. Carol moved over next to him. Taking her hand, he held it to his lips. "How long is this trip?" she asked.

"Three to three and a half hours' drive, cutting off the other side of Bozeman, heading for the mountains. It's sightseeing country; the scenery is fantastic," he said, smiling with a light in his eyes.

They were now leaving Highway 90, heading toward the scenic mountains. Climbing slowly on a gravel road until the grade leveled off, they turned off, coming upon a small lake, with a tepee sitting by the shore of the lake, a canoe turned upside down next to the tepee.

Big Bear pulled the truck up near the tepee, turning his pickup around so it would be facing out. He unloaded Babe, staking her out in the grass. He began unloading the supplies. Carol was standing and looking at what was a marvelous photographer's view. The picturesque lake glittered as the sun's rays danced on top of the blue water; behind were green-covered mountains.

What an enchanting place, a mysterious place, Carol thought. Maybe this is the place where Big Bear came to gather the strength required to live his disciplined life. Placing their supplies in the tepee, Big Bear looked at Carol, asking, "What do you think?"

"I don't know what to think. It's enchanting, so peaceful. How far are we from anyone?" she asked, seeing no neighbors coming up the mountain.

"There are others living up in the mountains; only a few find their way up here to be alone. Some are Indians," he said.

The tepee was large enough inside to hold a full-sized air mattress, with blankets, a large ice chest holding camping needs and a card table with two folding chairs. Big Bear watched for Carol's reaction. "All you need to camp for a week. Do you like camping?" he asked.

"I guess so. I haven't done much camping, but I guess I could get used to it."

"What is the real reason why we are here?" she asked, noticing his eyes dancing as if in another world. "I know something is going on."

"You're cunning, sweetheart, even knowing," he said, kissing her on her lips.

"We were directed here by spirits telling me to bring you here. You are the first to come here to the burial ground. We are here for the spiritual quest of our lives. We will stay here tonight; but in the morning, we will go up the mountain and wait upon them."

"What do you mean 'them'? Are you expecting someone else to come?" she asked, wanting to know whom to expect.

"Those who called us here will join us. Just be patient and you shall see, then you will know," he assured her, smiling at her.

"Big Bear, I know you come here for spiritual strength," she stated.

"Yes, about ten years ago, I came out of a relationship that I thought was going to result in marriage; then it fell apart. That turned out to be good for me, because it caused me to seek my spiritual life and my purpose in Mother Earth. That's when I found and bought this property, the best investment I've ever made; you'll see. Also, this is where I found out who I am in the spirit, knowing who you were in my life. As the legend goes, this is where Big Bear, the Crow warrior, brought Little Dove's and Black Kettle's bodies for burial. Big Bear stayed the winter here until Little Dove's spirit returned to him. This is sacred ground to us. Would you like to take a canoe ride on the lake?" he asked, blinking back the tears.

"Yes, that sounds good. This is something else. What other surprises do you have?" she asked, winking at him.

"Just wait and see; I have one more, but that will have to wait until you return from St. Louis. Come on, jump into the canoe," he said, pushing it into the water.

The water was smooth as they glided across with the wind in their back. Silently, Big Bear moved the paddle in the water, quietly moving with the rhythm of life. Carol relaxed, playing in the water and thinking What a wonderful way to spend one's life. Then she thought of what White Eagle had said, that he would be with her on the mountaintop, and thoughts about what Big Bear had said about coming close to marriage. That was the girl in the picture she had seen at the ranch house. Carol thought, I'm glad it fell apart. Then the most provoking thought she considered was the legend about this land where Big Bear's burial of Little Dove and Black Kettle took place. Little Dove's peace remained here and Carol could feel it. Big Bear had started his spiritual journey about the time she had started hers. Looking across the lake, she was no longer alone on this journey.

The night air was cool. They sat around the campfire sipping coffee, eating dried fruit and nuts. Carol looked at Big Bear thinking, He is the strongest man I know. Not even her father could match him. They silently took in their surroundings, enjoying every moment.

"Are you cold?" Big Bear asked Carol. "I can get you a blanket."

"Yes, please." The night was turning cold after the sun went down.

They retired early, going in the tepee and lying on the air mattress. Taking off their boots, they slept in their clothes. "I would like for you to wear your wedding dress and moccasins when we go up the mountain in the morning," he told her.

"Okay, if you want me to," she agreed, turning over, facing him. They hugged together, pulling the blanket up on them.

Morning's soft colors brought light into the tepee. Big Bear was up making coffee over the fire. Carol went to the lake, slipped out of her clothes, and waded into the water, washing her body and brushing her teeth. Big Bear stood shocked at this city girl standing nude, out in the middle of nowhere, just nature and her. The water felt cold at first to Carol, then she overcame the idea that it was cold water and enjoyed how refreshing it was. Big Bear came with a blanket and a cup of coffee, leading her back to the fire. Her wet hair was hanging about her face, her blue eyes blazing, staring at him. He put his arms around her, kissing her tenderly.

"We better prepare to go, the sun is getting high; the day will soon be half over," he said, helping her into the tepee.

Carol let the blanket slip from her body, as he left the tepee. The thought that one day they would run out of places to go, flashed pleasant thoughts across her mind. Then, with only her panties on, she pulled the doeskin dress over her head, combing her hair into a braid, placing the handmade moccasins on her feet.

Big Bear had his Native American clothes on and was ready to go. He took blankets, food, and water, laying the supplies across Babe's back in front of him. He held out his foot for Carol; placing her foot on his, she was able to mount Babe with his help. They began following a trail up the mountain. Looking back, Carol could see the tepee as they climbed. Astride surefooted Babe, Carol pushed her body into Big Bear with her arms locked around him. The scenery was breathtaking as she viewed the mountains and the valley. They continued climbing, never getting off the trail.

Carol felt as though the trail was familiar, almost as if she had been there before. As the sun was standing straight up in the sky, they reached the top of the mountain. Sliding down off Babe's back, Carol looked around, being able to see for miles. She could see the lake and the small tepee below. Her attention was drawn to the area where they were, and her eyes settled on a rock circle that looked as though someone had been building fires there.

Big Bear placed a blanket on the ground, then placed the food and water on the blanket. Then he began gathering wood, wasting no time, as he knew his job well. Carol sat on the blanket, watching him pile up wood next to the rock circle. She couldn't understand what he was doing, although he knew.

Big Bear started the fire, then used his voice to chant, the old Indian way of calling spirits to visit. He placed his whole being into the spirit world, as though he were in a trance, waiting for something to happen. Cold air came with nightfall. Carol rolled up in the blanket, as Big Bear kept the fire going all night.

Morning found Big Bear still working the fire, chanting to the spirits of old. Carol walked around the top of the mountain thinking, This will be a long day, but time passed faster than she anticipated. When night fell on the second day of their quest on the mountain, winds began to blow and lightning streaked across the sky, although there were no clouds in the clear Montana sky. Carol placed two blankets over herself; she didn't want her wedding dress to get wet. Gusting winds blew around them, but Carol felt no danger and soon she fell sleep.

She awakened to see lights. Big Bear was sitting at the farthest end of a blanket. There were two light beings sitting to each side of the blanket. White Eagle, in tangible form, was sitting in the middle of the blanket with a long peace pipe. The sacred pipe had five eagle feathers hanging to the side of it, and Big Bear was smoking the peace pipe. Carol unwrapped herself, moving quickly to the blanket just as White Eagle handed her the sacred pipe to smoke.

White Eagle held his attention on Big Bear, saying, "Why Big Bear summon White Eagle? Many moons have passed since Big Bear come to mountains to cry out for help in spiritual path of life. The Mother Earth has changed many seasons since Sand Creek Massacre, and Big Bear still carry anger in heart. Love cannot grow where anger is. Big Bear must let anger go and love all people, for all is Great Spirit's creation. Cannot hold past in present. Big Bear have heart to help Indian people, but must let go of anger first."

Carol held her face in her hands, weeping as she felt Big Bear's pain bottled up inside him, that he had carried for years for his people. He still blamed the white man for what had happened to his people.

White Eagle was saying, "It is the time for healing of all nations put on Mother Earth, time to study war no more, to live in peace and harmony. Come to edge of mountain overlooking valley, I will show you something."

White Eagle walked between Carol and Big Bear, moving to the edge of the mountain. They looked over the edge; there they saw a busy city of people going their way. Some were sick; others were heartsick, and some were dying. Drugs and sadness were destroying the lives of the people, who were striving to stay ahead of the rising cost of living, caught in a web, unable to find themselves. Then White Eagle pointed to a shining river flowing in the midst of all the troubles and heartaches. The water was crystal clear, shining as if diamonds were dancing on top of it. Some were trying to reach this river; some were in the water, but few were reaching the other side, where others were waiting for them. Those on the other side were coming down to the riverbank, helping others to cross over this river. Then White Eagle pointed to the place across the river, where they could see a garden held in perfect harmony, filled with happy people, with no sickness or death. Pain and sorrow had passed away; love ruled in this place, with Native Americans living in their land again. Big Bear and Little Dove bowed their heads to see such a place. How were they going to pass over to this paradise?

White Eagle spoke: "This river is the river of life, the pure love of Great Spirit, love to all mankind. I come to help Big Bear and Little Dove to immerse themselves in the waters of life. Keep yourselves in the river until ready to come up on other side, when ready to cross over to land of joy and peace, remembering nothing but love. You will enter consciousness of love, creating a life of love. Know love fulfills all desires.

"You go where there is no want. I, White Eagle, of the Brotherhood of Light, join Big Bear and Little Dove together for their purpose in life, creating life by giving life, teaching all Great Spirit give to them. 'No greater love hath any man, than he lay down his life for another.' Your conscious mind will never go back down; be nothing but love. You will help bring great changes in Mother Earth. We of spirit join forces with Big Bear and Little Dove to help them walk this path of light. He took their hands, joining them together. His departure was as sudden as his appearance, light beings following him. The peace pipe glowed, lying on the blanket.

Carol knelt on her knees, weeping with a broken heart for the people. Big Bear let out all his anguish and pain with a piercing yell to Mother Earth. He released all the anger held for generations in his people. He knelt with his hands in the air, reaching toward all the spirits that had passed on, held in this anger. He released them as he released himself from hatred. He finished, crying out to the spirits, then he comforted Carol, gathering her up in his arms. They stayed that way until the dawning light of morning. Then, wrapping the sacred peace pipe in a blanket, they mounted Babe and started down the mountain.

Carol didn't remember much of the view or ride coming down the mountain. At the base of the mountain, Big Bear removed the blankets from Babe's back, feeding her. Then he placed the sacred pipe in the truck. They spread a blanket next to the lake, Big Bear sat with Carol, tenderly removed her doeskin dress, then removed his clothes. They walked hand in hand into the lake, wanting to enjoy this time together. He held her, kissing her lips. After swimming in the cool water, they lay on the blanket, knowing each other in the fullness of manhood, and she received him with all her hunger. Later, in the water, they swam to the middle of the lake, racing back. He raced ahead of her, laughing good-naturedly at her trying to keep pace. They spent the remainder of the day knowing each other in the fullness of love. Night came soon. The night was spent under the stars, rolling up in blankets and in each other's arms, loving the night away.

Coffee was boiling as the morning light shone in Carol's eyes. She pulled the blanket over her head, not wanting the day to end.

Today was Sunday, which meant traveling back to another world. Why can't we stay just another night? she wondered.

Wrapped in a blanket, Carol sat gazing across the lake. Bringing coffee, Big Bear sat beside her. "Thank you," she said, smiling sweetly at him. "I feel like a new person, or born of a new world. Maybe the world out there is the same, but I have changed," she said, continuing to look at the lake.

"I feel complete. I know I've been lacking something for a long time, but now I'm complete in my spirit, mind and body. I feel as though my life's circle is complete finally and I want to help others find this completeness."

"We have to go; I hate to, but we must," he said, kissing her neck.

Taking one more breath of the air of the place where she had found her place, Carol raised herself slowly, packing up their belongings. Babe was loaded into the horse trailer. They went down the mountain, sitting close to one another, Carol loving Big Bear's beautiful spirit. He sang tender love songs to her. She would join in when she knew the song. They went down the road with their horse, singing country love songs.

The ranch was busy with people when they arrived, including Two Feathers' family and Walking Elk. They were glad to see one another. "Come, tell Walking Elk all about mountaintop. Did spirits come visit Little Dove?" Walking Elk was full of questions for Carol.

Carol left these questions to Big Bear to answer as he unloaded Babe from the horse trailer. "Please, Mom, don't bother Carol; I'll tell you about it." He then carefully removed the sacred peace pipe, wrapped in a blanket, from the truck.

Walking Elk just smiled at Carol, hungry for spiritual food. "Wait until we are all around the table, then I will tell everyone at one time. Then if you have questions, they can be answered," she promised.

They walked together to the ranch house for lunch. Carol was ready for some home cooking after three days of eating dried fruits and nuts. Yellow Bird had prepared food, so they added salad, Indian beans and rice with corn bread and drink.

Everyone looked at Big Bear, expecting something out of him, but Carol opened the conversation by saying, "This experience has opened up a whole new world to me. I heard the spirit world existed, but I never dreamed I would be part of it. This meeting with White Eagle has given me something above everyday life. I have Big Bear to thank and all of the wonderful Indian people for making this experience possible. I will let Big Bear tell you of our adventure in the spirit."

Big Bear started telling how they went up to the mountaintop the day after they arrived on the mountain. "The second night, the wind began to blow, lightning lit up the whole sky, but not a drop of rain came down. Little Dove was sleeping on the blanket when they came: four light beings. You could see light only in the place where they sat. Then there was White Eagle, sitting in the middle of the blanket, holding a peace pipe of old, with five eagle feathers hanging from the side of the pipe. Little Dove smoked the sacred pipe. Then he addressed me, concerning the anger in my heart and in all Indian peoples' heart. Past bitterness and anger has to go, so spirits held in this realm can be released." Big Bear stopped to wipe the tears from his eyes, and the others wiped their eyes.

"Then White Eagle asked us to walk with him to the edge of the cliff overlooking Mother Earth. He showed us people living in cities, trying to get their lives on an even path of life, despite all the heartaches, sickness, and death, with so many violent acts. Some people were being pushed to the river of life.

"White Eagle showed us the shining river of life, a pure river of the Great Spirit's love for all people, flowing down into the earth for all to immerse themselves into, giving life to themselves and all the world. It was a wonderful sight to see the sparkling river of life. White Eagle said he had come to help Little Dove and me to cross over this river of life, to the other side, where we would find perfect love, peace and our conscious mind would hold nothing but love, for ourselves and all creation. He said we will help others to cross over to the other side. He joined Little Dove's and my life together for this purpose in earth, helping every child we can to understand spiritual truths."

He looked at Carol, waiting for her reactions. Carol felt so unworthy, as she had felt on the mountaintop. Big Bear had spoken the words of White Eagle so plainly and truthfully. Feeling she had little to add, she said, "The words will speak for themselves; we are to help those trying to cross the river of life into a conscious mind of love."

Big Bear removed the sacred peace pipe from the wrapping of the blanket for all of them to see. All present, except Walking Elk, were spellbound, speechless. She said, "Walking Elk been to shining river, looking to other side, wishing to cross over. Now Big Bear and Little Dove show Walking Elk how to cross over, so she can walk in spirits of peace and love, wait for day all will be love, and old hates, bitterness will pass away. Walking Elk look for brighter day for all creations. When does Little Dove return from big city?"

"Just soon as I can. I don't want to go, but I must put that behind me. Parents are hard pulls on your spirit and life, so I must go through this; it's part of my crossing over," she said, looking at Big Bear, hoping he understood.

Big Bear understood more than Carol knew, keeping all quiet inside of his spirit. He was waiting for the day when she would return to be wholly his.

In the middle of the afternoon the company said good-bye, kissing Carol and wishing her a safe trip, hoping for her to return soon. Big Bear and Carol settled down to arrange their lives for Monday. She had clothes to clean, a suitcase to pack. Schoolwork was on Big Bear's mind.

They went to bed early, closing out a day of great impact on their lives. Carol and Big Bear held each other tightly, thankful for the night they had together.

Morning light came too early as Big Bear made coffee, waiting for Carol to have coffee with him before leaving for Billings. Carol came out in her jeans and T-shirt, sitting at the table, looking at him. How could she leave? she thought. She smiled at him, asking, "Will you call me every day?"

"No, I'll call twice a day; in the morning before I go to school, and at night when I come home. You're the first thing I will think about in the morning and the last thing at night. Please drive carefully, and don't be on the road at night. I know the spirit of White Eagle is with you. Heaven is at your call. I'm at your call, too; so if you need me, please call," he said, kissing her, and hanging on to her. "Just hug me one more time, then I have to go." They embraced with their hearts melting together forever.

Carol watched from the kitchen window as he pulled out of the yard. Tears flowed down her cheek. Her heart was breaking. She went back to bed, lying there and thinking, I have to get up, get things together and into my truck. Songbird was in the kitchen, cleaning, making noise. At 8:00 a.m. Carol had put off leaving as long as she could. She walked out of the bedroom carrying her luggage and camera case.

She set down her camera case and luggage, casting a longing eye around the room, picturing everything in her mind. Songbird watched her without a word, until Carol's tears started.

"Little Dove hate leaving Big Bear. Big Bear hate seeing Little Dove leave. Why don't Little Dove stay another day? Have plenty of time before September."

"This leaving will get no easier, Songbird. If I have to go, I have to go, whether today or tomorrow," she said, brushing the tears away.

The phone rang. Songbird picked up the receiver, "Hello, Songbird speaking. Yes, she right here," she said, handing the phone to Carol.

"Hello. Hi, no, I'm trying to leave now, but it's so hard. I can't bring myself to walk out the door. If I stay another day, I have to face it again in the morning. You will be home tonight, but not tomorrow night. It will be easier on you tomorrow night. Well, okay, I'll stay tonight, then tomorrow I have to go. I love you," she said, handing the phone back to Songbird, who took Big Bear's instructions, then hung up the phone.

Carol carried her luggage and camera back to the bedroom, thinking, I'll work on the article, then I'll take pictures of the front of the ranch, some of Babe. She kept herself busy so time would pass faster. Songbird was busy cleaning the house and doing laundry. They stopped around noon to have some salad and tea.

"Songbird glad Little Dove stay another night with Big Bear; he be lonesome when she gone. Will be happy when Little Dove come back to stay," she said smiling at Carol.

Taking her camera, Carol went out to the corral, calling Babe. Carol rubbed Babe's neck, then backed away to get a wide-angle exposure of Babe's beauty. Walking to the front of the house, Carol took pictures of the place where she would live, pictures to show her parents the ranch life of Montana. After finishing up the roll of film, she went in the house, looking at the clock: 3:30 p.m. Big Bear would be home around five. She would cook some vegetables and potato pancakes. Songbird had left for the day, knowing Big Bear and Little Dove wanted to be alone.

Everything was ready when he opened the door searching for her. "Come here, woman, give me a hug. I could barely get through this day for thinking about you. What will it be like when you go?"

Coming out of the hallway, Carol went straight into his arms, saying, "We both will be lost until this is past." She hugged him tight. Putting her arms around his waist and leading him to his chair, she said, "We have food; I hope you're hungry."

"Not now, all I want is to hold you. You sure you have to go? Okay, I'm pushing," he said, reaching for her hand. "You know, we could have a moving company take care of this moving for you, and have bank accounts closed by the bank here," he suggested, kissing her hand.

"In the morning, you will follow me into Billings. We will have breakfast there before you have to leave; maybe, it will be easier, if there is an easy way," he said, kissing her lips as she was trying to get dinner on the table.

After dinner he turned on the music; he danced with her, whispering love in her ear. Where did the time go? They lay in one another's arms, loving just to hear their hearts beating as one.

The morning shower was taken together, they dressed and were soon on their way to Billings, before the rest of the ranch hands started their day.

Breakfast was quiet. They gazed deep into one another's eyes, returning to where they had just met two weeks ago. A lifetime had seemed to pass. Here they were, lingering, knowing the depths of their souls. Carol wanted to dance; strange, thinking of dancing at 6:30 a.m. She smiled, thinking she had met the best dancer in the West.

Big Bear watched her with amusement, smiled and asked, "What is funny? Tell me."

"It's not funny; I'm just loving everything about you," she said, smiling back at him.

Big Bear reached in his pocket, pulling out a jewelry box and handing it to Carol. Carol reluctantly took the box asking, "What is this?"

"Open the box and find out, Carol. I want you to marry me. I don't think I will ever know you better than now." He was pleading with his eyes.

Carol opened the box in wonder, looking at the elegance of the diamond set in gold. She was caught off guard, never expecting a ring. "It's breathtaking, Big Bear. Why now? I'm leaving. I can't accept it; it's too much too soon. Let's wait until I return from St. Louis. Please try and understand I'm not saying no, just wait."

The rest of the time at breakfast was quiet; Carol could see she had hurt his pride by asking him to wait. He put up no argument, just yearning to understand. They got through breakfast, walked outside the restaurant, and watched the morning traffic.

"Seems everybody has somewhere to go," Big Bear said, taking her in his arms, kissing her lips. "I'll see you in about two weeks," he said, leaving her to walk to his truck.

She stood alone, watching his white Ford truck pull out into the main stream of traffic. Big Bear never looked back. Carol wiped the tears away and climbed into her Toyota truck, heading out on Highway 90.

CHAPTER FOUR

Home in St. Louis

The tears continued to come as Carol listened to the country music on the radio. Then she dried her eyes, thinking tomorrow was another day, and she would be in Denver, Colorado. She was intent on getting home, stopping only to gas up the truck and eat.

The sun was low in the sky with colors changing the sky to evening. Outside of Denver, Carol found a motel for the night. She ate dinner at the motel restaurant, thinking about Big Bear staying at the reservation for the night after teaching the adult class on agriculture.

Early morning Wednesday, Carol was through Denver before morning work traffic. She was now traveling east on Highway 70 heading to Kansas City, Kansas, with the truck radio playing country music.

Close to Kansas City, Missouri, Carol pulled into a gas station, deciding to call her mother, to let her know she was coming home.

"Hello, Mom. How is everybody? I'm in Kansas City; I hope to be home by dark," Carol said, waiting for her mother's questions.

"It's good to hear from you, Carol. I thought you were going to call before leaving Billings. Your dad called the Best Western Motel there, and they said you weren't staying there. Where have you been staying?"

"I'll tell you when I get home, Mom," she said trying to get out of answering more questions.

Hanging up as soon as possible, she took her sandwich and drink with her, driving on the ramp heading east on I-70, thinking, What made Dad call trying to find me? He had never done something like that before. With country music playing on the radio, Carol also wondered what Big Bear was doing. Maybe he was going home from school, riding the ranch and looking over the fields of grain and cattle. She would surprise him by calling tonight. Just thinking about hearing his voice made her feel good.

Darkness was approaching and the street lights were on as Carol pulled her dusty truck into the drive of the old two-story house in St. Louis. Her mother turned on the porch lights; she came out on the porch as Carol was getting out of the truck. Her mother said, "Well, it's time you returned. We have missed you and hoped you would call before leaving Montana. You're home now; that's all that matters. Let me help you with your luggage," she insisted, coming down the steps toward the truck.

Carol handed her the carrying case, saying, "I know, Mom; I should have called, but I was staying at a ranch with some Native Americans; well, time slipped by," she said, hoping that would satisfy her mother.

"Well, we knew you were staying somewhere else, after you called talking with Tony. Your father called the Best Western and discovered you weren't there. Whose ranch were you staying at?"

Carol thought, Oh, Lord, here come the questions. "I was staying at Big Bear's ranch, a Native American of the Crow tribe," she said, putting her camera over her shoulder.

Carol passed her mother, going on up the stairs with camera and luggage. Her room was just as she left it, with clothes on the bed. Carol put her camera and suitcase down. Her mother was right behind her, saying, "Just the way you left it. Tony is staying in his old bedroom; he and Sue Ann haven't worked out their problems yet. She is always calling here for him to give her money. So he went to a lawyer to draw up legal papers for separation. I don't think they will be getting back together."

"Mom, is Tony seeing somebody else?" Carol asked, watching

her mother's reaction. "No, I don't think so, not at night at least. He comes home, eats his dinner, goes to bed," she admitted, sadness in her tone.

"Mom, don't worry; things will work out. They always do. Now I want to take a shower, fix my hair, and get clothes down to the laundry room," she said, hoping her mother would leave.

Carol began thinking of what she had to do in the next few days. How was she going to tell her mother about cleaning out all of her stuff stored in the basement? When she finished her shower, she blow-dried her hair, slipping into a jogging suit. She gathered up soiled clothes, heading for the basement, hating to face those things of the past, but she had to. After placing clothes in the washer, she turned her mind to boxes of the past, dishes given as wedding presents, silverware, many other household items. What should she do, just leave this for Mom to sell or give away? Opening a box labeled PICTURES, Carol had no tears or regrets, only a job to get done. Carol could see the spirit of Walking Elk standing next to the wall. Carol looked, then turning her head, she thought, This can't be happening; I'm seeing things.

"Little Dove not seeing things, Walking Elk here to strengthen Little Dove, help face family. I will be with Little Dove until free, her spirit back with Big Bear, back with Indian people."

Carol knew Walking Elk was talking to her spirit. Carol could feel Walking Elk's strength. Carol thanked Walking Elk for coming to help her during this difficult time. Carol decided to talk with her mom about the stuff in the basement. If she wanted it, she could have it; if not, Carol would call one of those used-furniture places, selling it all at one time. She also decided, while all of the family was together tonight, she would tell them about Big Bear, and that she would be returning to Montana.

Carol could hear her mother coming down the stairs, saying, "What's taking you so long, Carol? I thought we would have time to talk while fixing dinner. I called your father at the office, telling him you are home. He was glad to hear that. He will be home soon."

"Mom, I have been thinking about this stuff of mine packed

back in these boxes. I'm getting rid of it; if you want any of it, your welcome to it. The rest I'm selling; I'm getting rid of it," she announced, watching her mother's face.

"You're getting rid of your fine china and silverware? Carol, what has gotten into you? These are your wedding gifts, gifts from your friends. Some day you will have your own place again, needing these things," she said, almost in tears.

"No, Mom, these things represent the past. I'm moving on. My life is not in these things. Just look through them tomorrow and see if there's anything you want. Let me know," she said, taking her clothes out of the dryer.

"Let's go up and finish dinner before Dad gets home," she said, putting her arm around her mother.

The kitchen was a large eat-in country-style kitchen with all of her mother's country decorations. Carol helped prepare the salad and set the table. The front door opened. Tony peeked around the corner from the living room. "What smells so good? Hi, Sis, when did you get back?"

"Late this afternoon. How are you doing?" she asked, wanting to hear it from him.

"Hanging in there; I've seen better days. How is everything with you?" he asked, looking at her.

"Everything is fine, glad to be home for a few days," she answered, walking over to the sink washing lettuce.

"Do you have another assignment for the magazine?" Carol's mother inquired.

"No, Mom; I'm not going on any more assignments for the magazine," she said truthfully. "We will discuss it after dinner, or I will inform the family of my decision."

"Where is my girl?" came her father's voice from the living room. Carol gave him a big hug, saying, "Good to see you, Dad; I've missed you." The family talked and remembered old times while enjoying Mom's fried chicken, potato salad and apple pie. Dad talked about the insurance business, and recalled that he couldn't contact her at the Best Western Motel.

Carol knew it was time to talk about her plans over apple pie and coffee, if only her mom would be quiet.

"Carol was staying on an Indian's ranch; that's why you couldn't contact her at the motel," she continued the conversation.

Carol's father looked surprised. "Is that right? Whose ranch is this?" he asked.

"The ranch belongs to Jim Nelson; Big Bear is his Indian name. We met at the Best Western Motel." Carol left out the part about the accident. "He invited me to go to the powwow with him and his family, afterward to stay at his ranch for a few days. Through him I got a first-hand look at the powwow and the Indian rodeo, which I enjoyed very much. Jim has a large ranch, plus he teaches school," she added, wondering if they knew what she was leading up to.

"Is he married?" her father asked, getting right to the point.

"No, not yet. We plan to get married as soon as I get back, if I'm ready," she said, seeing the shock in their eyes.

"Go for it, Sis; you're not getting any younger, and you've been waiting a long time to meet the right person," Tony said, backing her up.

"Thank you, Tony; I needed that. I love Big Bear very much and he loves me as much. Our life is planned together; that is how it's going to be," she said firmly, leaving no room for disagreement.

Carol's dad just sat there, saying nothing. Her mother broke the awkward silence. "You haven't known him very long. You really would move to Montana?"

"Mom, you can be with a person five, ten years and never know them. It's how your spirit feels that matters when knowing a person, not your mind. I know Big Bear by his spirit. It's a creative spirit of giving. When you meet him, you will understand and love him and his family," she said, having peace within herself. This was her life; she would live it to the best of her ability.

"Carol, I am confident you know what you are doing. We will stand by your decision, won't we, Mother?" her father said, looking at Carol's mother.

"Yes, of course, whatever makes you happy. That's what we want," she said, supporting her husband.

"Tony, I had to write the article on the powwow for the magazine. Will you please print it out on your computer for me? I have to get it in on September 8th," she said, asking for help.

"When did you take up writing?" Tony asked. "I'll be glad to help."

"I haven't; this was a must for the magazine, although I like the challenge. I'm going to see what happens. I may trade my camera in for a word processor. Come on upstairs, I will show you the article. Mom, I will be right back and help with the dishes," she said, going up the stairs with her brother.

"Your dad and I will put them in the dishwasher," her mother said, wanting to get them out of the room.

"Sis, I'm proud of you for standing up to Mom the way you did," Tony said, sitting on the bed as Carol looked for the article. The telephone rang. Carol put down the papers, picking up the phone, and heard Big Bear's voice. "Is Carol Fletcher there, please? Yes, just a moment," her mother answered.

"I have it, Mom. Hi, how are you? Yes, I made the trip with no problems. I miss you and can't wait to return. I'm going to place my film in the lab tomorrow. My brother, Tony, is going to print out the article for me . . . I know you would have helped me. Everything is going well. I have even had some help from Walking Elk; she is everywhere. I do love her. Call whenever you want to. I love you. I hope to get this finished up soon. Please take care of yourself, bye." Carol hung up the phone, looking at her brother.

"That was him, wasn't it? If you have found happiness, Sis, I'm happy for you. I can see love in your eyes. This must be a special man, considering how many you have turned down," he said, smiling at her.

"Yes, I can't begin to tell you how special he is . . . here is the article. Just print it the way it is; they will edit and format it. Thanks for doing this for me. When my film is developed I will show you pictures of Big Bear; he is so handsome," she said, wishing her brother could also find someone to love.

"Sis, let's you and I go out Saturday night. Then you can tell me all about this man. Who knows? There might be an Indian woman for me. Something sure has happened to you. I would like to be happy, too."

"It's a date, you and I at the First Street Bar and Restaurant Saturday night," she said, handing him the papers and beginning to sort her film.

Thursday morning, Carol was at the lab of the magazine early, putting in her film for development. She then made a stop at the editor's office.

"Come on in, Carol; have a seat. I will be with you in a few seconds," Mrs. Shell directed her. Carol took a seat, waiting for her to get off the phone.

Placing the phone down, the magazine editor looked at Carol, saying, "Good to see you. How was the assignment? And how was your trip? Hope you have some good shots and the copy. Do you have the article written?"

"Yes, the article is written and my brother is printing it for me. I will be able to view the negative sheet Monday. But there is something else I want to talk about. I've decided I'm giving my notice today. I'm not working on another assignment for the magazine," she said bluntly.

"What do you mean? Your quitting the photography business? I hope this assignment wasn't that hard. For heaven's sake, Carol, what is the matter? You're our best traveling photographer. Were these Indians too much for you?" she asked, frustration in her voice.

Carol thought for a moment before answering. "It's nothing like that; I'm strongly considering marrying one of those Indians. His name is Jim Nelson, or Big Bear, his Crow name," she explained, watching for her editor's reaction.

The frustration exploded out of her. She threw the pencil that was in her hand, hitting the wall with it. The Blackfeet Indian pencil bounced off the wall and rolled unbroken on the floor toward Carol. "Marrying an Indian! For God's sake, Carol, what in hell has gotten into you? There are plenty of good men in St. Louis. There's Steve in Advertising, for one. What in hell is wrong?"

"Mary, this is my life; I will live it my way. I'm a freelance photographer. I've been with you for the past two years. I have enjoyed it, but it is time for a change. I will be going back to Montana, probably to marry Big Bear. There are many good photographers out there; you will find someone else. If you will excuse me, I have things I must do," she said, getting up to leave.

"Wait a minute, Carol. I'm sorry for my actions, but it hasn't been the best of days. I'm sorry about my remarks about the Indian people. I'm sure they have their own thing going, but I just can't see you wasting your talent. Please listen to what I'm saying. What do your parents say about this?" she asked, cooling down considerably.

"My parents and my brother are behind me one hundred percent. They want whatever makes me happy. I'll have my article on your desk as soon as the prints are ready. Have a good day," Carol said, ready to leave.

She passed through the offices without noticing anyone. Why hadn't she seen this side of Mary before? Carol was money to her boss and nothing else. The only thing she was interested in was how much she was losing if Carol quit. Well, she felt pity for Mary and the other magazine employees, but they would find another photographer.

The elevator was going down and Carol could hear Walking Elk saying in her spirit, "Good for you, Little Dove; you're getting strong."

"You're right, Walking Elk; I'm getting strong, seeing things for what they are about: money." The mention of money reminded Carol to withdraw her savings and take a cashier's check to a Montana bank. She would have Big Bear, in Montana, help her. Carol went into the bank as thoughts continued through her mind about the change she was making. Carol told the teller she was closing out her savings account. Taking out her identification card, Carol asked for a cashier's check.

The teller retrieved her account file on the computer, saying, "Miss Fletcher, if you withdraw your money now, you will lose interest at the end of this quarter; by leaving it a few more days, you will receive your interest in full."

Carol thought, There is that money question again. She said, "I want to close the account today."

"Whatever you want, Miss Fletcher," the teller said. "It will take a few minutes to get you a check." She returned in a few minutes with the receipt for Carol to sign, handing her a check for twenty-six thousand, eight hundred sixty-five dollars and eighty-five cents ($26,865.85).

Carol had been able to save while living at home, and from her divorce settlement. She would use this money to help build a life with Big Bear. She thought of closing out her checking account, too, but she decided to wait until she received the last check from the magazine. Now to deal with the mess in Mom's basement, she thought.

While driving home, Carol noticed a sign: SALVATION ARMY THRIFT SHOP. She pulled her truck into the parking lot, walked into the store, asking to see the manager. She talked with the manager about the stuff she would like to get rid of, arranging to have them come by and pick up the items the next day around noon. Carol walked out of the store feeling as though a load had been lifted off her shoulders. If her mother wanted anything, they would pick out the items tomorrow morning before the crew arrived.

Carol's mom was sitting on the front porch. She greeted Carol: "Is everything going okay?"

Carol took a seat next to her on the porch and replied, "It's going well. I quit my job at the magazine, closed my saving account, and arranged to get rid of the stuff in the basement. The only things I'm taking, in addition to my clothes, are my portable sewing machine, my photography equipment and catalog of negatives and pictures. I want to learn how to quilt, Mom. Let's go to some material and craft shops before I leave. If there is anything you want out of the stuff in the basement, we will go through it in the morning. The Salvation Army truck will be here to pick up the stuff tomorrow around noon," she announced, the words tumbling out in a rush.

"Only linens, if they are usable after being packed up for so long. We'll check in the morning; maybe then I'll feel better about all this news. You haven't invited your father and me to the wedding yet. I hope you want us there," she said, sadness in her voice.

"As soon as I know the date, Mom, you will get an invitation. Of course, you're welcome to come, all of you," she said, putting her arms around her mother. "I know this is short notice, but believe me, Mom, I know what I'm doing."

"Have you had lunch?" Carol's mother asked. "I made tuna salad," she said, wanting to, but unable to say more at that moment.

"No, I'm hungry," Carol replied. "Come on, let's have some tea and tuna salad. Then I have to get my clothes sorted; some are going to the Salvation Army," Carol said, going into the house.

Carol ate her lunch quietly, saying nothing more. Finishing lunch, she went up the stairs into her room, cleaning out closets. She would take all of her warm sweaters and long-sleeved shirts. Jeans, western shirts and boots were a must. As for coats, some warmer coats, western style, could be bought in Montana. In cleaning out the closet, she found her wedding dress packed neatly with the accessories. What a difference from her doeskin wedding dress that Walking Elk had made for her. Laying aside the silk wedding dress, Carol thought, I wish I knew someone to give this dress to. Maybe someone who couldn't afford a dress otherwise, would buy it at the Salvation Army store. Carol put the dress in the bottom of the box of clothes that she was preparing for the people at the store to pick up.

Then there was footwear to sort: lots of shoes, winter boots, summer sandals, dress shoes. Carol picked through them, deciding to take her favorite winter boots and two pairs of dress shoes. Her life now would be lived mostly in western boots. After sorting the shoes, she started going through the chest of drawers and dresser containing underclothes going back five years. She set aside only those things she needed, placing the rest in the box. Old makeup she put in the garbage can that she had already filled and emptied twice. Why did people keep so many things? she wondered. Life is not in things; it's within people. It was close to five o'clock when Carol came down the stairs, nearly time for dinner.

Carol set the table, then made carrot salad as her mother took the meatloaf out of the oven. Carol thought she was being awful quiet, saying, "Mom, what is the matter? Talk to me. We have always been open with one another."

"Well, I heard something from Cora down the street. She said that your ex-husband is going with Sue Ann. I don't want Tony to hear this. Your ex was divorced about six months ago," she said, watching Carol's reaction.

"Oh, Mom, you know Cora is the neighborhood gossip. Don't pay attention to what she says. If it is so, what can you do about it? If it wasn't him, it would be somebody else. It certainly doesn't bother me if he is seeing Sue Ann, and I don't think it will bother Tony," she said, knowing her mother was trying to find out about Carol's feelings for her ex-husband. "I heard, before leaving for Montana, that Bill was divorced. Mom, he can't hold a candle to Jim. I never felt about Bill the way I feel about Jim. That chapter of my life is closed and will stay closed," she said firmly, placing the salads on the table.

Carol's mother answered her: "Carol, I only told you so you wouldn't hear it from someone else. You didn't tell me about Bill being divorced," she said, putting the bread in the oven.

"Mom, I hardly thought you would be interested in Bill's divorce," Carol said. She was glad to hear Tony come in the front door, "How is everybody?" he asked.

"Fine, how was your day? I have done a lot of cleaning out and cleaning up," Carol said, laughing at Tony as he nibbled on the salad.

"Well, I heard some news today at the office: Sue Ann and your ex are seeing each other. When they told me I thought that was the funniest thing I had ever heard. If any two deserve each other, it is those two. Don't you think so, Sis?" he asked, kissing her on her cheek. "Hey, Sis, let's go out tomorrow night, I have a softball game, then maybe a date Saturday night. Maybe this loving thing of yours is rubbing off on me," he said, heading up the stairs.

"Well you never know, I never thought he would take the news that well," said Carol's mother.

"Mom, God builds bounce-back magnetism into us; it always works, whatever we go through. It teaches us to be thankful and to appreciate people when we do meet the right one," she said, smiling at her mother.

"Is dinner ready? I'm starved," her father said, coming in the house. "It sure smells good—meatloaf," he sniffed, walking into the kitchen, kissing his wife and daughter. "You're the prettiest girls in town."

The conversation at the dinner table led back to Carol and her powwow experience. She told them about Songbird and Big Eagle, Two Feathers and Yellow Bird. Then she told them about Walking Elk and the doeskin wedding dress. Carol felt that was all she should tell them about their spiritual beliefs. Her family listened with great interest.

"I hope you don't get mixed up with this spirit stuff these Indians believe," her father said. "Some of them have some way-out ideas and rituals. When will I see some pictures of this Big Bear?" he asked, pushing back his chair.

"Monday, I'm viewing the negative sheets, then I will have all the pictures developed. There are pictures of the ranch, the ranch house, which is log and stone. There are beautiful horses, too; Jim gave me one named Babe. Jim breeds and raises the finest Appaloosa horses in the West. They are something to see. I love Babe," she said, thinking that she had said enough.

Tony took up the conversation, saying, "Dad, what are you and Mom going to do with this big house if Carol and I move out permanently? You sure won't need a four-bedroom house," he said, putting his plate in the sink.

"Are you planning on moving out, too? We're losing two in two weeks? his mother asked. "Your dad and I have held on to this house hoping to have some grandchildren to fill it up. But now they will live so far away," she said, looking at Carol.

"Don't look at me. I don't know if I will ever conceive children, thinking of the Indian children.

Carol's father finished the conversation, saying, "If we see this move of yours is real, we may talk about selling the place, but we will wait and see. Carol, it's your turn to clean the kitchen; Tony, you can help."

Carol and Tony cleaned up the kitchen, putting the dishes in the washer. As they were finishing up, the phone rang. "Hello, yes, how are you? Lonesome, that makes two. Things are going well here; I got a lot of things done today. I cleaned closets today, and I'm having the basement taken care of tomorrow. I plan to place my work on Mary's desk the third of September. So after that, anything could happen. Tell Babe I miss her, Songbird and Big Eagle, all the others. Just a few more days. I'll have my last check sent to your address, that way I can close out my checking account. I will have one day with Mom, shopping for quilt material and patterns. I have to have something to keep me busy during long Montana winters. I miss you, too, and plan to get out of here as soon as possible. I love you, bye." Carol slowly hung up the phone. She could see him hanging up the phone, looking so handsome in his western clothes, his beaming smile, smiling at her. I love you, Big Bear, she thought.

The kitchen clean, Tony asked her to go over the article with him. Up at his computer, they talked about their ex-spouses being together. They laughed about old times and funny things they had done as kids. The evening passed quickly and soon it was midnight. Tony gave her a reminder: "Don't forget; tomorrow night, we have a date around seven."

"I can't forget, good night."

Up early, having breakfast of coffee and toast, Carol was ready to tackle the basement. With her mother's help, she began pulling boxes out, each being labeled. Coming to the box of linens, Carol pushed it over to her mother. Taking things out of the box, she found everything in good condition. Taking a Coffeemate and the linens, her mother had everything she wanted from among the things packed. Then Carol turned to the pictures. Pictures of her wedding went into the garbage can, with all the pictures of her and Bill. Carol's mother was horrified that Carol could just dismiss this part of her life, including all the personal letters Bill had written her while in college. When she finished, Carol felt free.

"Mom, one thing Big Bear and I agreed upon is there should be no negative carry over from past relationships. We are starting our lives anew, free from all the old memories and heartaches," she said, smiling at her mom, hoping she understood.

"That's good, Carol, if you can do it," her mom said, smiling back at Carol.

"It's almost time for the men to pick up this stuff. We'd better get upstairs," Carol said, taking out a large garbage bag full of old memories.

The men were on time to pick up the boxes. After they carried out the last box, Carol felt that she wanted to treat her mother to lunch. "Mom, change your clothes; I will take you to lunch. Maybe after we will have time to shop at some craft shops."

The afternoon was spent looking at creative projects for Carol to do this winter. "Carol, I see how excited you are about your new life. I know everything will turn out well for you, for you will make it that way," her mom said on the ride home.

Arriving home, they had just enough time to warm up leftovers for Carol's dad. Carol hurried upstairs, doing her nails, soaking in a hot tub. She took special pains with her makeup. She chose her open-back, black cocktail dress. She pulled it over her head. The snug dress accentuated every curve of her figure. Then she donned black pumps and picked out her black evening bag, putting the finishing touch with pearls around her neck and pearl earrings. At seven, Tony knocked on her door.

"Hey, gorgeous, are you ready?" he asked.

Carol came out of the room whirling around in front of her brother. "Wow, you look great!" he exclaimed. I will be the envy of all the guys at the party. Sure wish you weren't my sister; I wouldn't let anyone else have you."

Carol hit him on the arm, saying, "Shut your mouth."

Dad instructed them as they went out the door, "You kids have fun, but be careful, and come home together," he said jokingly.

The First Street Bar and Restaurant was the place for working people to go uptown. After work and on weekends, they gathered to catch up on the latest computer technology and office gossip. Being seated, Tony and Carol looked around to see whom they knew there. There was Steve from the magazine; he was a First Street Bar fixture when he wasn't selling advertising for the magazine. Casting an eye around the room, Carol spotted Sue Ann and Bill sitting at a table together. She said nothing to Tony, knowing he would spot them soon enough. The waiter came over to take their drink order: red wine for Carol and beer for Tony.

"We will order later. I'm going to dance with my beautiful sister, so all these men can eat their heart out," he said, holding Carol's hand.

Tony held her tenderly on the dance floor. Carol said, "Big Bear always holds my hand," she said. "I love for him to hold my hand," she confessed, holding back the tears. She thought of having refused his ring; the way she had hurt him and that he had never said a word to express his great disappointment.

Tony turned her on the dance floor, but he wasn't the dancer Big Bear was. "Now, Sis, don't get mushy on me. Tell me about this wonderful creature; I know you want to," he said, smiling at her.

Carol loved the opportunity to talk about Big Bear. She told Tony how Big Bear taught school, helping young boys learn about Indian culture, teaching an adult agriculture class on the reservation. "His ranch is the pride of his life, yet he still has time for others," she said. Then she told Tony a little about Walking Elk and her family. After an hour of talking they decided to dance again. That's when Tony noticed Sue Ann and Bill.

"Of all the people to run into—are you up to this, Sis?"

"They don't bother me," she answered. "How about you?"

"I got over her before she wanted me out. Sue Ann just didn't know it. She finally did what I wanted to do. No, it doesn't bother me," he said, moving in time with the music.

"Let's order our dinner, eat and get out of here," she suggested.

"I think it's too late. They've seen us; they're coming this way," Tony said, pushing Carol's chair under the table after she sat down.

"Hi, Carol. You're looking good, real good," Bill said, admiring her. "Sue Ann and I were just having a few drinks, for old times' sake. Having been in the same family, you know how it is. What are you doing with yourself, Carol? Maybe we can have a drink some evening," he said, leaning over her chair.

"I don't think so, Bill. It seems you are busy with a new love," Carol said looking at Sue Ann.

"No, tell her, Sue Ann; we are just friends," he replied before Sue Ann could open her mouth.

Carol said, "You two are just alike. Please leave us alone, while we try and have an enjoyable evening," she said politely, but making herself clear.

"You must be hard up to be out with your brother. What's the matter, you can't get a date?" he asked, taking Sue Ann's hand, leaving with a smirk.

Tony rose up out of his seat, and Carol pulled him back down. "Don't, Tony, they're not worth it; they both need help, and I hope some day they realize it. All we can do is pity them. Let's eat our dinner."

Carol drove home, for Tony had guzzled one beer too many. "Tony, we have a whole new life; don't allow bitterness to hold you back from having a good life. Stop thinking of the past; think of the present, the future and how you can make it a better one."

"You know, Sis, you are wise. You will have a good life with this handsome Indian you have found. I just hope I can be that lucky. I've met this person who has just started working at the office. She is very pretty; all the single men will be hitting on her, but I got the first date. Her name is Sharon; she looks a lot like you: long blonde hair, with fascinating blue eyes. She's just out of college. You never know, Sis, at least I'm trying," he said, laying his head back on the passenger seat.

Parking the car, Carol took Tony's hand, leading him up the steps onto the porch. Then the lights came on and the front door opened. "Mom still waits up, can you believe that? Carol asked. "Good night, Mom," they said heading upstairs.

Carol went to sleep thinking of Big Bear and of leaving for Montana. She had little left to do after getting the article and pictures to Mary. Maybe she would leave early Thursday morning, being able to reach Billings Friday afternoon around five, about the time Big Bear would be returning home. Could she do this without him knowing what day she would be home? She wanted to get there as soon as possible and surprise him.

Carol and her mother spent another day looking at quilt material and crafts. She was really becoming interested in country crafts. Carol's mother was enjoying herself being a part of Carol's newfound interest. "I'll have a couple of days before leaving, Mom; you and I can figure out how to put one of these quilt patterns together, and start cutting out the pieces."

"I would like that. We could work on the dining room table. Then we could leave the pieces in place without moving them. My grandmother used to quilt; in fact, I have one of her old quilts in her trunk in the basement. We could take it out of the trunk and look at it. We might get some ideas," she suggested, engrossing herself in Carol's project.

"I would like that," Carol said. "I have never seen a quilt in the basement." Carol's mother said, "It's in the old trunk that was my great grandmother's, then my mother's."

"That's something, Mother; you never told me. I'll go down and find the old trunk," she offered, heading for the basement stairs.

Carol found the old trunk packed away in a corner. Opening the lid of the musty trunk, Carol found old letters and pictures dating back to the 1800s. To her surprise, she found one of a proud woman sitting with a dark man who looked like an Indian. Their sober faces told of the times when surviving off the land was a struggle. Carol looked through the trunk, finding pictures of little girls in long dresses and stockings. Carol was getting a strange feeling some of her ancestors were Indians. Why hadn't her mother told her?

Then Carol found an old book of Indian history. Slowly, she opened the yellowed pages. She flipped through the pages to the description of the Sand Creek Massacre, reading: "On December 28, 1864, troops led by former clergyman, Colonel John M. Chivington, carried out a raid on the peaceful Cheyenne and Arapaho camp. Out of the mutilated bodies of 123, nearly 100 were Indian women and children." Carol laid aside the small book and wiped the tears from her eyes. She felt so helpless as she thought, What the Nazi holocaust was to the Jewish people, slavery to the African-Americans, Sand Creek Massacre was to the Native Americans.

Carol could feel the presence of Walking Elk as she wept for the Indian people. "Little Dove weep over past; let go of past and live for today, be answer not part of problem. We now have crossed over shining river. Walk with love in heart for all people. Indian people quiet, they will inherit earth."

Carol wiped her eyes over and blew her nose as she heard her mother coming down the stairs. "Carol, did you find the trunk? I know the old quilt is in that trunk. Ah, you have found it and the old pictures. Carol, your great grandmother married an Osage Indian; my mother, your grandmother, was part Indian," she said, wishing she didn't have to explain.

"Mother, why didn't you tell us? I knew my grandmother was a little dark, but she died when I was so young. This is something; does Tony know?" Carol was carried away with the idea that she was part Indian on her mother's side of the family.

"No, Carol; nobody knew since my mother died, and now her sister is gone. Carol, you don't understand; back in those days, it was improper to marry an Indian or black person. If you did, you became an outcast."

"Mom, that is ridiculous; people can't control who they fall in love with. I wish you would have told me about my great grandmother. Now I can understand why I'm attracted to Native Americans. I feel more like they are my people," she said, looking at her mother's shocked face.

Carol pulled out the old quilt, with its holes and ragged edges. The old quilt was, nevertheless, a work of art. Each piece was stitched by hand.

Carol's mother handled the quilt gently, saying, "Let's take it upstairs, then put it outside to air out."

In the light upstairs, Carol was able to see the quilt better. Maybe her grandmother had slept under that old quilt, keeping herself warm during frigid Missouri winters. Carol had touched her great grandmother's spirit and what the Osage Indians had gone through to follow their heart. Thank goodness, prejudice against nonwhites had decreased since that time, but many people still had to learn to judge others by their character, not by the color of their skin.

Carol set up her craft project on the dining room table, cutting out patterns for her first quilt. She looked at the old quilt, wondering if she could make a quilt like her great grandmother's. Then the voice spoke, "Sure you can, I will help you." Standing next to Carol's chair was the pioneer woman she had seen in the picture. "I will help you make the quilt, and with the changes in your life. I, too, followed my heart, marrying an Indian. Our love kept us, giving us a good life. You, too, will have a good life."

Carol's mother came in, saying, "Who are you talking to?"

"This quilt has stories to tell," she replied. "I'm listening with an open heart," was all she said, knowing her mother didn't understand.

"Your father and I are going out for dinner tonight. We want you to come with us," her mother insisted.

"No, Mom; I have to stay. Big Bear will be calling, and I don't want to miss his call. You go ahead; I will be fine, cutting out my quilt pieces."

"If that is what you want, we will be home around nine," she said, leaving to get ready.

Carol was busy cutting her patterns when Big Bear called. "Hello, yes, I'm missing you. I've finished up almost everything. No, you don't have to come after me. I will soon be there. Guess what I found out today? My great grandmother married an Osage Indian. Yes, I just found out. My mother knew all the time. I found this old quilt in a trunk my grandmother left my mother. In the old trunk were these pictures of my great grandmother with an Indian man. Isn't that something? No wonder I love the Indian people so much; they are my people," Carol said, waiting for his response.

Big Bear listened, waiting for a break: "That doesn't surprise me, but your people in Montana miss you. Please tell me you're leaving tomorrow," he said, loneliness in his voice. "This house is so lonesome without you. Carol, tell me when you'll be here, so I will have something to look forward to."

"Darling, as soon as I can, I will be out of here. I don't know yet when the pictures will be ready. I will know Monday. Can you wait until Monday night?" she asked, hoping he wouldn't think she was putting him off.

"No, I can't wait another minute, but I guess I will have to. I love you and miss you; please hurry home, bye," he said, hanging up the phone.

Carol was almost in tears when her mother and father came down the stairs. "Carol, are you sure you don't want to go with us?" her mother asked.

Wiping her eyes, Carol said, "No, thank you for asking, but I would like to stay at home."

"So you can call that man back, telling him you will soon be out of here," her dad said, reading her mind.

They left and the old house was quiet. Carol thought about

what her dad had said about calling Big Bear back. Maybe she would call before going to bed. She started to concentrate on her quilt, then the doorbell rang. She put her pieces down, went to the door and turned on the porch light. There stood Bill.

"What are you doing here? I'm busy," she said, shocked to see him standing at the door. At first, Carol thought that she shouldn't let him in.

"May I come in and talk with you? You wouldn't have a drink with me, so here I am," he said, standing in the doorway.

"Sure, Bill; come in," she said, stepping back out of his way.

"I don't know what you think we have to talk about. We said all we had to say five years ago in court. Why do you want to talk now, because you are feeling sorry for yourself?" Carol was on the defensive.

"Carol, do you realize we could have a son or daughter three or four years old if we could have made it? You always wanted kids, but I was too busy getting rich. Now I don't have children, a wife or a home. What is the matter with me, Carol? You seem happy with your life," he said, pacing the floor.

"Bill, you always wanted to build your life on the wrong things. Money is to meet your needs, not to make you happy. Happiness comes from inside when you like the person you are. You can't be happy if you don't like yourself. You can do something about this, if you want to. You are the only one who can do this," she said, watching him pace.

"Carol, do you think you can help me make this change? If I had someone to care for me, I know I could change for them," he said, a pleading tone in his voice.

"No, Bill; you have to do this yourself. I can't be around; I'm leaving for Montana. I'm getting married," she told him, seeing him turn around upon hearing her words.

"You're kidding me!"

"No, I'm not kidding you. I'm marrying a Crow Indian named Jim Nelson. He is a rancher and schoolteacher. I love him very much," she said, allowing him to know her plans.

Bill walked slowly toward the door, saying, "You sure took the life out of me. I hoped we could get back together. I thought you were still available. I was obviously mistaken; well, have a good life," he said, reaching to kiss her. Carol turned her head, and he brushed her cheek with his dry lips.

Locking the door behind Bill, Carol continued cutting her quilt pieces, thinking about Bill and his problems. She hoped, for his sake, that he could find someone to help him find himself. Thinking further, she decided to call Big Bear, to tell him if they could get her photos ready by Wednesday, she would turn the work in, leaving that morning, arriving in Montana late Thursday night.

The phone was ringing, "Hello, Big Bear; this is Carol. I think I can finish up here Wednesday and be out after I turn in the article and photos to the magazine. If I get the photos from the lab, that is, and if we don't have to much cropping to do. Tony will printout the article tomorrow. I will try real hard; I want you to know I'm trying."

"I know you are sweetheart. I'm sorry if I made you feel pressured. But I know your place is here with me. If you come Thursday night, I will have a room reserved at the Best Western. We can spend the night in town. How does that sound to you?"

"That's fine. I know I will probably be late arriving in Billings," she said, feeling better.

"I will call to reserve the room. Just ask for Jim Nelson's room. I will leave word at the desk you're coming in. I should be there around nine. I can't wait to see you, and hug you. I love you."

Carol said good-bye just as Tony came in from his date. "You look happy," she observed. "How did your date go?"

"Everything went real well, Carol. We did a lot of honest talking to each other. She has been married, has a three-year-old son. Her mother takes care of him while she works. I think we may have something going, at least I hope so," he said, lying down on the couch.

"You look pleased about something; what is going on? That

man called again," Tony guessed, smiling at Carol.

"No, I called him, telling him I'm leaving Wednesday morning, if I can get this work to Mary. When can you print my article?" she asked, hoping it would be soon.

"I will print it in the morning after breakfast, when my head is clear. I don't want to hold up true love," he said, laughing at her. "I'm going to bed." He headed for the stairs, saying, "See you in the morning."

"I'm going, too; Mom and Dad must have gone to a movie," she replied, turning out the lights.

Lying awake in her bed, Carol was wishing she was in Big Bear's arms. The morning came, with the family gathering around the breakfast table, talking and laughing. Carol hated to tell them her plans, but she had to.

"I will be leaving Wednesday, if all goes well with the photos."

"We know your heart is there, so do what you have to do," her father said. "Your mom and I know this, and we are prepared for the news. We played cards with some friends last night, after seeing them at the restaurant. They have a daughter, who married an Englishman and moved to England. After talking to them we figure Montana is not that far away, if they have airports," he teased, pinching Carol's cheek.

"Of course they have airports, one in Billings, about fifty miles from where I will be living. Come visit any time," she said, getting up from the table.

Carol wanted to get her stuff ready to load in her truck while Tony was available to help carry it. She worked repacking the boxes, her luggage, cleaning out the closet and a filing cabinet with photo negatives and photos. She finished packing coats and shoes, taping up the boxes. Tony came in, waving her article in the air. "This is good, Sis, you may become a writer yet. Can I help you with these boxes?"

"I thought you'd never ask. I want you to bring my truck around to the back door. It will be easier going out the back with these boxes."

"Where are the truck keys?" he asked, looking at the mess on the bed.

"In my purse on the bed, if you can find it," she said, pushing things aside.

They loaded all the boxes and luggage, except the one Carol needed on the trip. Tony pulled down the topper, locking it. "Wait, Tony, we forgot the sewing machine; it's in the basement."

Tony loaded the sewing machine and a box of photos from the basement, moving the truck back around to the front of the house. Carol walked through the room, looking to see if she had missed anything. She needed to vacuum the bedroom rug, but she would wait until just before leaving.

After lunch, Tony left to meet his new girlfriend. Mom and Dad lay down to take a nap. Carol went up to her bathroom, soaking in a hot tub, doing her nails. She thought, I'm going to be at the lab first thing in the morning. Things had gone well, faster than she had anticipated. It occurred to her that maybe Walking Elk had something to do with that.

Monday morning at nine o'clock, Carol walked into the photo lab. "We have your negative sheet to view. There are some spectacular shots in these negatives. These people believe in wearing bright colors. Where do they gather those feathers from? I thought gathering feathers was illegal. I don't think much cropping is necessary. You pick out the prints you want, and they will be ready by noon tomorrow," the photo lab technician said. Carol couldn't believe her ears.

"That would be wonderful to pick all of them up at noon tomorrow. You can make me one print of all the negatives. I will mark the ones I want for the magazine article. See you around noon; thank you," she said. Carol's heart was singing as she left the lab.

Carol could get out early Wednesday morning, arriving in Montana Thursday afternoon around four. She knew Big Bear was going to be happy to hear this.

Carol quietly helped with dinner as her mother went on and

one about her friend having a daughter living in England. Carol only wanted to get through dinner, so she could call Big Bear about the news of leaving early Wednesday morning. Her dad was carrying on about her getting a cell phone. "Being on the road, you need a phone," he said.

Carol kept saying, "No, I'm not ready to have a cell phone. I've got my own protection."

When Big Bear called, they talked about her leaving, when she would be in Billings. "Go to the Best Western and I will meet you there," he said.

Carol was counting the hours until she could pick up those prints at the lab, then make her presentation to Mary. Carol vacuumed her room, changed the sheets, did the laundry, and cleaned up everything. She ate a light lunch with her mother, then left for the lab.

The prints were spectacular, particularly Big Bear riding the bronc, and Andy and Billy in the horse races. Seeing the photos of the children dressed in their Native clothes, Carol had to clear her eyes of tears. She asked the lab technician to help pick out the best shots for the magazine article. They decided on ten that would give Mary the best overall account of the powwow.

Mary was available to see her as Carol walked into the office. "You have done some fast work, Carol," she said. "I hope all of it is good. Let me see what you have," she said, taking the large envelope from Carol's hand. Mary slowly viewed each picture, saying, "These are exceptionally good; you really enjoyed your work. This is Big Bear on the bucking bronc? Well, he's quite a man. I'm pleased with your pictures, as always. Carol, I hate to see you go, but I know that is what you want." She read over a few pages of the article, laying it down. "This is good. Why don't you try freelance writing? I could use you," she said, hoping for a positive reply from Carol.

"I don't know what I will be doing yet, Mary. I will leave my address at the accounting office. It's been good working with you. God bless and keep you," she said, shaking Mary's hand.

Carol went to the bank, closing out her checking account. She had arranged to have the last check from the magazine sent to Big Bear's address in Montana. She made a last stop at the craft shop, where she bought more thread for her quilts. She had placed the old quilt with her belongings. Her mother said she could have the old thing. Carol would cherish the old quilt and all its memories.

That night, Carol viewed the pictures of the powwow at dinner, especially those of Big Bear and family. She broke the news that she would be leaving in the morning. The family took the news well, wishing her the best.

"I'll say my good-byes tonight. I will be leaving early in the morning, before the work traffic gets heavy," she said, kissing her mom and dad, then Tony. "Please take care of yourselves; I'll leave Big Bear's address and phone number by the phone."

Big Bear called: "Hello, Carol; I'm counting the hours until you arrive back in Montana. Everything is arranged for us to stay at the motel Thursday night. I will meet you at the motel at four or five. Have a good trip; please don't be on the road at night. I love you, and I miss you. Good-night," he said, hanging up the phone.

Carol was so keyed up she couldn't sleep, thinking about being back in Big Bear's arms. Finally, as morning was coming, she went to sleep. She was awakened out of a sound sleep when she saw a light in her room. Standing close to her bed were two young Indian girls smiling at her. They looked to be about two and four years old. They came closer to her bed, touching her hand. Carol reached out to touch them; then they were gone. She sat up in the bed, longing to see them again. Were they spirits? Carol lay back down. It was four a.m. She was wide awake thinking, What did this mean? If Walking Elk were here, she could tell her. Carol was taking a shower when the knock came on the door. She went to the door in her bathrobe, and there stood her mother.

"I've made coffee for you; when you are ready, I will be downstairs," she said, quietly going down the stairs.

Carol couldn't shake the vision of the small girls, their big dark eyes and long black hair. "Mom, I wish you would have stayed in bed. I could have gotten coffee down the road, but thank you," Carol said, pouring the coffee in her travel cup. "I will call you soon after I get there. Please, don't worry; I'll be fine. Kiss Dad for me; I love you."

Carol had the truck running and was backing out of the drive when she saw the two Indian girls sitting in the front seat with her. They smiled as if they knew where they were going. Carol thought, Well, I'm going to have company on this trip. She was on her way to Denver, planning to stay overnight there. The next day she would leave early to be in the Big Sky State, Montana, and her true home, as soon as possible. Big Bear would be waiting.

CHAPTER FIVE

Home in the Big Sky State

Carol looked at her truck's gas gauge as she drove down Main Street in Billings thinking, I better get gas before going to the motel. She knew there was a Texaco station on the right just before the motel. That is where she would get gas. Coming close to the station, Carol saw a white Ford truck that looked like Big Bear's. Someone was pumping gas on the opposite side of her with his back turned to her. Carol came around lifting the pump off the hanger, about to put it into the tank when she asked, "Can someone show me how to pump this gas?"

"I will show you, pretty lady, and pay for it if you will give me a hug," Big Bear said, hanging up his pump nozzle and coming around the concrete island, hanging up her pump.

He grabbed her, lifting her off her feet, hugging and kissing her. "You beautiful woman. Come hold my hand as I pump this gas. How are you? Your trip—was it good? I thought of you last night. I've thought of you every second while you have been gone. No more leaving now; if so, we both go," he said, placing the pump nozzle back, still holding on to her hand. They walked hand in hand to pay for the gas. He placed a credit card down on the counter. "I want pump four and five put on the card," he said. He signed the receipt and they walked outside. "Billy Joe is with me. He is taking my truck back to the ranch, helping Big Eagle with the cattle tomorrow. We're selling steers at the cattle sale; they're bringing a good price. I'll go with you to the motel. We'll eat, then you're going to school with me," he said, walking to the truck.

Big Bear then spoke briefly to Billy Joe, who left with his truck. Big Bear opened the door for Carol, saying, "I'll drive; I know you are tired of driving." He smiled at her, showing his white teeth.

Carol thought, Seeing his handsome face, and feeling his love make me complete. They drove a short distance and parked at the Best Western Motel. Entering the lobby, Big Bear walked over to the counter, picked up the key to the room, and they continued into the dining room. They placed their order with the waitress, never taking their eyes off each other. "I can't believe you're back here with me," Big Bear said. "We will never be parted again. I bought you something at the jewelry store yesterday, a homecoming gift," he said, reaching into his pocket, taking out a ring case that contained a dazzling blue sapphire and diamond ring. She was breathless looking at the stunning ring. "Oh, Big Bear, I can't believe anything could be so beautiful," she managed to say, allowing him to slip the ring on her finger. "It's a perfect fit. How did you know the size?"

"I just guessed, but it was a good guess. Do you like it?" he asked. "Better than the other one I offered you?" he commented with a smile on his face. "You do know that is an engagement ring?"

"Yes, it's beautiful. Thank you; I love it," she said, holding the ring out and looking at it. Carol kissed the ring. "It's just that I'm overwhelmed," she admitted.

They ate their baked potatoes and salad, finishing up with conversation about her trip back home and the magazine. Carol told him about the pictures of the powwow and the rodeo. She would like to give some to the boys in the races, Walking Elk and all the others.

"I'm sure they would like pictures of the powwow and the rodeo. Do you have any of yourself in your wedding dress?" he asked, his dark eyes dancing.

Carol thought of the two small Indian girls coming into her room, riding with her on the trip to Montana. Since she had arrived in Billings, they had made no appearance. Maybe they knew she was safe with Big Bear now. Big Bear and Carol walked to the motel room before leaving for the adult class at the reservation. She wanted to stay at the motel room, hoping the girls would make another appearance. Carol knew Big Bear wanted her to go with him, so she would accompany him.

In the room Carol decided to tell Big Bear about the Indian girls. "Honey, I had an experience back in St. Louis; I don't know what to think of it," she began, wanting answers.

"Tell me about it," he said, sitting down on the bed.

Carol placed herself beside him on the bed. "Do we have time? I can tell you later," she offered, holding his hand.

"We don't have to leave for another hour, so tell me what is bothering that pretty head of yours. I'll fix it for you," he said, pulling her close to him as they lay on the bed.

Carol pulled his strong arms around her, saying, "When I was back in my bedroom the night before leaving, two small Indian girls came into my bedroom, coming up to my bed and touching my hand. Their ages looked to be about two and four years. It was so real. Then the next morning they were with me in the truck, staying until I reached Montana. I keep feeling their presence," she said, sitting up on the bed looking around the room.

Rolling over on the bed, Big Bear took her in his arms, saying, "Put your head here on my arm and listen to what I'm going to tell you. Your spirit is making contact with the spirit of children that are in trouble or need someone. Their spirit is able to communicate with yours because of your love for them, your ability to feel their pain. They had to pick up two little girls on the reservation because their parents were using and selling drugs. They have been placed in a foster home until the court can arrange adoption by a member of the family. The Indian people like keeping Indian children with an Indian family. But I will check and see what has happened to them. Will that make you feel better?" he asked, kissing her hand.

Tears were coming down Carol's face, thinking those little girls' spirits had tried to contact her to help them. "Please, Big Bear, check and see if there is anything we can do," she said, her heart aching for the children.

Big Bear tenderly wiped the tears away, kissing her eyes, then her mouth. "I sure will; for you, I will do anything, my Little Dove."

They lay quietly until it was time to go. Carol fixed her makeup, slipping on her denim jacket. They walked hand in hand to the truck, holding their love in their hearts. The drive to the reservation was quiet. Carol was deep in thought, concerned about the little girls. Big Bear broke the silence with his comments, "Don't get your hopes up about those little girls; if they have grandparents, they usually take them."

"I know. Just find out if they are okay for me," she said, choking back the tears. It was hard for Carol to speak.

"At the next council meeting I will inquire about them, my love. I promise. Give me a smile," he insisted, holding her hand as they pulled in the parking lot outside the adult classroom.

Big Bear taught in the government agriculture building on the reservation. They walked in to the classroom, which smelled, Carol thought, a bit like the ranch where she had stayed. He placed his briefcase down on the desk. Carol took a seat in the back of the room, with a few students already present.

Big Bear's class was on cattle diseases. He walked to the blackboard, writing a list of diseases. The room was filling up with his students, mostly older men, some in their twenties. Soon there were about thirty men in the class, Carol being the only woman.

Carol found a book on horses. She was reading the book as the class progressed. In an hour they took a break. That's when they asked who the visitor was. Big Bear asked Carol to stand and give her name.

"If you're wondering what she is to me, and I hope you are, she is my sweetheart," he said, handling the situation with ease. "Now back to the lesson. How many have completed the assignment with the veterinarian?"

The response was good, with most holding up their hand.

These Big Bear allowed to come to the board, writing the cure or treatment for the disease. Then he discussed the process of treatment. Big Bear was a good teacher because he knew the material and was dedicated to his students. The class was over at nine, but Big Bear took a few extra minutes with his students. Then he excused himself, returning to Billings with Carol by his side.

That night they lay in each other's arms, talking about the class and the children, as well as about their lives and what they wanted out of life. They were like newfound friends.

At six a.m., they received a wake-up call. "I have no clean clothes. I can take a shower, but I have no clean clothes," Big Bear grumbled as he went into the bathroom.

Carol heard him talking about having no clean clothes. She knew this bothered him, for he always looked so neat. Carol never thought of clean clothes for him. He seemed to always have everything under control. "You will survive wearing a suit of clothes two days," she teased him.

Big Bear came out of the bathroom with only his jockey shorts on, pulling the bed covers off her. "What was that smart remark? Say it again; I dare you. I dare you," he repeated, kissing her over and over on her lips.

"You better let go so I can get dressed, so we can get to the restaurant for breakfast," she said, swinging her legs off the bed.

"Okay, go, but one of these days our rushing will be over. Then I'm going to get enough of you," he vowed, kissing her as she slipped by him.

"Big Eagle and Billy Joe will be hauling two loads of cattle to the auction today. On their return trip they will leave my truck with the cattle trailer in the schoolyard for me. Billy Joe wants to stay in town," he added, pulling on his boots, ready to go.

Carol finished applying her makeup, pulled on her boots, and was ready for the day. "Whatever you want to do: I could drive back and pick you up after school. This is Friday and the Labor Day holiday. I have you three days all to myself," she said, taking his hand.

The coffee tasted good to Carol at seven a.m. in Billings, Montana, because she was with the man she loved, but the thought of going out to the ranch without him made her feel lonesome. The thought of Songbird being there soothed her thoughts. Big Bear was talking about doing something over the weekend.

"I have a place to take you, to the mountain, not to stay in the tepee this time. I have a surprise for you; I know you will love it," he said, always sounding mysterious when talking about the mountain.

"It's too cold to stay on that mountain at night," she said, sipping her coffee.

"We're not staying on the mountain, in the valley; you'll see," he said, smiling at her. "We better load your stuff in the truck and go. I can't be late." He pushed back his chair, helping her.

Carol hated dropping him off at the school. She watched him walk in the door before she pulled out into the traffic, heading west toward the ranch.

The sun was up and shining brightly as she pulled into the yard of the ranch. She could hear the noise of the cows being loaded. Carol looked around the familiar yard. Her eyes rested on Babe and Quickfire in the corral. They lifted up their heads when Carol closed the truck door. Songbird came out, offering to help with the luggage. "Good, Little Dove home," she said. "Everybody ask when Little Dove be home. I tell them Little Dove home to stay," she said, picking up two suitcases.

"Yes, Songbird; I'm home to stay. If I go again, Big Bear goes with me. We can't be separated any more; we love one another too much," she said, taking the steps up onto the front porch.

The house was warm with a fire going in the fireplace, the aroma of cornbread filling the air of the large comfortable room. Carol set her load down breathing the smell of home. Everything looked the same, except for a card on the table with her name on it. Carol picked up the card, carefully opening the envelope. The card had a picture of Montana's big sky and rolling plains with a ranch house in the background, a cowboy on his horse, and his cattle. As Carol opened the inside of the card, a credit card fell out onto the table, a Visa gold card issued by the Bank of Montana. Carol wiped away the tears in her eyes.

These words were written in Big Bear's handwriting. "We are one; what I have is yours, and what you are is as much of me as breathing. We shall live again in all that spirit brings forth out of our life. I shall know all your desires; you are all my desires. Just small things makes a difference in our lives: to know your love for children is my love, to be able to go dancing, holding you, singing a love song while holding your hand, to pick wild flowers in the spring, wading the brooks in the summer, riding the hills; most of all, being joined for our spiritual quest. I love you; I always have, and always will. Please accept this card with my love," signed Big Bear.

Wiping her eyes, Carol admired the card. She had never had anyone love her so much, wanting to share his live completely with her. Carol placed the credit card in the greeting card, putting it in her purse.

Songbird returned to the room, taking the things Carol had left behind. Carol took the card out of her purse, reading it again. Over and over the words rang in her ears, as though Big Bear were there speaking them to her. I love you, Big Bear, she thought; I always have and always will love you.

"Little Dove found Big Bear's card. Big Bear lost without Little Dove," Songbird said, watching as Carol wiped the tears away. "I think Little Dove lost without Big Bear, too."

"Yes, I was lost without Big Bear, but I have found him; I will never be lost again," she said, smiling through her tears.

Carol unloaded the truck with Songbird's help, placing her things in the guest bedroom. Big Bear had bought another dresser for their room. Carol placed her underclothes in the dresser, hanging some of her clothes in the closet, moving some in the other room, making room for her shoes. Carol worked to find a place for her sewing and quilt makings. She thought of the card, and the wonderful feeling of loving and being loved filled her heart. She cleaned and reorganized the room, stopping long enough for some of Songbird's beans and cornbread. Then she moved her sewing machine into the guest bedroom, organizing her quilting material, threads and other accessories.

It was past four before Carol could say she was finished. Songbird looked at the clock, saying, "Big Bear be home soon. He clean cattle trailer; cows make big mess. First Big Bear clean trailer, makes Big Eagle clean trailer every time," she said, watching Carol as she stared out the kitchen window.

The trail of dust covered Big Bear's truck coming up the lane to the ranch house. Carol watched from the kitchen window as he pulled up behind her truck. Big Bear hurried onto the porch, carrying a dozen red roses. Carol met him at the door, taking the roses, and kissing him. He picked her up, taking her over the threshold into the living room. Carol laid the roses down on the counter, giving her full attention to him. Holding on to each other, they kissed, Big Bear saying loving things: "I missed you; I didn't know I could miss someone as much as I missed you. You, young lady, will never leave me again," he said firmly, caressing her face.

"I don't plan on leaving, unless we go together. I'm sorry, but you're stuck with me. I know I'm stuck with you in my heart," she said, kissing his neck.

"I hate to, but I have to clean that cattle trailer," he said, lifting Carol off her feet. "Why don't you come out to the barn with me?"

"I'll be right out. Just let me change my boots. I'll slip my rubber boots on," she said, heading to the bedroom after putting her roses in water.

Carol watched him out the window as he circled the truck around, backing the trailer to the water hose. He placed the pressure nozzle on the end of the hose. Carol continued to watch with wonder in her heart. What if she woke up and found she was dreaming? If so, she could at least say she had met the man of her dreams.

Carol joined him as he cleaned the cattle trailer of the mess, and his truck of the dust. It was a dirty job, but they jumped right into the task, getting the job done as quickly as possible. Carol held the hose while Big Bear took a shovel, pushing out the dung piles. When they completed the job, he unhooked the trailer and parked the truck back in front of the house. Songbird and Big Eagle drove up as they walked up on the porch. The sun was going down, with vivid colors painted across the Big Sky of Montana.

Big Bear held Carol in his arms as Songbird and Big Eagle came up on the porch. The cool air gave the evening the feeling of early fall, when the leaves would turn their rich color. Carol remembered this was the time of the year when Big Bear had been trying to find Little Dove, so they could be married. Her heart felt sad just for a moment, then Carol's inner voice spoke, "No more sadness. They have made it through all the stars and lights to find that great love that was theirs in the very beginning. Never again will they be parted; their love shall shine in all eternity."

Soon they all were talking and eating. Big Bear held Carol's hand, letting go only when he had to. Songbird watched saying, "Big Bear and Little Dove is love birds, Big Eagle and Songbird in way."

"No, don't go," Big Bear said. "Let's build up the fire, take the chill out of the room, sit and talk about our Indian ways. I'm sure Carol would like to hear some of the stories of our people."

This satisfied Songbird who, with Carol's help, cleaned the kitchen while Big Bear and Big Eagle placed more wood on the fire. The fire cast a warm glow in their dark eyes. The four of them sat on the floor. Big Bear and Carol looked at each other, knowing their lives were joined for a purpose in Mother Earth. Each was ready to do his/her part, but not apart; they were one that night as they sat around the fire, searching the depths of each other's soul.

Big Bear broke the silence with his announcement: "I haven't told Carol I have sold the ranch. We finished up the sale on the ranch this week, will finish the sale of cattle this week. We have to the end of July to have everything moved over to the mountain ranch. I have worked and dreamed of this day for twenty years, when I would move to the mountains, in our new home with my love. Then the children will come. I know all of this is new to Carol, but I'm here to answer questions as they arise," he said, turning his attention briefly to the fire, using the fire poker. Big Bear then looked at her. "Are there questions you would like to ask?"

Carol was stunned, and it showed on her face. Big Bear gathered her in his arms, saying, "My precious Little Dove thought this was her home; now she has to move. I plan to take you this weekend to show you your house."

"All things work for our good. Whatever you want to do is good for all. I can adjust anywhere you are, as long as we are together. Where we live doesn't matter," Carol said. She whispered in his ear, "I love you, not your house."

Songbird lay in Big Eagle's arms thinking and saying nothing in the discussion of the move. Songbird's eyes rested on Little Dove, seeing Little Dove in spirit rising in the smoke of the fire. Little Dove's spirit was strong, wanting to care for the little Indian children. Songbird saw Little Dove standing with two small Indian girls. Songbird gazed at Carol, seeing the love she had for the Indian people. Songbird hung her head, weeping softly; her heart ached to think of such love. The others watched Songbird on her spiritual quest.

Songbird came out of the spirit realm with a smile, saying, "Little Dove will be mother to many nations, raising many children in spirit way, to love Mother Earth."

As Songbird was speaking, Carol could see the little girls again. She began to weep over the Indian people and their suffering. Carol knew for every bit of suffering there would be joy, for every injustice there would be justice, for God was a just God. For everything taken, something would be given. God had a balancing wheel that would move through this land balancing all things again. Then it would be up to mankind to keep out the prejudice, finding no place for it in the heart of God. If only she could have a small part in this great change, Carol thought. She could understand why Big Bear was selling the ranch, quitting teaching in public schools. There were greater needs for Indian children to have parents. Beautiful children needed to have loving parents. Carol's heart broke as she listened to her spirit. Please, God, help me to help those I can, loving those I can't, she prayed silently.

"I'm planning to take Carol up the mountain tomorrow; we'll be back Monday. Big Eagle, you and Songbird stay close to the ranch," Big Bear said, holding Carol in his arms as the fire danced in their eyes, casting one shadow on the wall.

When the morning light was reflecting the day to come, they pulled onto the highway heading to Bozeman. They stopped at the outskirts of Bozeman for breakfast, eating and talking about the move. "The day you bumped into me at the Best Western Motel, I was there to meet and talk with the man buying the ranch. He is one of my partners in the Best Western Motel. Three of us were partners building the motel. It has been a good investment. I have made a few more good investments. Carol, financially I have no worries. I invested in two Indian casinos with good returns. With the ranch being sold, we can afford to do what we want to. We can work with children without needing any help to manage the finances. This is what I have dreamed of for twenty years and the day I decided it was time. You came along, making my dreams complete. You are so loving and kind; I can't believe you're mine," he said, holding Carol's hand while drinking his coffee.

They listened to country music, loving each other in their thoughts on the rest of the trip. Carol knew Big Bear was a man of means, but she had no idea he was rich. He certainly never gave people that impression. Carol thought that her thirty thousand in savings was small in comparison. Maybe she would just take the money to the bank. No, she would ask him to take care of it for her, Tuesday after the holiday.

They started to climb after turning off the main highway. "Carol, I want you to come into town Tuesday, meet me at the Bank of Montana. I want to put your name on some accounts I have," he said, releasing her hand to make a sharp turn going down into a valley.

How does he always know what I'm thinking? she wondered. "Okay, I have some money to deposit in a checking or savings account, whatever you think is best."

"We'll just put it in checking, so you can spend it anyway you want to. We will need to buy some furniture for the new house," he said, stopping the truck at the top of the hill then descending into the valley.

The greenery of the valley was unbelievable, with the promise of fall with leaves turning their colors. The road came down into the valley, leading up a hill to a two-story white house with dark-blue shutters. The front porch faced the road with a colonial front. A white board fence enclosed the yard around the house, extending down the road to a barn with a creek running through the pasture. Fruit trees and a garden spot were to the right of the road. The grounds conveyed the impression someone was living there; everything was so neat and kept. Carol could feel the peace that comes from transcending life, beyond daily life. She couldn't explain the feeling. This was the place she had always seen in her spirit.

Following the white fence leading up to the side of the road, they came upon a garage built separately from the house. A small travel trailer was parked next to the garage.

"Well, what do you think? This will soon be your home, all six hundred and ten acres of it. The lake where we stayed is to the north over the ridge," Big Bear said. Then he pointed to the southeast, saying, "There are the pastures that will hold our Appaloosa horses. There, up in the trees, you can see Big Eagle and Songbird's cabin. They will be moving, too. There is something else I better tell you. Mom wants to move in, helping with the children when they arrive. If that is all right with you," he added, opening her door, taking her hand, smiling and showing all of his white teeth.

The land and the house were just too much for Carol. She just stood there, looking around the yard at the fields where horses would run free. She, too, felt free and loved; her spirit was riding Babe across the green fields, looking forward to the day she would move into the house, making a home for Big Bear and all the children that would come to her.

"Carol, I have to take these supplies over to Running Deer in the trailer. I'll be right back; go on in," he urged her, gathering the bags out of the back of the truck.

Carol walked in the side entrance next to where they parked, entering a large room made into a classroom. A blackboard and desks with computers were built into the walls. In the front left corner was a large wood-burning furnace. Carol noticed the tiled floors; how neat and clean they were. From there, Carol entered a hall with a bath on the left and a utility room on the right. The hall opened into a breakfast room with bay windows, the breakfast room being part of the large country kitchen. The colors were white and blue, white cabinets with blue tile countertops. The modern appliances were easily accessible from a center cooking area.

Sitting at the round oak breakfast table, Carol looked around. There she sat when Big Bear came in, looking at her. Walking over, he took a seat next to her. "If there is anything you want to change, just tell me, sweetheart. I can get somebody up here before the snow sets in," he offered.

"No, darling, I just can't believe my eyes. All of this I have seen in my spirit before, thinking I was daydreaming. I just can't get over this. The spirit told me everything was prepared; now I know what the spirit was talking about," she said, wiping her tears away.

"Don't be sad, my Little Dove, everything has been prepared for you because of your love. I love you so much. This is a small token of my love. Each day you will see what I mean," he said, kissing her face where the tears were running. "Let's look at the rest of the house."

Taking her hand, Big Bear led her into the large open room. A huge stone fireplace had been built at the end of the room coming out of the breakfast room. The room was open from the front entrance all the way to the back entrance. Big Bear said the room was 20' by 60' for a large living room. Halfway on the left side of the large room were stairs leading to the second story. Facing the front to the right were two rooms: the first room was a library and a study. The other was a bedroom with its own bathroom across the hall. Then to the left of the large room was a spacious dining room opening into the kitchen. There was a hallway leading into a room off to the right of the main part of the house. The bathroom for the bedroom was on the right in the hallway. Coming into an oversized open glassed room, Carol stood surveying her surroundings: the green pastures, fruit trees, places to plant summer flowers leading up into the tall pines.

A king-sized oak bed sat in the middle of the room on oak floors partially covered with Indian rugs. Big Bear's clothes hung on the back of an overstuffed chair. There was a pair of boots next to the chair. To the right of the room, upon entering it, was a large walk-in closet. When he opened the closet door, the light came on. There was a gleaming bathroom with tub and shower, cabinets circling the walls of the bathroom. The walls were paneled with virgin pine paneling. Big Bear sat on the bed, watching her survey every inch with her eyes. The house was truly a masterpiece. Who but Big Bear could have constructed anything so perfect? she thought.

Carol sat down on the bed beside Big Bear. "What is the square footage of this house?" she asked. "It must have cost a fortune to build. How long did it take you to build it?" She was full of questions.

"Over two years. Every time I made money from my investments, I would put it into this house. All of this is paid for; not a dime is owed," he spoke proudly of his accomplishment. "See, Carol, I have a dream; that is, to do something for my people. If I do my part to the best of my ability, the Great Spirit will do the part I can't do. That was finding you and drawing you to me," he said, gently pushing her back on the bed, kissing her hard on the lips. "Come on; we have to see the upstairs. There are four bedrooms, three baths. They climbed the solid wooden stairs and went into the upper large rooms that looked much like the ones below them. On each side were two bedrooms, with one bath on one side, two on the other. Big Bear opened the door to the left of the stairs. "This will be Mom's room with her private bath. There is room for her sewing and other crafts. You and she will have plenty of room for whatever you want to do," he said, holding her hand. They looked briefly at the other rooms, then he led her back down the stairs.

Carol was so overwhelmed with the house she forgot it was past lunchtime. Big Bear had the refrigerator stocked with fruits and vegetables. When did he have time to do this? she wondered. He could accomplish more than any person she had known. Carol made a green salad, cooked frozen spinach, baked a potato for each of them in combining lunch and supper.

The afternoon was spent going from room to room, making a list of furniture needed for the house: long couches for the living room, with recliners and a coffee table, a love seat and table for the entrance. The library would have leather furniture. They walked through once again making sure everything was thought of for furnishings.

"I have a baby grand piano stored in a warehouse of a furniture store in Billings," he said. "We'll have that moved up here."

Day was turning to night when Big Bear asked Carol is she wanted to take a walk up the mountain. "You better put on a sweatshirt under your jacket; it's cold after the moon comes out."

Carol pulled a sweatshirt over her head, then her denim jacket over the shirt. Feeling warm enough, she joined Big Bear, who was waiting on the north side of the house. He took her hand and they passed through the gate into the pasture in back of the house. The full moon had crested the treetops, enabling them to see clearly. They found the creek, following its bed until reaching the back pasture fence. Their path was clearly marked by the creek. They climbed, following the flow of water descending out of the mountains into the valley.

Carol held Big Bear's hand as he led the way higher. The stream began to widen the higher they climbed. The water came tumbling down over the rocks, emptying into the rich valley below. Carol could hear water rushing down as in a waterfall.

"Is that a waterfall up ahead?" she asked Big Bear as they stopped to catch their breath.

"Yes; it's just ahead. We're coming upon a pool of water. The waterfall spills into a pool. That is why I brought you up here, to see something that is unbelievable, that is, if they are here tonight. I think they will be, for the moon is full. From here on, you can't talk. Walk as quietly as you can; stay in my path," he directed her, releasing her hand so she could follow him.

The noise of the waterfall grew louder as they came closer to the pool that received the generous flow of water coming out of the mountains. Big Bear was cautious in his steps, as quiet as a mountain cat. Carol tried to follow just as quietly, finding it impossible to do so.

They stood, staring down into the pool. The water glowed with a golden haze of illumination over the surface. From gold the haze became a blue and purplish color turning to deep pink as it ascended into the heavens. Carol stood in amazement at what she was watching. There were four Indian people playing around in the water as kids would. They were young, with no blemishes on them; their skin was as youthful as that of babies. Big Bear took Carol's hand as they stood together watching the Indians playing in the nude.

One of the playful visitors noticed Big Bear and Carol, motioning them to come in. Carol looked at Big Bear, but he only held his finger up to his lips. They proceeded to remove their clothes and boots. Holding hands, they entered the pool of gold, a perfect world of joy with water warm as bath water, energizing their bodies, filling their hearts with love. They lost consciousness of the cold and time, playing and loving with their companions.

What time the light beings left the pool of gold only the moon knows, hanging high in the Montana sky. Carol and Big Bear watched as they disappeared into the night without a word. The water suddenly felt cold. Big Bear helped Carol out of the water. They hurriedly pulled on their clothes and boots, walked quietly down the mountain and through the pasture gate into the house.

Immediately, Big Bear built a fire in the huge stone fireplace. Carol made coffee, they pulled the mattress off the bed, laying it on the floor in front of the fireplace. The flickering fire reflected their image on the wall. They sat drinking coffee in the large empty room. Big Bear was in his jeans, with his arm around Carol. Carol kept her sweatshirt on, covering her legs with an Indian blanket. She didn't understand just what they had seen and participated in, but it had been an ecstatic experience, filled with love and warmth she had never felt before. "That is the first time they asked me to come in the pool with them. It's because of our love. The more love you have, the brighter your light, the more spiritual companions you will have. These are the Bird Tribes returning to help people spiritually, especially children," said Big Bear.

"Tonight they asked us to join them," he repeated in wonder, setting his cup down and pulling Carol into his arms. "Carol, they led me to buy this property, telling me to build this house for you and the children. They are the ones I asked to bring you to me, my precious Little Dove. Your love shone brighter than all their light. I love you so much."

Carol's heart was so full she wept on Big Bear's arm. "I was lost without you; I couldn't find myself. You gave me that part that was missing," she said, kissing the strong, smooth chest that covered his heart.

They finally closed their eyes at the dawning of morning. The sun was past its highest point in the sky when they awakened in each other's arms. "I can't stop thinking about the light beings we saw last night. I don't understand why they picked us to come to," Carol said. "Big Bear, I know you are a spiritual person, knowing about spirits, but I know nothing."

Big Bear pulled the covers over their heads, smiling at her. "You don't have to know anything about spirits to be spirit. That is what you are, Little Dove; you are spirit, the spirit of love. Only the highest of the spirit world placed this great love in your heart for my people. That love is light, meaning you are a light being, too," he said kissing her lips, drawing her closer.

Carol answered Big Bear. "There is no greater love than you have for your people," she said. "So our light together makes a brighter light, and the vibrations of our hearts in the heavens and earth bring great joy. These spirits of the same light and vibrations are descending to help with our purpose in Mother Earth. I understand now what you are talking about," she said, responding to his kiss.

Lying in each other's arms, they talked about the night before. Then the subject changed to the house and moving, getting settled.

Carol made more coffee, walking around unconcerned that she was in her sweatshirt and panties. Big Bear pulled on his boots and shirt, kissing her on the back of the neck as she made bran muffins. Canned peaches, bran muffins and coffee made up their breakfast. They drank in each other with their eyes as the radio played "Unchained Melody" as recorded by LeAnn Rimes. "Do you want to dance?" Big Bear asked Carol.

"I thought you would never ask," she answered.

He took her in his arms, and they danced around the kitchen, losing themselves in the larger space of love, holding on to each precious moment of life. The song ended, but they continued to dance. "Tonight we dance and then we go to bed," Big Bear declared.

Carol soaked her body in the warm water, feeling good. She shampooed her hair, and without using her blow dryer, she let her hair hang loose. She put on clean clothes and her boots, then walked outside in the sun. Big Bear had gone to see Running Deer about some work on the ranch. Meanwhile, Carol sat in the sun thinking of the strange things that had happened to her since she met Big Bear. Maybe this spiritual life was in her all the time, but it had taken Big Bear's spirit to bring all of it out of her. They had planned to spend the day walking over the ranch, picking out a place for the herb garden and more fruit trees.

When Big Bear returned, they walked hand in hand, planning their life, talking about children, how to care for them in spirit and body, discussing the boys Big Bear would bring to the ranch, teaching them. All their plans were wrapped up beside the fire, as the sun kissed the day away, with brilliant colors splashing across the sky.

The fire cast a dimmer light across the room, as they danced to country music, holding each other tightly. They both knew that tomorrow was another day, with a lot to consider, but they pushed that thought away, holding on to the joys of today. They kissed and whispered love in each other's ear, lying in front of the fire, making love slowly, completely.

Morning sun rays danced across the room. Big Bear kissed Little Dove tenderly. They continued to hold so tightly to life, thinking this love happens only in dreams. He freed himself, entering his spirit. He saw himself and Little Dove racing across the sky on their beautiful Appaloosa horses, free to enter the moonbeams, becoming the drops of rain, the first snowflakes, their blushing faces in the early spring as the first flowers opened to their great love. They ran through the fields, playing in the streams, spreading their love over all the earth. They sang their enchanting love songs to the birds, who echoed their words. Big Bear touched Little Dove with his spirit, and she opened her eyes. He was propped up on his elbows, looking at her.

"What is the matter? Should we be up and getting ready to go?" she asked.

"No; I'm just thinking how much I love you, how I have always loved you, will always love you," he said kissing her lips gently.

"I love you, my darling, always have and always will. These promises we don't have to make, for they were made for us," Carol said, kissing him. "I think we better get up now, make coffee, free ourselves for the day."

"You're right, but there is something I want to talk with you about. While we have coffee I'll tell you," he said, pulling off the blanket. He grabbed her and they rolled around on the mattress, laughing and kissing.

Big Bear went to make coffee and Carol went to the bathroom, taking a quick shower, putting on her makeup, and coming out ready for the day. Big Bear handed her a cup of coffee, with a kiss. "Now, what do you want to talk with me about?" she asked.

Big Bear started the conversation by saying, "As you know, the winters are awfully cold and long in Montana. So last year I bought a place in Arizona for a winter home. It has two hundred acres, with a small three-bedroom, three bath house. Next winter when we are there, we can add two or three bedrooms, another bath or two, whatever we need. "Why are you looking that way at me?" he asked, taking her hand.

"I knew I would be spending my winters in Arizona," she said, laughing at him.

"Well, that is part of it; there's something else. During the winter when I'm teaching, I stay for weeks in Billings, to keep from getting snowed in and missing school. I just take a room at the motel for two or three months. There I have my meals and laundry done. What I'm trying to say is that I would like for you to work at the school, too, staying in town with me. Also, I have been talking to the vocational supervisor where I teach on the reservation about you teaching a photography course this winter. I know you would have many students sign up for the course. I know your heart is set on making quilts this winter, but you have too much to give to children to sit home making quilts," Big Bear said, looking into her eyes as he talked to her.

"What makes you happy, makes me happy. I'm not staying at that ranch without you. If you stay in town, I will stay in town. If I can teach a course in photography, I would love that. Can we work this out so I can teach the same night you teach your course? I would also like to work as a teacher's aide with first or second grade children. Can you arrange that, Big Bear?" she asked, smiling at him.

"I have already set up an appointment for you Tuesday morning at ten. You have an interview with a first grade teacher. She had a teacher's aide who left recently. Hearing about the job opening, I looked into it for you. You staying out at the ranch, while I am in town just wouldn't work. Hope you don't think I want you to work, but these winters are long. It's best you have something to do," he said, waiting for her to respond.

"Don't worry about it; we will wait and see how everything works out. I would never think anything but loving thoughts of you. I understand what you are doing, looking out for me; thank you," she said, picking up the coffee cups.

They sang love songs to each other while driving back toward the ranch. The country music was ringing in their hearts. "You're getting good with that singing," Big Bear exclaimed. "We can sing this winter in the lounge at the motel."

"I don't know about that," she said, laughing at him.

"Just for me, you could try. We have Friday and Saturday night shows in the lounge. I hope you will be a part of it," he said, kissing her hand.

"No promises; we will have to wait and see about this singing business," she said, kissing his neck.

The drive back home was short, like the weekend they had together. Arriving home, they greeted Songbird and Big Eagle, who were glad to see them again. Songbird asked, "How good you feel being in mountains? Did light beings come for Little Dove and Big Bear?" She wanted information on their encounters with the spirits on the mountain.

Big Bear fielded the question before Carol could answer, saying, "Yes, they came, inviting us to swim with them. This is the first time they asked me to join them. It was because of Little Dove's love, I'm sure. We had a wonderful time with them. What has been happening around here? There are a lot of truck tracks out front."

Big Eagle looked at Songbird before answering. "They came out, looking around. I stayed with them, Mr. Fowler and wife with another couple, wanting to know if you would sell the Appaloosa horses, especially Quickfire. I told him to see you. I said I have no authority to sell anything on the ranch. I don't like them coming around when you're not here."

"Don't worry about it, Big Eagle. It will not happen again. I will speak to him tomorrow. You did good," Big Bear said, thanking Big Eagle for his judgment on the matter. "Let's all of us get some lunch, then go for a ride."

"Sounds good to Songbird, long time since ride ranch," she said, joining in with Big Bear.

Taking Carol's hand, Big Bear teased, "I want to race Carol. She can't beat me at swimming; let's see if she can beat me riding."

"That's not fair. How long have you been riding? I have been riding only for a short time. But I will take you on, down to the sign and back," she agreed, holding tightly to his hand.

The lunch was simple, with boiled chicken and rice for Songbird and Big Eagle. Carol and Big Bear ate a large green salad with baked potatoes. They all laughed over things that had happened in their lives and their Indian ways, telling stories of old, hoping to be together for many years. They had already been together for twenty years. "When I came to this ranch, or I should say, when I came to this land to make a ranch out of it, Songbird and Big Eagle came with me, living in a small trailer, until five years later, when we built this ranch house, setting them up in a larger trailer to live in. Those were hard years, but we made it," Big Bear remembered.

Big Eagle picked up the story, saying, "Because of our determination, Big Bear would go off to teach school. Songbird and I would stay at the ranch for weeks without seeing anyone in the wintertime. Then in the summer, when Big Bear was out of school, he would work from daylight to dark making the ranch what it is today. We need each other. It has been a good life, and the best is yet to come. We all have a purpose in what is coming in the earth. We are ready to help mankind with this change, especially the children. Songbird and I never had children; now we want some children we can help," he said with tears in his eyes.

Big Bear took up the conversation. "We don't have children of our own, but we have all the children in need. We have prepared ourselves for what is ahead of us; this is what we have been doing. With Carol coming, the circle is complete. June and July will be spent with Carol and me taking a trip, moving and getting everything ready for all the children we can get. I know Andy will be coming for a year, then I will teach him about horses and himself. We have twenty brood mares and two stud horses. These will keep Andy busy in addition to his education. I feel new life coming in all of us for this calling we have accepted. We don't have to do this; it is our choice. Who can be happy without fulfilling their destiny? I know I can't deny myself," Big Bear said, holding Carol's hand.

Carol thought, He was always planning, and what a perfect plan it was. Since she had been back the past few days, Big Bear had not said a word about a wedding date. Yet this didn't bother her; she felt that she was already married to him—always had been and always would be. She loved him so much, particularly when he planned for the children. In her spirit she could see them dancing around with the children, running in the green fields, picking wild flowers, playing in the creek, going barefoot in the summer. She awoke from this trance at the sound of Songbird removing dishes from the table.

"Songbird woke Little Dove out of trance—good place to go. We ready for horse race, dishes can wait, Songbird get ready," she said, aware of Carol's experience.

"No, Songbird; you get ready. I'll put the dishes in the dishwasher. I'm ready, and Big Bear can help me," she said, kissing his lips.

"Sure we will, meet you at the corral in a few minutes; go on, get ready," he told her, helping Carol remove the dishes from the table.

Big Bear and Carol had four horses saddled and waiting when Big Eagle and Songbird returned. Songbird laid out the race course, saying, "Here is the race: from front of the barn to the Double B

Ranch sign and back. The loser has to buy dinner Saturday in town. Songbird not race, too long since Songbird ride; I judge race," she said, climbing in her saddle.

They all mounted, placing Carol in the middle of Big Bear and Big Eagle. Songbird shouted, "Go!" Off they went, with Babe keeping up with Quickfire, running hard to the sign, Big Eagle only a few paces behind. As they made the turn heading back to the barn, Carol and Babe left time and space.

Little Dove, in her wedding dress, dismounted Babe, standing beside the river on the reservation. She saw two little girls playing close to the water. They were playing around having fun, but when one of the little girls pushed the other, she fell into the swift-moving water. Jumping in the water, Little Dove pulled the girl out. Taking the two girls aside, Little Dove told them of the danger of the river, asking them not to play close to the water. She asked them their names, picking them up and carrying them away from the water. They promised Little Dove they would never play close to the water again. Their names were Carrie and Molly. They waved at Little Dove as she mounted Babe, and returned to the barn.

"Where Little Dove go?" asked Songbird.

"I really don't know. I was here, then I was on the reservation by the river where two little Indian girls were playing. One fell into the water, would have drowned if I hadn't been there. I was wearing my Indian wedding dress. Now I'm back," Carol said simply. They stood staring at her in disbelief.

Big Bear asked, "Has this happened to you before, Carol? I know you were here, then gone the next minute. You were close on my tail, then you were gone. How do you feel?" he asked with concern, taking Carol off Babe.

"I'm fine, just as if nothing happened. It's no big deal. It's you people—anything can happen around here. The names of the two little girls are Carrie and Molly; they were dolls. I wanted to bring them with me," she said, sitting down on the grass. "Now let's finish our ride."

Remounting, they rode toward the hayfields, taking their time. The day was a day Carol would always remember: in love, every hill echoing this love. Right then, she had enough love in her heart for the whole world. She would help everyone she could find, thinking of the little girls. Thank God I was there, she thought. Riding to the back acreage, they turned to go home, urging their horses into a gallop.

Songbird and Carol went into the house, fixing something to eat, while the men unsaddled the horses. "Little Dove, tell Songbird about spirit trip. Someday Songbird will love enough to go this way. This is great light. Songbird knew medicine woman once that could translate body."

"I really don't know what else to say about it. To me, I was needed, and the spirit wanted me there. Thank God I was available," she said, hoping Songbird understood.

They finished up the meal without any more talk about Carol's experience. Songbird and Big Eagle left for home. Big Bear and Carol settled themselves on the couch, listening to music. Big Bear hugged her close, saying, "Don't forget, tomorrow at the school, ten o'clock, at the principal's office. The elementary school is on the right coming into town; I teach in the building on the left. Then I will meet you at twelve-thirty in the motel restaurant. We will stay overnight, so bring clean clothes; if you don't mind, please bring me a clean suit," he said, kissing her hand.

"Honey, I will be glad to take you some clothes. Do you think they will put me to work Wednesday?" she asked, wanting more information.

"I'm sure they will, you beautiful doll. Come on, let's go to bed," he said, picking her up off the couch.

CHAPTER SIX

Crossing Over the Shining River

They slept in each other's arms. Morning came to them at five. Big Bear tried to get Carol to stay in bed while he prepared himself for the day, but she got up and made coffee in her oversized T-shirt and panties, fixing him fruit and cereal. "Big Bear, did you ever find out about those two little girls at the reservation? Were they placed in a foster home? I know those are the two little girls that I went to at the river."

"Yes, they were placed with grandparents on the reservation. We have a council meeting this Friday night. I'm going to ask more questions about them then. I'll find out even if I have to go and see for myself," he said, kissing her lips. "Believe me, precious, I will let you know."

After Big Bear's departure Carol slipped back into the warm bed, trying to sleep. When she heard Songbird in the kitchen, Carol slowly arose out of the bed, taking a shower, dressing for the day. She joined Songbird for coffee, saying, "Good morning, Songbird; it's a beautiful morning. I have a lot to do today. I may be getting a job, at least I hope so."

"Little Dove think she like working at school? Big Bear likes work at school with kids. Songbird thinks he miss kids when he quit. Hope he has more children to teach," she said, drinking her coffee.

"I have every confidence Big Bear has planned all this out. He seems to have it all under control. I will help him, whatever he has set his heart to do," Carol said as she sipped hot coffee.

"Little Dove good wife for Big Bear, he lucky to find Little Dove."

"No, Songbird; I'm the lucky one to find Big Bear. He is my life," she said, thinking of him. "I have to get some clothes for Big Bear and myself for tomorrow. We will be staying in town tonight. If I go to work, I'll be back home Wednesday night with Big Bear. I don't want to forget his toothbrush," she said, setting her coffee cup in the sink.

Carol packed the clothes they needed, hanging Big Bear's pants and shirt with hers in the truck. She left the ranch for the school, playing country music on the truck's radio.

At 9:55 a.m. she walked into the principal's office. Betty Davis was part-Indian, middle-aged and a serious person, taking her job with the children as her life quest. "Carol Fletcher, I'm glad to meet you," she said. "You come highly recommended for the job. We appreciate people taking an interest in our school. Our goal here is the learning welfare of the child. Their school environment is just as important as their home environment. I'll take you down to meet Nancy Johnson, one of our best first grade teachers."

Carol followed Mrs. Davis down the hallway to Classroom 1, as indicated on the door. Nancy Johnson came to the door, inviting them into the classroom. It appeared that with thirty-five students, she had her hands full, but everything was under control.

"Nancy, this is Carol Fletcher, applying for the teacher's aide job. I would like for you and Carol to step out in the hall and talk for a few minutes while I stay with the class," Mrs. Davis said.

Carol was in shock as she saw that Nancy Johnson was no doubt, the Indian woman in Big Bear's picture. Why hadn't he told her this or at least prepared her? Why should I have any reaction to this? she asked herself. That is part of his past.

Nancy looked Carol over, saying, "Miss Fletcher, you have no experience working with children; how do you know you can do this job?"

"Because I know in my heart I can do this job. I love children and they love me; other than that, I have no qualifications. But

I'm willing to learn and work with you for the children's sake," Carol stated her position firmly.

"Well, you came highly recommended by Big Bear. He seems to know an awful lot about you. Big Bear and I went together for about a year, right after I came here to teach. I was a fool for letting him go. If I had it all to do over again, I would never let him go. He is a good man; I hope you appreciate him and don't make a fool out of him," she said, making herself clear.

"Mrs. Johnson, I came here to discuss a school job, not Big Bear," Carol replied, looking straight into Nancy's dark eyes.

"You're right, Carol, school first. I'm going to take you on as an aide. I know we can work together for the children," she said, extending her hand to Carol.

Carol followed Mrs. Davis back to the office to fill out papers for her employment. "You know, Miss Fletcher, Nancy was involved with Big Bear at one time. Is this going to be a problem for you? If so, I can place you somewhere else. With her marriage breaking up, this is a difficult time for Nancy. I hope you can work with her for the benefit of the children," Mrs. Davis said, with concern in her voice.

"I can work with Nancy. She needs me; the children need me, too. When a person is going through difficult time emotionally, it is hard to concentrate. Yes, I will be a friend to Nancy," she said, filling out the papers. When Carol completed the paperwork, she was told to report to Mrs. Johnson's class for work tomorrow.

Carol sat drinking coffee at the restaurant when Big Bear came in looking for her. He slid in the booth beside her, asking, "Well, how did the interview go? Listen, Carol, I'm sorry; I should have told you about Nancy, but I thought you wouldn't go for the interview if I did."

"I got the job and I like Nancy," she replied. "I'm sure I can learn much from her about teaching children. This is the reason I'm there, that and being a friend to Nancy at this time of trouble in her life. The spirit always knows where you can be of help," Carol said, holding his hand. "Now, we'd better eat so we can go to the bank before you have to return to school."

Big Bear stared at her. "Is that all you have to say? You're right; there is nothing else to say," he decided, closing the subject.

"I'm to be there tomorrow at seven-thirty sharp. I'll be there, ready to work with the children. Your name will never be mentioned by me. This is for the children; no tension can exist between Nancy and me," she insisted.

Big Bear nodded in agreement, then ordered lunch for them.

Carol took out the cashier's check, depositing it in Big Bear's checking account. He put her name on his checking and saving accounts; his ranching account was with Big Eagle. "When we move I will close out the ranch account, transferring all in checking, moving the accounts to Bozeman. You are something else, Carol. I love you," he said as they got into the truck.

"I love you, Big Bear, and always will," she said, leaning her head on his shoulder.

He left her at the motel while he returned to school. Carol took this time alone to shampoo her hair and do her nails, but most of all to listen to her spirit.

Carol felt good about accepting the job, knowing the spirit was pleased with her handling of the situation with Nancy. Carol could have only love for Nancy, because she realized that we all make mistakes in our lives. Nancy made a mistake when choosing something else or somebody other than Big Bear. Now she was trying to recapture what she thought they had, but that just didn't work in the present. We must create a new day for ourselves, releasing ourselves from emotional ties, freeing ourselves to send forth love vibrations into creation. To give love is to receive love. This will be manifested in our lives, if we stay on the right track. Carol was still resting in her spirit when Big Bear opened the motel door.

"We have two hours before leaving for the reservation; let's go dancing," he said, putting down his briefcase, lying on the bed with Carol. "I want to hold you and move around and around with you in my arms. My beautiful Little Dove, I love you so much; come closer."

Moving her body closer, Carol could feel his heart beating. "I love you always," she said, kissing his mouth, feeling his passion.

"We won't be able to get out of here if we don't get going," he said, helping her off the bed. "Let's have some fun," Big Bear insisted. "I have waited a long time for this."

Carol dressed, watching Big Bear brush his teeth and change his shirt. He seemed to be a teenager, so full of life to share with her. How could she refuse him anything?

Gliding across the dance floor to the rhythm of the music, they were reminded of the first time they met. They listened to the music and the voice of LeAnn Rimes. What a voice the young woman had. The song "I Will Always Love You," captured their hearts, and they softly whispered their love to one another. Big Bear kissed her hand, moving Carol smoothly around the floor, continuing to play his favorites on the jukebox. "I love you, Carol; I will always love you," he told her. "This is written in the heavens, established before we became flesh. I know that you know this; you can feel this oneness we have." She melted in his arms, not saying a word.

Big Bear wanted to dance the night away. "Together Again" came on, with Big Bear moving his body with the music, Carol fitting in his arms and moving with him. "We have to go," Carol reminded him at the end of the song. She coaxed him off the dance floor and out of the restaurant.

Big Bear returned to the room, gathering his briefcase and material for the class. Joining Carol in the truck, they were on their way to the reservation. "Carol, Mom wants you to come stay with her Thursday night while I have class. I told her I would ask you. You can see Allen, the director of continuing education, about the photography course tonight. I doubt the class will be starting for at least two weeks, allowing time to run an ad in the paper. You'll know after tonight; do you feel comfortable with that?"

"Yes. Whatever happens, let it happen. I would love to spend Thursday night with your mother. I love Walking Elk, and the wisdom of the years she has. We'll call her tonight, tell her we will see her Thursday to spend time with her. I know that will make her happy," Carol said, holding his hand.

Big Bear's class consisted of a test on cattle diseases and treatments. Carol sat in the back of the room, waiting for Allen to have time for her in his office.

Allen came in and directed Carol to his office, saying, "Carol, I'm happy to have someone to teach photography. I would like to see some of your pictures and qualifications, names of magazines you have worked for. Then we can run an ad for the class in the paper. As soon as I get this information, we can get started. I will set the course up to start in two weeks. I hope this complies with your plans. You will be teaching two nights a week, just like Big Bear, at the same time. I expect you will have young students, high school age or those just out of school. We can enroll twenty-five, maybe more if they come. Can I expect this material on your qualifications Thursday?" Allen asked.

"Yes. I can't be here Thursday night, but I will send it with Big Bear. I thank you, Allen; I'm looking forward to teaching the class. I'll see you next Tuesday when I come with Big Bear."

"How did Big Bear get so lucky, finding someone like you?" Allen asked. "He has always been such a loner. He sure got lucky; maybe it's not too late for me," Allen said, flirting with her, squeezing Carol's hand.

"It's never too late to love, Allen," she responded, by squeezing his hand in return.

"You can never tell; I may become one of your students," he said, smiling at Carol.

"I better go; Big Bear's class is almost over. You'll get the material Thursday night," she said, walking out of Allen's office.

She walked back to Big Bear's classroom thinking, I will have to keep Allen at arm's length, or I will have to deal with him. She decided that she would cross that bridge when she came to it. Maybe it was best to talk to Big Bear about Allen now rather than later. Opening the door to the classroom, she saw the class was breaking up for the night.

"How did your interview go?" Big Bear asked.

"Two weeks from tonight the class starts. Big Bear, tell me about Allen; what is his problem?" she asked, getting into the truck.

"What is the matter, Carol? Don't teach the class if you're not comfortable with Allen. He has been divorced for two years, had the reputation of hitting on women. If you have a problem with this, just let me know. I'll talk with him, nice and sweet, but I'm sure you can handle him," Big Bear said, holding her hand.

"Yes, I can take care of Allen. I have seen thousands of them, men who don't understand what No means. That is enough on the subject. I have school to think about tomorrow," she said.

Carol held on tightly to Big Bear's hand, thinking out loud, "I have to get material for Allen to advertise the course in the paper. Will you please take the material to him Thursday night? I will be with your mother, so I told him you will drop off the material at his office."

"That's fine. I'll be glad to give your material to Allen," Big Bear said, parking the truck at the motel.

Then they were quiet about their daily lives, losing themselves in one another. There were no problems when they were together, holding the world outside, loving each other.

Big Bear and Carol had breakfast at the motel restaurant, then they went their separate ways with Carol driving her truck to school. She arrived at 7:25 a.m., ready to go to work. Nancy had the day planned out, giving Carol a program for the day. Carol could understand her part in the program; her name was written next to each task she had to do. Nancy had done a good job, making each detail described plainly for Carol. Carol studied the program, visualizing each activity. The day went quite smoothly. The kids' outdoor recess was Carol's favorite time with them, when she felt closest to them. She helped with art class and clean up, read to the children, helping them with their numbers and writing their names. Carol had a good day, working in harmony with Nancy.

Carol drank coffee at the restaurant, waiting excitedly for Big

Bear. She kept her eye on him as he walked toward her. "Hi, how was your day? I thought of you all day, how much I love you and always will," he said, kissing her hand.

"You lovable creature," she replied. "I had a wonderful day; everything went very well. Nancy is a good teacher; she really loves children. I'm lucky to get to work with her," Carol said, smiling at him, holding tightly onto his hand.

"I know what you learn from Nancy will help with teaching the children we take. You see, I had an ulterior motive for you working with Nancy, knowing you could use the training. You loving darling," he said, kissing her hand.

The waitress watched Big Bear kiss Carol's hand. Blushing, she asked, "Mr. Nelson, can I bring you some coffee?"

"Yes, some coffee and two large green salads, the kind I usually get, thank you," he said, turning his attention back to Carol. "Do you want to stay in town tonight? We'll have more time to dance."

How loving and carefree his heart was, Carol thought, saying, "Honey, I can't; I have that material to prepare for Allen and Nancy tomorrow. Nancy asked me to bring pictures of the powwow and animals to show the class. All this is due tomorrow, but another night I will be available," she said, winking a blue eye at him.

"I forgot we are busy working; thank goodness this is the last year. We have Saturday night in town, staying over, going back to the ranch Sunday morning. One night for fun. Is it a date, Miss Carol?" he asked, winking back at her.

"You have a date, Mr. Nelson. Saturday, it is, a night of fun."

They finished their salad and coffee, hating that they had to drive in separate trucks home. Carol pulled out first with Big Bear behind her. Her thoughts were on all she had to do: find her photography certificate, books, list of magazines she had sold photos to, photos for Allen and some for school. Maybe Big Bear would help her pick out the photos for the school children and Allen, she thought.

When Carol arrived home, Songbird met her at the door, saying, "Little Dove got call from St. Louis today, think mother of Little Dove. She wants Little Dove to call."

"Oh, my goodness, I have forgotten to call them," Carol realized, putting down the suitcase. She picked up the phone, dialing the family's number in St. Louis.

"Hello, Mom, how are you? I'm fine, doing well. I'm sorry I haven't called, but I have been so busy. I'm working at the school as a teacher's aide. I will start teaching a photography course at the Indian vocational school, where Jim teaches. How are Tony and Dad doing? No, Mom, no wedding date has been set yet, but I will let you know when and where. Mom, I'm extremely happy; that is all that matters. Let's leave well enough alone. Yes, I will call or write more often; take care of yourself. Yes, Mother, I will, bye," Carol said, hanging up the receiver. Her mother was always worrying about her, especially about when she would get married.

"Little Dove's mother wants her marry by white man's law; don't she know Little Dove married by Indian law?" Songbird asked, getting right to the truth as usual.

"It's tradition, Songbird, and I respect it, but right now I'm happy living the way I am. This marriage thing Big Bear and I will work out for ourselves. We can't be pushed by other people's opinions. We have our life, and it's a happy one, why change it?

Carol carried the suitcase and clothes to the bedroom, taking out the soiled clothes. She turned her attention to the boxes in storage in the other bedroom. In the box labeled Photography, she found her diploma from the school in St. Louis. She selected photos of the powwow, picking out some for the course, then some to show Allen as samples of her work. She looked through animal pictures for the children. She was still looking at photos when Big Bear came looking for her.

"I can help if you need me; if not, I'm going out to the wheat field with Big Eagle. The wheat is ready for the combine; a crew will be in there tomorrow," he said, noticing the pictures on the counter. "I bet Mom would love to have some of these; take her some tomorrow night, okay?"

"I will. I know she would like to have some of you and Two Feathers in the rodeo. Then there is Billy on Babe; they are good pictures. I'll see that she gets the ones she wants. Sweetheart, you go with Big Eagle; I have this under control. Wish I had time for a ride, but duty calls," Carol said, kissing him on the lips.

"I should be back in an hour or so; maybe you will be done, then we can listen to music," he said, kissing her.

Carol sat at the typewriter, thinking of what to include on her resume. Words began to come. She listed the magazines that had purchased photographs from her, her years of experience, naming some of the places she had traveled for photos, the name of her school, year of graduation. Soon she finished the resume, placing all the material in a large envelope. Then she placed the photos for the children in another envelope, marking it Children. Then she went to take a bath before Big Bear returned.

Carol soaked in the warm water, taking time to refresh herself. Music was coming from the living room as she pulled her oversized T-shirt over her head. Carol knew Big Bear was back, music being as much a part of him as eating or sleeping. Carol began putting herself into the music, music being the rhythm of the soul. Certainly Big Bear had a soul that often found its expression in music. Carol smiled to herself, thinking about Big Bear and his love of music.

"When are you coming out to dance with me?" he asked, looking into the room for her.

"Dance? I have on a nightshirt. I'll be right out," she said.

When Carol came in the room, Big Bear was looking over the photos again. "These are real good," he said. "I know Allen will be pleased to see them. Mom will love these of the rodeo and the horse races. Do you have extras for her? If not, we can drop some off at the photo lab, pick them up after school," he said, placing the photos back in the envelope.

"We could do that. I showed the pictures to them, but none of your family asked me for pictures of the powwow. I will have her copies made and just take them to her. I know she would like that. What was that you said about dancing?" she asked, smiling at Big Bear.

Slow, soft, loving music filled their hearts. In his arms Carol danced around the living room. They continued to dance, losing track of time, realizing they were together for always. At ten o'clock they decided to shut off the music and go to bed.

Carol jutted her face forward toward the daylight that shone down upon the new day. She sat on the deck in back of the ranch house, gazing across the fields. The late-September morning was cold and frost was coming on. What a day to be alive, being a part of God's great plan for mankind, she thought. Pink clouds burst forth with a gold cast, sending a reddish glow across the sky, a photographer's dream. Carol wondered where she would be if she had accepted her next assignment for the magazine, but quickly she dismissed the thought, knowing there was no use in considering "what if." Hearing Big Bear in the kitchen, she rose to join him for breakfast.

Then they placed clothes in the truck, as they were spending another night in town, and they were off to school.

Carol greeted the children with joy, happy to be a part of their lives. During the school day Nancy came to her, thanking her for being such a help to her and the children. Carol pinned her pictures up on the bulletin board, telling the children where the pictures were taken. When the children were gone, Nancy and Carol started cleaning up the classroom. Nancy asked Carol, "When are you and Big Bear getting married?"

Carol thought for a moment before answering. "We are one; we are already married," she said, leaving it there, saying no more.

Carol was waiting in front of the school when Big Bear came to pick her up.

Later, Carol lay on the bed wanting to rest, thinking of Nancy. There was something Nancy had wanted to tell her, but Nancy had been unable to get it out. Maybe when they knew each other better, she would trust Carol more. Big Bear and Carol rested in their room until it was time to eat. After dinner, they drove out to the reservation.

Walking Elk was glad to see Big Bear and Carol. They gave her the pictures, and she laughed to see photos of Big Bear and Two Feathers at the rodeo, proud of them as sons. Big Bear's stay was a short one before having to leave for his class.

Kissing Carol and his mom, Big Bear left the two women together. Carol looked around the humble dwelling where one room functioned as kitchen, dining and living area. There were two bedrooms with one bath, small, but clean. Walking Elk moved papers from a chair, saying, "Little Dove, sit by Walking Elk. You my daughter; Walking Elk had no daughter. Little Dove alone so we talk. How Little Dove like Nancy Johnson? She go with Big Bear long ago."

Walking Elk had caught Carol off guard with the question. "She is okay, a good teacher; the children like her. Anything else would be unfair to say. I don't know anything about her. I know she was a part of Big Bear's past, but that doesn't bother me. I have an ex-husband; Big Bear never asks me questions about him, our lives are now," she said, wondering what Walking Elk was getting at.

"Nancy have two boys, one ten, and one eight; one ten she says is Big Bear's. When she and husband have trouble, she tell everybody boy is Big Bear's. Big Bear ask her for test, she refused. Big Bear pay no attention, say boy born to her husband, raise by husband, not Big Bear's son. Little Dove should know, before gossip catch her," Walking Elk said, studying Carol's reactions.

"This doesn't shock me. Big Bear thought they would marry. These things happen; it's no big deal, Big Bear can handle this in his wisdom. If the boy is Big Bear's son, then we will love him. But there is no use upsetting the child's life because of his mother's past. Help me pray, Walking Elk, an end will come to this," Carol said, smiling at the old woman.

"Little Dove have good heart. We pray Great Spirit work out for boy, what best for him," Walking Elk said, satisfied with Carol's reaction to the news about the boy. "Little Dove teach photography course, maybe Walking Elk take course," she said, laughing at herself.

After nine, Big Bear arrived to pick Carol up. Riding back to the motel, Carol was quiet. Big Bear held her hand, asking, "What is the matter? Mom told you about this business with Nancy, but there is nothing to it. If so, I would have told you myself. This is somewhere in her fantasies; the boy is not mine. I tried to have a test to proof parentage, and she refused. Her husband doesn't need this; he loves that boy and is a good father to both of those boys," Big Bear said, holding on tightly to Carol's hand.

"I believe you. Nancy is going through a difficult time, but things will work out. I know if you thought for one minute that was your son, you would be the first to say so. Let's drop the matter, and let her know this is nothing to us. I think quietness will put a stop to all of the confusion," Carol said, kissing his neck.

"You're right. If we raise issues from the past, things will only get worse in the future. Let's not mention it again; such things rob us of our joy," Big Bear said, turning on the country music.

Never again was the subject of the boy mentioned by either of them. Friday came and went with school, then staying late for Big Bear to attend the Tribal Council meeting. Carol stayed at Walking Elk's while Big Bear attended his meeting. Walking Elk and Carol talked about the Indian way of life, enjoying each other's company. Big Bear picked Carol up around ten and they headed toward the ranch.

They held hands, listening to country music, loving each other. "I found out about the little girls tonight," Big Bear said. "They are living with grandparents on the reservation. Their mother was white and her parents wanted nothing to do with the children. Now they hope this will work out with the other grandparents, but it is a slim chance. I asked if I could go and visit them, to see how they are. They agreed, if the social worker approves of these visits. I plan on going out soon, seeing about their welfare," he assured her, holding Carol's hand tighter.

"I hope for the sake of the girls all will work out well. If we are to care for those girls, things will work out that way," Carol said, laying her head on his shoulder.

They were late getting to bed, and Carol was late getting up. What time Big Bear left, she didn't know. Looking at the clock, she realized it was nine, and out of the bed she came. She had a hundred things to do before tonight, including clothes to wash and work on the photography course.

Carol proceeded into the bathroom to gather dirty clothes for the laundry, but there was no clothes. "Songbird, what happened to the clothes in the hamper in the bathroom? I'm going to do some laundry," Carol said, looking around the room for dirty clothes.

"Little Dove call Songbird?"

"Yes, where are the clothes from the bathroom?" she called from the bathroom.

"Little Dove look in closet, will find clothes. Songbird do job, why Little Dove yell at Songbird?"

"I'm sorry, Songbird; I got up thinking I had to do laundry. I'm used to doing everything for myself. Thank you. Say, can you saddle a horse?" Carol asked, thankful for the free time.

"Songbird can saddle buffalo if he stands still," she replied, laughing at Carol.

"As I don't have to do laundry, let's take a ride before noon," she said, coming out of the bedroom carrying her boots.

"Songbird ready, have beans cooked for lunch," she said, laying aside her work. They left the house to have fun. Songbird was right; she could saddle a horse as well as a man.

"Songbird, will you teach me how to saddle a horse?" Carol asked, watching carefully as Songbird handled the saddle.

"Next time, Little Dove saddle Babe," Songbird said, mounting her horse.

They rode through the fields to the wheat field. Big Bear and Big Eagle stood watching the crew in the field. Then they noticed the women, waving at them. Carol and Songbird rode up to where they stood. Big Bear went over to Carol helping her down, saying, "What have we here? Two lost girls, asking to be kissed." He pulled Carol into his arms and said, "I missed you this morning; there was no one to have coffee with me."

"I'll make it up to you, I promise," she said, kissing him.

"All right; everybody heard that promise, she will make it up to me," he said, joking with her. "What are you girls doing out here?"

"Little Dove have no work, want to take ride, ride good for her. But we don't race," Songbird said, laughing at Carol.

"We were ready for home," Big Bear said. "We need some food and drink. Hope something is ready; instead of cooking, the women are out riding around," he teased, pulling Carol closer.

"For that remark, we're not coming home for the rest of the day. Songbird and I will teach you not to take us for granted," she said, holding him tight.

"Big Eagle, you better help me; I'm in trouble," Big Bear joked, kissing Carol on the neck.

"Big Eagle stay out of mess; these women could quit cooking," he said, laughing at Big Bear and Carol.

"Big Eagle, take the truck back to the barn. I'll ride back with this pretty girl, if she will let me. We have a date tonight, remember?" he said, taking Carol's hand, helping her in the saddle, and swinging his leg up behind the saddle.

They took off at a gallop toward the house, Songbird in the rear. Big Eagle followed them slowly in the truck. At the barn was a truck with a man awaiting them. Big Bear noticed the man, saying, "Fowler—wonder what he wants. I'm too busy to fool with him. Carol, you and Songbird go into the house. I'll unsaddle the horses."

Stopping at the barn, Big Bear dismounted, helping Carol down. Songbird and Carol just nodded to the elderly man, leaving the three of them to talk.

The women cooked rice, making a green salad to eat with the beans. They were putting the food on the table when the men came in. After washing their hands they sat down to eat. "Big Eagle, Carol and I are going out tonight to have some fun; do you and Songbird want to come along? I might allow you to dance with Little Dove," Big Bear said smiling, showing his white teeth.

Carol said, "You handsome man; you will allow it, huh?" laughing at him.

"We will be leaving around seven. Meet us at the motel lounge, okay? Carol and I will clean the kitchen now. Go home and make yourself beautiful, Songbird," he said, tapping her on her head.

"Big Bear in good mood, what he been drinking? Songbird is beautiful, no have to fix up," she said, poking him back.

Songbird and Big Eagle left, agreeing to meet about eight at the Best Western lounge. Carol and Big Bear talked about schoolwork while Big Bear worked at his computer. Carol studied her photography book, outlining lesson number one. At six they began getting ready for their night out. Carol dressed in a new western outfit she had bought in Billings. She had also bought Big Bear a shirt to match. Big Bear dressed in his shirt and western pants, looking handsome as always. then he came out with something in a box, laying it on the bed. Carol opened the box, seeing a western suede jacket with Indian bead work on it. The jacket was a rich brown suede with a turquoise and white bead pattern, fringe hanging on the sleeves and across the back. "It is so becoming, Big Bear; where did you find such a jacket? Thank you," she said, kissing him.

He took a matching jacket out of the closet. They were a striking couple in their suede western jackets, playing and singing their love songs on the way to Billings.

Big Eagle and Songbird sat waiting for them in the parking lot. "What take so long? Night soon be over," Songbird joked.

They picked a table close to the bandstand, ordering a glass of wine. A young group was performing on stage, playing and singing modern country music. Big Bear took Carol's hand, gliding over the dance floor with the music. Carol spotted Nancy sitting with an Indian man across the room. Big Bear saw them, saying nothing. He just kept time with the music. By the time they had sat down, the music would start again. Big Bear would swing Carol back on the floor. At the intermission, they played on the jukebox, LeAnn Rimes' recording of "Unchained Melody," their favorite song. Around and around they danced, lost in each other's love, enjoying the music and the feel of their bodies moving together.

Then they took time out for some wine and conversation with Big Eagle and Songbird. They watched Nancy and the man with her make their way to the table. Big Bear squeezed Carol's hand. "Carol, I want you to meet my husband, Robert; this is Carol," Nancy said. "I have told him what a good teacher's aide you are. How are you, Big Bear, Big Eagle and Songbird? Robert and I are getting back together, or trying to make it," she said, smiling at Big Bear.

Carol held her hand out to Robert, saying, "Pleased to meet you, Robert. I enjoy working with Nancy; she is an excellent teacher." Carol could feel Robert's eyes looking deep into her heart.

"I'm happy Nancy has someone like you to help her. I plan on taking your photography course. Well, we have to go pick up the boys. Nice meeting you, Miss Carol, hope to see you again," he said. They walked away, saying nothing to Big Bear.

After the encounter with Nancy, no comment was given by anyone. Big Bear said nothing of the matter, only asking Carol to dance. Carol couldn't forget the look in Robert's eyes, his obvious resentment of Big Bear. Carol asked the Great Spirit to take this resentment out of Robert's heart, to give him a happy life with Nancy and their boys.

At twelve midnight, the evening came to a close, with big Bear and Carol going to their motel room, Big Eagle and Songbird returning to the ranch.

Big Bear ordered coffee from the restaurant first thing Sunday morning. At nine, he sat down on the bed beside Carol with coffee in his hand. He wanted to talk about the night before. "Carol, I will be glad when we go to the valley. It's not fair to expose you to all this garbage. This has nothing to do with you. I'm sorry you had to be caught in the middle," he said.

"Big Bear, put your coffee down and take your boots off; lie up here with me for a few minutes. I want to talk with you about this Nancy and Robert stuff." She pulled back the covers for him. "First, darling, you can't go around protecting me from negative vibrations; the world is full of them. But we can erase these with positive vibrations, giving love and life. White Eagle told us we would cross over from negative to positive, when we are put into a situation like that with Nancy and Robert, if all we think of is love. This will erase those negative vibrations and positive ones will take over. We cross over to come back clothed in light and love. We know why people act the way they do, so we don't react to those spirits. We hold ourselves in that love, regardless of what happens. All we have to do is send out love and understanding, giving it time to work out," she said, tenderly kissing his lips.

"What did I ever do to deserve you? You're right; all of this will work out for the best as long as we think good thoughts. Let's go out to the reservation, see Mom and Two Feathers before going back to the ranch," he said, reaching for the phone.

"Hello, Mom. Carol and I are coming out for a while before going back to the ranch. Yes, we stayed in town last night to do some dancing. Yes, we will have lunch with you. That's fine, anything you have; we should be out in an hour," he said, hanging up the phone.

Carol was in the bathroom preparing herself for the day and thinking, What else was there outside of love? She was looking forward to seeing Walking Elk and Yellow Bird.

The radio was playing their favorite songs, and they sang them to one another, making love with their eyes while riding to the reservation. The sounds of the song "I Love You So Much It Hurts" filled the truck, with Big Bear singing along. "Do you ever get tired of music or singing?" Carol asked Big Bear.

"No, I have always loved music. I could always find my deepest feelings in music, being able to reach my inner self through music and singing. I hope you enjoy it as much as I do," he said, kissing her hand.

"I guess my soul wasn't in tune. I never thought much about music until I met you. The way you love music, I want to hear it all the time. I enjoy listening and singing along with you," Carol said.

"Look, doll; the leaves are turning. Soon yellow and brown will take the green away; snow will cover the ground. It was this time of year that Big Bear was searching for Little Dove. I know his feelings for I, too, searched for Little Dove. Now that she is mine, I will never lose her again," Big Bear said, pulling off the road, pushing the truck's gearshift up into Park. He took Carol in his arms, kissing her on the lips tenderly, then kissing her again. "I love you—always have and always will have this deep love for you."

The rest of the way to his mother's house he kept kissing her hand. All of the family was waiting for them. They joined in the family conversation, talking about ranching, teaching, Carol's new job at school and the upcoming photography course. Walking Elk was her usual jolly self, cooking Indian beans and cornbread, adding cabbage and strong coffee and tea. Big Bear enjoyed spending the afternoon with his family. After lunch, he took out his old guitar and began playing some old songs from his college days. They joined in, singing with him, all having a good time.

"When Little Dove start course at reservation? Walking Elk wanted to know.

"One week from Tuesday, if Allen has everything set up. It should be in the paper this week. Why don't you take the course, Walking Elk? Then you could take good pictures of the powwow next year, sell your pictures to tourists, make a lot of money," Carol said, placing her arm around Walking Elk.

"What Walking Elk do with lot of money? Don't go nowhere to spend money," she said, laughing at Carol.

Big Bear and Carol later told them all, "Good-bye, thanks for a good day." Music played in their hearts as Big Bear and Carol headed for the ranch. The sun was setting in the big sky of Montana, changing colors with the promise of another day.

They walked hand in hand to the house, seeing smoke come out of the chimney. Songbird and Big Eagle sat around the fire drinking hot tea. "Big Bear and Little Dove have a big night and big day. We build fire; night air is cold. Fall is here, soon be winter. Lots of snow, more snow than St. Louis, Carol see," Songbird said, moving away from the fire. "We go home, see you tomorrow."

Carol said good night, and Big Bear followed them out on the porch. He talked for a moment, coming back in with a piece of wood. "I'm going to take a shower, put on my night clothes, take a blanket and lie by the fire. Will you join me? Do you have work to do at your computer?" she asked Big Bear.

"I have about an hour's work to do at the computer, then I'll join you on the couch," he answered her turning on soft music.

Carol's shower felt good, then she made herself some herbal tea. Wrapping herself in a blanket, she lay on the couch looking into the fire, thinking how peaceful this place was. She would miss the place, she thought, watching the fire flickering and popping. So much of her had changed recently. This is where her life took a major change, with Big Bear. She sipped her tea, listening to the soft music. She set her empty tea cup on the coffee table, closing her eyes. She was truly blessed, she realized, and then she went to sleep.

Big Bear's strong arms were under her, taking her to bed. After showering, he joined her and they slept in each other's arms until five in the morning.

The electric heat came on while Carol was putting her hair into a French braid. She donned her work clothes: a long denim skirt with a denim shirt and jacket, then pulled on her boots. Big Bear turned over in bed, feeling for her. She bent over, kissing him on the lips, saying, "You better be getting up, tomcat."

He grabbed her, pulling her into the bed. "What did you call me, huh? What was that name, tomcat? I'll show you what a tomcat is," he said, pulling her under him. "What are you doing with all these clothes on?" he asked, releasing her. "Okay, I'm up; you ruined my fun."

"All I want is one week with you; no, make that two weeks. I want to love you until I can't move, calling me tomcat. I'll show you then who is a tomcat," he said, talking while going into the shower.

Carol made coffee, setting out cereal and fruit, waiting for him. She was drinking coffee when he came out talking to himself, "Calling me a tomcat; I'll get her for that," he said, laughing at Carol and pinching her on the buttocks. "Let us plan a vacation after getting out of school, say the second week in June. We could spend two weeks in Colorado camping and fishing. Do you know how long it's been since I took a vacation? Except for school conventions, it's been about twenty years, not counting powwow."

Carol sat listening, thinking, This man has gone ape. I can't hold him down. He is flying too high. Carol just listened to him, realizing he was free, free to love and be all God created him to be. She watched him enjoying his freedom, loving him as he stretched his wings, flying away to new heights. She held onto him, agreeing to his idea. "I would love to go on a trip after school, up in the Rockies. How soon can we leave?"

Big Bear was stunned by her answer. "I can't believe you didn't give me some excuse why we can't go. Any other woman would have said, We can't," he said.

"I'm not 'any other woman.' If you want to go to Africa, I'm ready. Hey, that would make a good photography trip," she said, now laughing at him. "You're the first man I have met who would gladly spend his money to do something spontaneous. Maybe there is hope for you yet."

"Now you have gone too far," he said, kissing her as she passed. "If you want to go to Africa, just say the word, and we'll go to Africa. They have children there; maybe we should travel the world, helping every child we can. That would be something, to have children from all over the world—every color and race."

As they traveled to Billings, Big Bear was playing his country music on the radio. Carol thought, He's just not talking; his spirit is speaking. This love God has put in his heart is for all children. He is broadening his horizons. Carol was watching his spirit soar, passing this realm into a whole new world, just as she had to take her flight. But she had to hold him. He was an Indian and could get wild, she thought, laughing to herself as he stopped the truck in front of the school building, dropping her off with a good-bye kiss."

Her day at school was uneventful and she eagerly awaited Big Bear's arrival after school. He picked her up at 4:30 p.m. They rode home, talking in general conversation, then Big Bear changed the tone of his voice, saying, "Little Dove, this calling is far greater than I can imagine, so let's go with our feelings and trust them. I'm going to see those little girls, to determine whether I can help them to stay with their grandparents. They need their family. We have to travel; there are things we need to learn and do. Only when this freedom came did I realize how selfish I have been, thinking only of Indian children. Maybe we will travel for two or three years before we get tied down at home. What do you think of this?"

"Big Bear, you're a wise man. Leave yourself open to come and go as the wind. I'm with you, finding your wings," she said, holding his hand. "But don't get so free you just wander, accomplishing nothing," she advised him. Tuesday night at the Vo-Tech school, Carol met with Allen. The photography class was to start the following Tuesday night at seven p.m. Carol was ready for the class, planning to start with the mechanics of the camera. She had prepared by using her lessons from photography school; using them as an outline made the teaching easier. Carol could visualize her hand extending to children all over the world. She and Big Bear would be helping children wherever their travels took them.

At the ranch that night, the fire was sending sparks up the chimney. Big Bear wanted to dance. After supper Big Bear fed the fire, and it sent warmth over the room. They settled on the couch, holding each other. "I have never felt so free, loving every moment of life," he said. "Carol, don't obligate yourself to teach this course next year. We may not be here next year. I don't know, my spirit is so free. How would you like to go to Hawaii?"

"Okay, with me; I have you and Babe first in my life. Where you go, I will go. Let us go to bed now. I love you, Big Bear."

Big Bear picked her and the blanket up together, taking her to bed. He placed her gently on the bed. After showering, he joined her in bed.

Time passes—where it goes, no one knows. Snows already covered the cold ground and December was coming on.

Carol's photography class included twenty-three students, Robert being one of her prize students, learning a new profession. Carol was especially proud of him. He had overcome his resentment, blossoming into a beautiful flower. Walking Elk was also taking the class, learning things that excited her spirit, becoming one of the best photographers in the class.

Carol and Big Bear moved into the motel for the winter, going home when they could. Carol loved the snow, so pure and white, and she enjoyed taking long walks in the snow.

Big Bear worked out each day in the gym. Carol walked from school to the motel, despite Big Bear's fussing that it was too cold for her to be out.

Carol's spirit waited for the time when she could gather wild flowers, see trout running in the streams, sitting outside by the light of the summer fires. Until then, they sang their love songs for the lounge crowd. She like the feel of the music, singing with Big Bear, knowing this pleased him. She put no limits on herself, flying into realms she had never known. She loved the old songs of Patsy Cline, learning and singing her classic songs. The lounge had standing room only, with many being turned away on Friday and Saturday nights. Carol started a fund for Indian children with the proceeds from their singing. People came and gave whatever they could. Big Bear was free to do his heart's desire, singing and playing music. Carol watched him proudly as his spirit soared.

Spring came with love on its wings. Carol made plans to move to the mountains. In April they moved back to the ranch. Carol was glad to see Babe, who was expecting a colt. Because April was Carol's birthday month, Big Bear planned a huge party for her at the Best Western Lounge. On her birthday, he sang all her favorite songs, even "Love Is So Beautiful." Big Bear then took Carol by surprise by his announcement, "I'm asking Carol to come up on stage for I want to ask her to marry me."

Carol ran up on the stage, kissing him; then he slipped a diamond ring on her finger. "Little Dove, I have always loved you and waited a long time for our spirits to be reunited. Will you have me?"

"Yes, yes I will marry you in the fall when the leaves are turning. Our life circle is complete," she said, kissing him with tears in her deep blue eyes.

Walking Elk was there with her camera, taking pictures as Big Bear and Little Dove sang "True Love," Carol wearing her Indian wedding dress and Big Bear in his Native American buckskin clothes.

Carol sang "Always" with Big Bear joining in, singing their vows to one another. "I'll be loving you always, a love that is true, when the plan needs a helping hand, I'll be there always, always, not just an hour, not just a day, not just a year, always, as always, but always." Carol moved smoothly into another of Patsy Cline's songs.

"I fall to pieces each time I see you, I fall to pieces, how can I be just your friend? You want me to act as if we never met. You walk by and I fall to pieces, each time someone mentions your name. Time only adds to the flame. You tell me to find someone else to love. You walk by and I fall to pieces." Carol moved into one song after another, loving Big Bear as he followed her, supporting with musical backup.

At the intermission the jukebox played. Carol and Big Bear danced, holding onto the years they had loved each other in another life. Big Bear loved her, she loved him and heaven waited for them to be free of all life ties, to soar in the spirit of life. He guided her across the dance floor. They laughed and kissed each other on the lips. Everybody watched, wondering how they could be so free and full of life.

Nancy and Robert were the first to congratulate Big Bear and Carol on their wedding plans, asking to be invited to the wedding. Nancy said to Carol, "I will miss you. Today, I knew you wouldn't be back next year to work at the school. The whole universe belongs to you; you have too much love to stay in one place," she said, placing her hand in Carol's hand. "I love you, Carol. Your life has changed mine; please, always be my friend." Carol took Nancy in her arms, embracing her.

"I'll always be close when you need me; just call my name, I'll be there," Carol promised Nancy.

It was time for Big Bear to get back on stage. He started singing "I'll Always Love You." They sang it together, bringing down the house.

May was the month Big Bear and Carol shopped for furniture for the mountain home. They moved some from the other ranch house. For each room, they took their time, ordering just the right colors. The store in Bozeman delivered the furniture to the house. Songbird and Big Eagle moved to the mountain home, getting settled.

Their weekends were spent in the mountains. Big Bear and Big Eagle built a barn for hay and the horses. The crisp air welcomed spring flowers as they stuck their heads out of the ground. Carol and Big Bear would take long walks in the woods, searching for certain flowers for Carol to dry.

School was coming to a close. The horses were moved to their new home. The grass was now tall and green, the streams running with trout to cook over the summer fires. Big Bear and Carol lay under blankets watching the stars, waiting for the full moon, listening for the whippoorwill calling his mate. The lovers chased fireflies, laughing and rolling in the grass, making love under the moon.

The first week in June, they finished moving. On the last day of school Big Bear and Carol stayed in town, closing out the year of teaching school there and their time singing in the lounge.

Andy came to stay with Big Eagle and Songbird at the mountain home. They treated him as if he were their son. Big Bear knew it was good for all concerned.

After packing up all their camping equipment and Big Bear's fishing gear, Carol and he headed for the Colorado Rockies for two weeks' vacation. They began to relax and take their time, making camp in Wyoming for a few days and nights, enjoying being outdoors. They hiked, following the streams, holding hands. Big Bear fished and Carol took pictures of the beauty of the majestic mountains. Hating to leave this incredibly scenic area, they followed Highway 25 south to Denver.

CHAPTER SEVEN

Love, Was, Is, Always Will Be

Camping in the Pike National Forest, Colorado, lay quietly on her cot in the tent, thinking What am I doing in Colorado? The tent became illuminated with light; the light became brighter. In the light Carol could see a heavenly figure with a flowing white gown; gold trim glittered in the light. The brightness of the angel caused Carol to cover her face. The kindness and love showed was beyond expression. The angel came closer to Carol, removing a small black book from beneath her pure white gown. She spoke with the voice of heaven and, in a heavenly chorus sang, extending this book to Carol. "In this book is written your life; take and read it. You ask, 'Why am I in Colorado?' You are here to set spirits free, so they can cross the shining river. Those that lost their lives at the Sand Creek Massacre are being held in that terrible day; your spirit has come in love and understanding to release these spirits so they can cross over the shining river. Don't ask why, for your life will always have a purpose." Then the angel left, leaving behind a sweet scent of roses.

    The grandeur of the moment left Carol numb; she had never thought of spirits being set free. When she could function again, she picked up the small black book from the tent floor, beginning to read. "Your life was love in the beginning; it is, and always will be. Love spoke your life into existence; it is, and always will be. Love speaks, light creates. Everything is created out of love; love holds all in harmony. There is a love so great nothing can stop it. This is the love of Big Bear and Little Dove. Years of separation and many light years apart, this love continued on through all the stars. There is a love that lives forever, giving life to all that touches this love. Nothing can stop your love, neither time nor space; it will complete its circle, living on in the hearts of your children and others you come in contact with. Your love is the fragrance of the flowers, the wetness of the rain and the purest snow of winter; you are the life energy of all things. You are the conscious mind of all things created, giving forth the life to complete life's full circle.

Carol's tears wet the small black book, the precious Book of Life. She stared at the place where the angel had stood. Making this journey to Colorado to set spirits free, Carol set all this love in her spirit free, a love she had held for many years for the Indian people and Big Bear.

Big Bear opened the tent flap, eager to tell her, "Little Dove, I had a vision today on the river; we are joining forces with those working in the spirit. We're becoming one with the same purpose. The spirit ones are returning more and more to help those wanting to cross over the shining river."

"I know what you are talking about. I had a visitor today. She informed me we are here to release spirits in this area who were victims of the Sand Creek Massacre. Big Bear, I don't understand it all, but I know if they are trapped here because of that great injustice, we can help by loving them," she said, holding his hand. Someday she would share with him what the angel said and let him read the Book of Life.

A friend of mine who heard me sing in Montana asked me to come to his club in Denver. "We have this date at the club in Denver, best we get things packed up," he said. "We will have just enough time to look for a motel."

"Big Bear, do you miss the ranch?" Carol asked.

"The ranch, some, the time clock, no. I know Carol, we had to make this trip to release our people. There is a love that reaches beyond this life. With you, this life is complete," he said, kissing her as they lay in their tent in Colorado.

Tears came to Carol's eyes as she thought of the anguish the

Indian people must have suffered at Sand Creek. Now she and Big Bear could love them in the spirit, helping them to cross over from the negative to the positive side of God's love. We were here to help, she thought. They held each other tighter, wrapped in their love.

That night, they sang in the lounge in Denver, talking with Big Bear's friends. Carol wore her Indian wedding dress; Big Bear performed in his Crow buckskin outfit. They finished the night's show singing "Always," watching the people dancing and enjoying each other's company. The club manager wanted to book them the following weekend, but Big Bear said, "No, we won't be around."

When time came to leave, Big Bear's friend gave them a check for the children's fund, telling him to stay in touch. "If you ever come this way again and want to sing, just give me a call," White Deer said. Big Bear agreed, shaking hands with his friend before parting.

Carol was quiet as they were leaving Denver. Big Bear knew something was on her mind. He asked, "What is the matter? Is all of this too much?"

"No, darling. I was thinking of the angel that came to me in the tent, giving me the Book of Life to read. I didn't tell you then; I wanted to wait." She pulled out of her purse a small black book. Reading this book made me realize that every life is here for a higher purpose, coming into the light of their spirit, a life-giving flow of spirit, being born of the spirit of love. To be filled with love should be the goal of all who begin their walk on the spiritual path: to love every person equally, judging no man based on his color or creed, seeing God in all. Every person must know his own heart, seeking to cleanse that heart and asking for a heart of love. If we ask, we receive; when we seek, we find; if we knock on doors of opportunities, they will open to us.

"Big Bear, nothing makes me happier than thinking about the children. This is our door of opportunity. We are knocking on that door, and now it's opening. Let's go home and see the little girls. I don't like organizations, but we may have to set up something for the children's fund. Please talk to an attorney and find out how to do it right," she urged him, holding his hand.

Big Bear was astonished at the things Carol told him, saying, "I knew you were different that day in the tent; why didn't you tell me?" Big Bear took her hand, kissing it. "We're going home tomorrow to see the little girls. I want you to go with me to see them."

"I wanted to tell you, but I had to wait until the right time. I just want to live a quiet life at home with what we have, teaching those children who come our way, and those we find in need of help. I hope you can understand that I have no desire to travel around making a name for myself, singing when we want to. Right now, the needs of these children are more important to me. Sometimes you have to reach the flesh, before you can reach the spirit. We have to help them to become healthy in body and mind to reach their spirit. I just can't give up trying to do that," she said, wiping away the tears.

Big Bear held her close, saying, "This trip has showed us what we have, a dream of our own—a dream we will make come true, a home for many children. Yes, darling, we will walk this path together," he said, kissing her tenderly.

"Carol, we came to Colorado, finding our true spirit, the spirit within us to be what we are. Let's take these lessons we have learned and use them to help others. Let's begin some serious loving and living," Big Bear agreed.

They drove out of Colorado into Wyoming, spending the night in Casper, Wyoming. The next day in the afternoon they passed through the Crow Indian reservation. Big Bear said, "Carol, why don't we go to the home of the girls and try to see them?"

The open, rolling land of the reservation is where the small trailer sat in which the family lived. A weary old woman opened the door, glad to see Big Bear, who introduced Carol. He asked to see the little girls. Carrie, the older one, sat looking out the window; little Molly was in the hospital with bronchitis. The woman kept going on about how she was too old to raise kids again. Carol sat holding Carrie, with tears in her eyes. Carrie's clothes were dirty and she needed a bath. Dirty dishes were piled in the sink, the floors needed cleaning, papers and clothes were scattered all over the small trailer. "My husband is at the hospital," the old woman said. "We don't know how long Molly will be there. We don't have money for a hospital bill. I don't know what we are going to do, maybe get some aid."

Big Bear reached for Carrie, taking her on his lap. "Mrs. Boles, do you care if Carol and I go by the hospital to see Molly? I will talk to the hospital administration about the bill and I will take care of it for you. When Molly comes out of the hospital, Carol and I would like to take her and Carrie home with us. We can take care of them for a couple of weeks. Do you think this is possible?" he asked.

"I don't see why there would be a problem, taking them for couple of weeks. I'm not able to care for them. I'm sick and my husband is not well. I'll have their clothes ready and I'll call you when I know she is getting out of the hospital. It is awful kind of you to do this for the girls," she said, wringing her hands and looking off into the distance.

Carol noticed the garbage can full of beer cans, realizing what took most of the grandparents' time. Saying nothing about the situation, Carol hugged little Carrie, wiping some of the dirt off her face.

As they were leaving the trailer, Carrie kept waving until the old woman closed the door. Then Carol started crying as though her heart would break. Big Bear comforted her, saying, "Honey, please don't cry; it will be okay. This experience has convinced me. I'm going to see if they will give us custody of the girls. I know they will. The old folks really don't want to be bothered with them. Now give me a smile; it will all work out. Come on; dry those blue eyes and kiss me," he said, reaching for her to come closer.

That night Big Bear telephoned Songbird. "We're at the Best Western, spending the night," he said. "We have to go to the hospital tomorrow, then we will be home. How is everything?"

Carol listened as Big Bear talked to Songbird, hoping he would ask about Babe, to find out if she had given birth to her colt. It seemed so long to her since they were home. "Did they say anything about Babe? How is she?" Carol asked.

"They had the vet out yesterday to look at her. She's doing fine. It will be another month at most. I love you, darling; I'm glad to be home with my family. I have to get Andy busy with his studies if he is going to college this fall. We have a garden and flowers to plant, too," he said, kissing her on the neck.

"It's good to be back home with you. There are a lot of words spoken out there, but actions are always louder than words. I love you and our life together. I wouldn't trade it for any other place. We have to do whatever we can for Carrie and Molly. I love them so much. If I have to, I will sit there every day and night to see those girls are taken care of," she said with determination.

The hospital was a busy place the next morning. Molly was doing better, and was glad to see Big Bear and Carol. She immediately took to Carol, wanting to go home with her. Carol hugged and held on to the sick little girl. Molly was improving and would be able to return home in few days.

Big Bear informed the hospital staff to call him when Molly could be picked up. Carol and Big Bear spent some of the afternoon buying new clothes, boots and play shoes for the girls. Carol purchased all new underwear, socks and sleepwear for the girls. She came alive while matching colors of shirts and pants for them to wear. Big Bear tagged along, picking up small boys' clothes, looking at them. Nothing would satisfy them except saving these children.

Arriving home, Big Bear and Carol saw all the changes, the results of hard work that Big Eagle and Andy put into the place. Big Bear felt guilty for being gone, but there was still plenty to do. He took the supplies through the schoolroom. There he stopped, looking around. He could start Carrie and Molly on beginner's books and number games. These thoughts were going through his mind when he heard the phone ringing. Setting the groceries down on the counter, he answered the phone. "Yes, this is Jim Nelson. Yes, I can be in your office at ten. Two boys, five and six? Okay, we'll be there," he said, hanging up the phone.

Carol stood there, shocked at the conversation over the phone. "What's this about two boys coming?" she asked. "How did these people know about us?"

"That was a social worker in Bozeman, wanting to know if we would take two boys as foster children. What do you think? I talked to the head of the Child Welfare Department in Bozeman about taking foster children when I decided to stop teaching and move up here. We'll go and listen to what they have to say," he said, kissing her lips.

Carol took the clothes for the little girls into the bedroom next to hers. Taking each suit, she carefully placed them on hangers, folding each undergarment and placing it in the dresser drawers. She placed Indian dolls on each twin bed. She had had twin beds put in each room, except Walking Elk's. Carol liked this room with pale pink bedcovers for the beds and matching curtains covering the window. Each girl would have her own dresser and a large walk-in closet. Then Carol thought, I have to call Mom.

She thought, I have been too slack in my correspondence with the family, only taking time to make short phone calls once in a while. She had called her family when Big Bear gave her an engagement ring, then when they took a few days in Colorado. Now she had to share the joy of getting the children.

"Hello, Mom, how are you and Dad? We are fine, doing real well and very happy. I have some news for you; we are making you and Dad grandparents. No, Mother, I'm not pregnant; we are taking in two small Indian girls. I don't know if we will be able to adopt them yet, then we are going to see about two boys tomorrow as foster children. I know this will be a lot of work, but Mom, I have help. Songbird and Walking Elk will be here to help. No, Babe hasn't had her colt yet. No, we haven't set a date yet, but soon, sometime this fall. Mom, how is Tony? I want him to come to my wedding, please tell him I miss him and will call him. Love to all, Mother; yes, I will let you know what happens with the kids. Bye." She hung up the phone, thinking her mother didn't sound too excited about the children.

That night, they built a fire in the stone fireplace and Big Eagle, Songbird and Andy came over for supper.

"Songbird have to go to work. Big Bear back to stay, Songbird hope," she said, winking a dark eye at him.

"We're here to stay until it's time to go for the winter in Arizona. We may be getting two girls and two boys; we're going tomorrow and find out," he said, holding Carol's hand. "Andy, be over early to start your studies. I can get you started before going to Bozeman. Before you start college, I want you to go to school for half the day and work the other half-day."

Carol smiled at Big Bear. He was back, taking charge of the situation and his family. She could tell Songbird and Big Eagle were glad to have him back. They sat around the fire, talking about the work on the ranch and the part each would play in the lives of the children. That night, all was well in the valley. Carol snuggled close to Big Bear, who hugged her, kissing her lips.

"I don't know what, Carol, but I feel we have just gone through something that was trying hard to pull us off our path with these children. We will listen tomorrow, make our decision about the boys. I love you, darling, always have, always will. There is no time in love; it was, is, always will be. That's what it is all about. You're the sweetest person I know. Now tell me what you think about having these boys with us."

"Honey, I would love having the boys; not for a short time, but forever. They will be our boys, our girls, our family, I hope we have at least ten children. I love you, you handsome man," she said, kissing him.

At ten o'clock they were sitting in the office of the social worker, listening to her complain about not having enough money to do the job for the children. They needed more foster homes desperately, the social worker stated. Would Big Bear and Carol consider their places as a foster home? she wanted to know. Big Bear didn't answer, but instead asked to meet the two small boys. Brian was the younger of the two. His skin and eyes made it obvious that he was a full-blooded Indian. Scottie, being the older and fairer, held onto his brother's hand. Carol thought that it must be humiliating for them, being paraded before people to see if they were wanted.

Big Bear asked Brian to sit on his lap. Immediately, he took to Big Bear. Carol took Scottie on her lap, with him keeping his eye on Brian, being his protector. The boys were soon taken out of the room by the social worker. Big Bear asked for a few days to think this over with Carol, knowing what their answer would be.

On the way back to the mountain home, they talked about the situation with the boys. "Carol, I would like to adopt the boys, so they will know they are loved and wanted. How terrible a child must feel not knowing when they will have to leave, what they will have to face next," he said, holding her hand. "What do you think?"

"I'm thinking the same; if I had to give them up, it would kill me," she admitted.

"Okay, darling; we will ask to adopt the boys. I have a good attorney in Billings who will handle the legalities, but we will visit and get to know the boys until this takes place."

The next day, when Big Bear and Carol were preparing to go to Billings to pick up Carrie and Molly, the agency called, wanting to see them. On their way into Billings, they stopped by the agency to see what they wanted. "Mr. Nelson, those two boys have been put up for adoption; I thought you would like to know," the social worker told them the good news.

Big Bear and Carol couldn't believe their ears. "When did this happen?" he asked.

"The day after you were here. As of now, we don't have anyone filing for them. I thought you would like to know about the boys," the lady spoke softly.

"What do I have to do to file for adoption of the boys?" Big Bear asked.

"You can file through your attorney, notify the agency and

petition the court. Your attorney will know all the steps involved. I will give you the boys' full names and the name of the agent who will be handling the adoption. We will rush our end of the work. I know there will be no problem qualifying you," she said, handing Big Bear a piece of paper with names on it.

They drove down the highway, with country music playing on the radio. "Carol, in just a short time we could have a family," Big Bear said. "We crossed over the river of life; now we are returning to this side, helping to erase the negative vibrations, helping as many children as we can. I better call Mom from Billings, tell her to get packed and ready to move, for the boys will be coming," he said with a smile, showing his perfect teeth.

That night, the mountain home in the quiet valley was filled with new sounds, the joyous sounds of Carrie and Molly running and playing. Big Bear and Little Dove settled down for the night with two little Indian girls in their king-sized bed. Carol had insisted on this, saying, "They have to sleep with us until they get used to the place."

How could Big Bear refuse her, his eternal love? Theirs is a limitless love. As they often tell each other, their timeless love was, is, and always will be.

CHAPTER EIGHT

The Wedding of Big Bear and Little Dove

Peace filled the valley in which Big Bear and Little Dove settled down with a family, living their everyday lives. The fields were a lush green, with the horses wading through the tall grass and cool mountain streams. The mares waited to foal with their colts, including Babe, who was watched carefully by Big Eagle and the family each day. The garden was peeking out of the ground, giving forth tender sprouts. Flowers burst into bloom. Carol would take Carrie and Molly each day to help in the vegetable garden and flower garden each having their row of flowers they had planted. Molly loved the outdoors, especially planting and gardening, but Carrie had more love for animals, wanting to be around the horses and dogs. She ran after Big Bear when he would go out the door, so he started taking her to ride with him. When the boys went riding Carrie tagged along riding with Big Bear.

Late in June, they summoned the vet for Babe, as she was in the barn waiting for her time to give birth. The day was also drawing near for Big Bear to go back to court for the final adoption of Brian and Scottie. On the morning of June 27, Babe gave birth to a stud colt. He came out kicking and immediately tried to stand up. His thin legs were wobbling, and he had to try over and over until he was able to stand. He was beautiful and, with his markings, had the look of a prize Appaloosa. Carol stared at him with tears in her eyes, holding Carrie's and Molly's hands. All the family was in the barn for the event. Brian and Scottie watched Big Bear as he helped the vet. Soon they had Babe up on her feet, cleaning up her baby. Big Bear reached for Carol's hand, saying, "What are you going to name him? He's a beauty."

"I don't know; I'll ask the children to name him."

Carrie said, "Call him Star."

"What kind of star, Carrie? There are many stars," Carol said.

Walking Elk walked around the stable watching the new colt. "Name him Evening Star for he is a mystical horse that will love night. One will come that will conquer Evening Star; she will be small, but mighty," the wise woman prophesied.

Carol listened to the old wise woman, agreeing, "His name is Evening Star, by the prophesy of Walking Elk and Carrie."

Big Eagle agreed the name fit the colt well. Big Eagle stayed with the vet while Big Bear went to clean up and prepare for the court date in Bozeman. He wanted Carol and the boys to go with him. They had traded Carol's truck in on a Toyota van to have room for all the family. "Let's bring all the family, including Mom. She is some kind of lady."

Carol hurried with the girls getting them dressed. Walking Elk took the boys upstairs, cleaning them and helping them put on their handsome western clothes with their matching boots. They all piled into the van, going to Bozeman for the hearing. They had time for lunch in Pizza Hut before the court session at one o'clock. The children were so excited about being in town and getting to eat out. Big Bear and Carol were proud to take their family out in public. Molly always hung on to Carol while Brian always clung to Big Bear. Carrie and Scottie acted so grown up and busy helping with the younger ones. Carol thought of how well they had settled down in their new home.

After the lunch of pizza, they made their way to the courthouse, proceeding into the courtroom. Carol and Walking Elk took their seats toward the front, just behind Big Bear and his attorney. The judge came in looking sternly at the spectators seated in the courtroom. The court clerk read the court case and number. The judge asked if anyone had anything to add to the case. A heavy silence filled the room and Carol spoke a silent prayer.

The judge continued: "If there is no legitimate objection to this adoption, I grant this petition for adoption of Brian and Scottie Stewart to Jim Nelson. This gives me great pleasure to place these children in a home where they are wanted and loved; I can't say this about every case. I want to congratulate you on having a generous heart to care for children. I would like to meet the boys and the rest of the family," he added, his eyes fixed on Carol and the children.

Big Bear stood up, asking Carol and the children with Walking Elk to stand. "Your honor, one year ago I met the woman of my spirit and dreams; her name is Carol Fletcher. We will be married this fall. She is the mother of these children, and without her it would have been impossible for me to take them in. She is my life. The two girls with her are Carrie and Molly Boles; we are waiting to find out if we can adopt them. Next is my mother, Walking Elk, the young men with her are my sons, Brian and Scottie Nelson." With that, Brian broke loose, running to Big Bear. "We hope this is just the beginning of our family." He picked Brian up in his arms.

"Mr. Nelson, if at any time I can be of service to you and your family, please call me. Court is dismissed."

Carol wiped the tears from her eyes, as she and Big Bear hugged. The lawyer congratulated them on the adoption of the boys and offered his help with the girls if needed. Big Bear said he would call.

In the van everybody was talking at once, then Big Bear asked how many wanted ice cream. All said yes and they headed to the ice cream parlor.

Carol made plans for a wedding in the fall when the leaves would be turning and the ground would be white with frost. Their children settled down with their school program and activities on the ranch. Carol called her parents, letting them know the wedding date of September 6, during Labor Day weekend, one year after Big Bear had brought her to the mountain home. Her life had changed a lot since that sweet day when she saw her future home. She was now a mother with four children and making plans to marry the greatest man alive. What else could she ask for?

The month of July came with outdoor activities with the boys learning how to handle a horse and fishing and camping with Big Bear, Big Eagle and Andy. Big Bear would take the group up to the tepee on the lake, teaching the boys to swim and make campfires, and about safety in camping. Carol would stay home with Carrie and Molly, but Carrie didn't like this; she wanted to go with Big Bear.

In the month of August came a surprise phone call from Carol's parents, saying they were coming out and staying about a month, or until after the wedding. At first Carol was caught off guard when her mother said they were coming and staying a month before the wedding. Carol was to pick them up at the airport in Bozeman August 10. That night Carol talked to Big Bear about the upcoming event.

The moonlight beamed through the windows of Big Bear and Carol's bedroom. Carol broke the serenity of the moment of being alone together. "Mom called, saying they plan to come August the tenth; that's only nine days away. I don't feel good about Mom coming and staying that long, but I will pray everything will be okay. When are we going to the powwow?"

"Even if they come in on the tenth, we leave the fourteenth for the powwow. Do you think they will want to go? If so, I will take the tent for the boys and me. I hope they like the Indian way of life," he said with a good-night kiss on Carol's lips.

Carol lay awake thinking, Why do I feel this way about Mom coming? No matter what we face, we will do it in love. Our life together is what we want. I hope they can be a part of it. I'm looking forward to seeing them.

Big Bear felt her restlessness, saying, "Honey, I think you are worrying where there is no reason to. I'm looking forward to getting to know your parents. There is fishing, swimming, gardening and plenty of sewing to be done before we leave for Arizona the first of December. Maybe your parents would like to stay in Arizona for the winter. Little Dove, quit worrying," he said, caressing her face.

In the month of August, Walking Elk was busy making trips up the mountains, hunting herbs and roots to make her tea and Indian medicines. After school every day, she was busying doing something. Carrie and Scottie would follow her up the mountain, carrying their bags for leaves and roots. Returning late, they would dry their roots and leaves and long bark strips. Then Walking Elk, with the help of the children, would transfer their herbs into jars with labels. The bark strips were taken up to Walking Elk's room. Carol wondered what was going on. She would rest in the afternoon with Molly and Brian while Big Bear and Big Eagle worked out on the ranch. At nightfall the entire household was tired, after an active day of work and play.

Carol and Big Bear waited with the children at the arrival area of the airport. Carol lifted Molly into her arms as she spotted her mother and Dad. "Hi, Mom; hi, Dad. How are you? How was your flight?" Carol hugged them, still holding Molly.

As Carol's mother came closer, Molly clung tighter to Carol's neck. "Mom and Dad, I want you to meet Big Bear, my love and my life."

Carol's parents extended their hand to Big Bear. "You're just as handsome as your pictures," Carol's mother spoke, looking Big Bear over.

"Pleased to meet the man that was finally able to capture my daughter's heart, but I see you had some help," her father said. "These are fine boys; what are their ages? Look at this pretty little girl," he added, sticking his finger under Molly's chin. Molly hid her face under Carol's hair.

"She'll be okay when she gets to know you; let's go and get your luggage, then we can have some lunch," Carol suggested, continuing to carry Molly down the escalator.

The luggage was placed in the van and the family filled the

remaining space in the van. Big Bear placed Brian next to him, buckled up, then he helped Carol place Molly in her seat. Carol's mother sat beside Molly, then her father, Carrie and Scottie in the backseat.

"The children are well behaved, but Carol I don't see how you manage four little ones at one time," Carol's mother said with concern for her daughter.

"Mother, I have help; Big Bear usually has the boys most of the day. Then Walking Elk, Big Bear's mother, has Carrie and Scottie in the afternoon. I have Songbird to help with the cooking and housecleaning. We have everything organized and working perfectly. Our home is filled with peace and love; that makes it easy on everyone." Carol was firm with her answer.

"Now Helen, she seems to handle the situation well, but I would never have dreamed of Carol as a country girl, especially married to—," Carol's father stopped before finishing his statement.

Carol looked at Big Bear, then at Brian and Molly. Thank goodness they couldn't understand prejudice and she prayed they would never have to face prejudice. If so, she was sure they were beginning with their grandparents; they would only react with love to the ignorance of others.

Big Bear parked the van at the restaurant, helping Carol with the children. Carrie finally allowed her grandparents to take her hand. The children ate their vegetables and potatoes, the same diet Big Bear and Carol ate. The grandparents were shocked to see the children eating no meat. Although they said nothing, they wanted to lecture the parents on their children's need for more protein.

On the way home, the children were tired; in fact, Molly and Brian were already asleep. "Mom, can we go with Walking Elk today? Mom, do you think Walking Elk is waiting for us to go up the mountain? Mom, I hope she waits for Brian and me," Carrie said, wanting not to miss her trip up the mountain.

"I'm sure Walking Elk will wait, Carrie; she knows you and

Brian look forward to your trip up the mountain. I think she has a special lesson for you and Brian today. We will be there soon." Carol comforted Carrie with her words.

They left the main highway, climbing up into the mountains. The van was quiet, with each passenger lost in their own thoughts. Carol's parents gazed outside the windows, as they started descending down into the valley. They could see the beautiful home, the fields, a garden and fruit trees. Carrie pointed her finger at her vegetable row, then her flowers. Big Bear drove slowly up the lane to the house. The horses ran to the fence to see who the visitors were.

Big Bear parked the van, got out, picking up Brian and handing him to Walking Elk. Carol took Molly out of her car seat, making room for the rest of the passengers to get out. Big Bear opened the back of the van, taking luggage out. Andy walked up, to help carry the luggage inside. Carol stopped Andy to introduce her parents, "Andy, these are my parents, Mr. and Mrs. Fletcher; Andy is one of our boys, studying to go to college this fall."

Carol's parents nodded at Andy, passing on into the house. Carrie and Scottie ran to find Walking Elk, while Carol placed Molly on her bed. Brian was put downstairs on one of the girls' beds. Big Bear excused himself to go out to the barn with Big Eagle.

Carol led her parents upstairs to a large comfortable room with a private bath, with their own sitting room. Carol's mother looked over the room, saying, "Where is the TV? Your father has to have his news every morning and night; now that he is retired, he watches more TV."

"I'm sorry, Dad; you will have to read or something; we don't have TV for the good of the children. We don't want them watching TV; we teach them to read. You are welcome to use the computers in the schoolroom. We teach the children to be outdoors and do active work and play also. At night, they are tired and ready for bed. We teach them a healthful lifestyle; they have their animals and chores. We love our life here in the mountains and we love one another and respect each other as a person. I hope you like it here and enjoy your stay. I wish Tony could have come with you." Carol wished she could see her brother.

Carol brought the luggage into the room. "Carol, can we talk a minute before you get too busy for us? I know you are busy. How long do you think you can continue this type of life, with all these Indian children and Indian people? I thought you were to be living in Billings, not out in the wilderness. Before you get married I want you to think about this type of life. It's so different from how you were raised," Carol's mother stated.

Carol looked at her father, asking, "Is this the way you feel, too? I was concerned when you called saying you were staying a month. Mom this is a different life than the way I was raised. These are different times, and I love my life and family. These people are my people and it is time we accept people for who they are, not according to the color of their skin or their culture. Mom, the Indian people are free, loving people. They don't try and change me; they accept me. I don't want to change them; I accept them. This way we are not competing, but giving to each other to live in peace. Now this is my life and these are my and Big Bear's children, and you are their grandparents, if you want to be. This is your privilege, but I will not tolerate the first thought of prejudice against my family or people; if so, this is not the place for you," Carol insisted. The conversation hurt Carol, but she knew her feelings were true.

Carol's parents sat looking at her, thinking it was unbelievable that these words could come out her mouth. "Well, I guess we know where we stand. Carol, we would never do anything to hurt you or the children. We love you; we're only thinking of you," her mother said.

"Mother, you don't understand; if you hurt anyone I love, you hurt me. Can you accept these people for who they are? If you can't, then your thoughts are prejudiced and they hurt. Please love each one and enjoy being here with us. "We will be getting ready for the Crow Powwow, leaving Friday to stay two days. This is part of my children's heritage. You will stay with me and the girls in the trailer. Big Bear and the boys will camp in their tent. We're going to have fun with our friends and family. Now you can clean up or rest; we serve supper at six." Carol reached over and hugged her parents.

Carol came down the stairs feeling strong enough to move heaven and earth for her children and Big Bear. When she came in the kitchen, there stood Walking Elk at the sink, washing her collected roots, with Carrie and Brian helping. They had stories to tell of what they saw up on the mountain. "Mom, today we saw a fox, two raccoons and the tracks of a wolf. Walking Elk said we would go up early one morning see the animals drinking at the stream. Can we go early one morning?" Carrie asked, her eyes dancing with excitement.

"Sure you can, darling, just be sure you go to bed earlier the night before." Carol turned her attention to Walking Elk, saying, "Your spirit was with me this afternoon."

"Walking Elk ask Great Spirit to make Little Dove strong, yet fill heart with love for parents. They to cross shining river; Walking Elk already cross over." Walking Elk spoke with understanding.

Carol watched Walking Elk with her herbs and leaves and different barks. "Walking Elk, what are those bark strips you are drying? What are you using them for?"

"Little Dove ask too many questions. She know when time right," Walking Elk said, removing her project material from the counter. "Walking Elk take Carrie and Brian upstairs to help." Gathering up her stuff, she handed some to the children.

The children followed Walking Elk up the stairs, and Carol turned her attention to preparing supper. Songbird had boiled chicken earlier, for chicken pot pie. Carol knew this was her father's favorite dish. Songbird entered the kitchen, ready to help. "Songbird take Molly and Brian outside, while Little Dove cook. Little Dove good cook."

"That's okay with me, Songbird; I hear Molly now, and Brian

will soon be up. I will cook; if Mom comes down, she can help. They are part of the family while they are here," Carol said while taking out a baking dish.

Songbird took the children outside to walk down to the horse barn. Carol's mother came into the kitchen, looking refreshed and eager to help. "Carol, what can I do to help?"

"The lettuce and tomatoes and other fixings are in the refrigerator for salads. We will eat at the big table in the dining room; we have twelve chairs in there. I hope you were able to rest some; how is Dad?" Carol was concerned about her parents.

"We rested, spending the time talking about your wise words. It used to be, we thought parents were smarter than the children; now the children are smarter. They are coming into a higher understanding of life and a different set of values, which is good, Carol; your father and I are proud of you and your family. Big Bear is a wonderful man and will make a good husband and father. We can see how much his loves you and the children. He is a good provider, and that means a lot to a woman. We are a family and we will love and accept each person for who they are. Who couldn't love those adorable children? Where are they?" Carol's mom looked around; there stood Walking Elk behind her.

"Where did you come from?" Helen was surprised by Walking Elk's presence.

Carol laughed when she saw Walking Elk. Carol knew how quiet Walking Elk could get around. "Mother, this is Walking Elk, Big Bear's mother and our best friend."

Carol's mother extended her hand to Walking Elk. They shook hands, then Walking Elk excused herself to help the children with the roots outside.

There was a rule in the house: everyone was to be at the table at six p.m. sharp. At six o'clock, the high chairs were set up for Molly and Brian, and the rest of the family were present around the table. The conversation started about the powwow coming up, then to the horses Big Bear raised. Carol's dad said he wanted to do some fishing and Big Bear promised to take him up to the lake.

The rest of the time was spent discussing their plans for the powwow. Big Bear took charge of the plans, saying, "We will take the tent for the boys and myself; Carol and Molly can stay in the trailer with Mr. and Mrs. Fletcher. Mom and Carrie can stay with Two Feathers. Andy will be with Songbird and Big Eagle. We will only be there Friday and Saturday, coming home Sunday. That will give us enough time to enjoy the powwow with our family and friends. We have a wedding to prepare for; that is the most important event this year," he said, smiling at Carol and showing his perfect teeth.

Carol touched Big Bear's hand. She sat next to him at the head of the table. "We have to pack the trailer with clothes. We never take unnecessary things, just two suits of clothes, one pair of shoes. I will take care of Molly's and Carrie's clothes; Walking Elk, you take care of Brian's and Scottie's clothes—you better take an extra suit for Scottie; you know how he loves water," Carol said, winking an eye at Scottie.

The children had been taught to never speak when someone else was talking. Carrie couldn't wait until Carol was finished, saying, "Mom, I want to take my sleeping bag to stay in the tent with Daddy and Brian and Scottie; can I, Daddy?"

"What do we say, boys? Can a girl fit into our tent?" Big Bear watched the big tears come up in Carrie's dark eyes.

Scottie spoke up; "Sure, she can; we will have plenty of room."

That was settled. Carrie would sleep with Big Bear and the boys in the tent. After supper, the family settled down to an evening of preparing the children for bed, while Big Bear and John Fletcher talked about fishing and ranching. Carol and her mother talked about sewing and the children. Walking Elk retired early to work on her project. That night, Big Bear and John planned an early fishing trip.

Carol was up twice during the night hearing Molly coughing. The second time Walking Elk heard her and she came downstairs, offering her help. She took her herbs out of the cabinet, brewing some tea for Molly to drink. Walking Elk told Carol to go back to bed; she would stay with Molly. She rolled Molly in a blanket holding her on her lap, spooning tea into her mouth, then sitting in a rocking chair with the child until Big Bear woke her.

Big Bear took Molly out of Walking Elk's arms, taking her to her bed. Walking Elk went to the kitchen to make coffee for the early-rising fishermen. John came down the stairs, surprised to see Walking Elk. "You plan on going fishing, too?" he said to Walking Elk.

"Walking Elk no time to fish, have surprise for Little Dove and Big Bear to finish before wedding day. Wedding day big day for Little Dove and Big Bear," she answered. Her eyes glistened as she talked about the wedding day.

Walking Elk placed breakfast on the table in the kitchen. The men ate hot oatmeal with fruit, wheat toast and coffee. They left in Big Bear's truck for the lake. Carol was up soon after they left and her mother joining her. "Carol, we have to shop for a wedding dress and other articles you will need for your wedding," Helen said, wanting to help her daughter.

"Mother, I have my wedding dress that Walking Elk made, ready for me to wear. Walking Elk is drying flowers for me to wear in my hair. Big Bear said he would take care of everything else; I don't know what he has planned, but I'm sure it will be a wonderful surprise," Carol said with a smile on her face.

"Do you mind if I see this wedding dress?" Carol's mother asked.

"Of course not mother; it's in my closet." The women walked into the bedroom where Carol opened the closet door. The light didn't come on, yet there was a glow in the closet and an Indian maiden stood there wearing the wedding dress. Carol and her mother stared at the beautiful sight of the dress glowing with radiant colors. The maiden spoke: "This marriage of Big Bear and Little Dove has been made in the stars and will endure forever." Then she disappeared. The dress was left hanging on the hanger in the closet.

Carol carefully removed the dress. Her mother had backed up

and sat down on the bed. "What was that, Carol? I have never felt such love and peace. It was like the feeling I had when we came up the valley. Carol, this must be a special place for the spirits." She looked a little pale.

"Mother, you never talked to me about spirits before."

"I know it would upset your father, so I put it out of my life. But I used to listen to my grandmother talk about spirits. You see, Carol, I have Indian blood in me, too." Helen spoke proudly. "The dress is beautiful and fitting for the occasion; that Walking Elk is talented."

They could hear Songbird in the kitchen starting the day. They prepared the children's breakfast, then Carol took them in the schoolroom to do Big Bear's teaching for him, as he had gone fishing. The day finished with packing the trailer for the powwow.

Friday morning, after breakfast dishes were cleaned and put away, Big Bear hooked the truck and trailer up pulling it out front. The boys were riding with him; Carol, the girls and her parents would ride in the van. By nine o'clock they were all on their way.

The powwow was busy on Friday for it had started the previous day, Thursday, but Two Feathers had reserved a parking place next to them so the family could be together. They could feel the excitement of the family coming together. Big Eagle was bringing Andy and Quickfire to race. Things were happening so fast, Carol thought, only a year ago she was here taking pictures for a magazine. This year, she would take pictures of her family.

Carol introduced her parents to Two Feathers and Yellow Bird, while the men worked to get the trailer hooked up to the utilities. The children ran off with Billy, their cousin. Carrie was the children's leader. They loved being with the other children. Carol settled Molly down inside the trailer. Each one found his way to go and enjoy the powwow. Carol knew they would return at eating time.

Big Bear set up the tent for himself, the boys and Carrie. Then he was off to the horse corral, where he picked up the children and brought them back for lunch. The lunches were just sandwiches and salads, with cereal and fruit for breakfast, so the cooking would be made easy for Carol and her mother. Night arrived soon, and the lights came on over the arena, with the crowd gathering with blankets and chairs. Carol placed her camera under her chair and wrapped Molly in a blanket, holding her in her lap. Big Bear seated the boys next to him. John and Helen had Carrie. The drums were beating and Crow youths were singing in their native tongue. Carol noticed Big Bear was getting anxious to be on stage. Carol forgot to tell her parents that Big Bear was a country music singer. The announcer called for Big Bear to come up and entertain the crowd with his songs. Big Bear took Brian by the hand, taking him along up on the stage. He sat Brian on a stool beside him, then he took a guitar and begin to sing, "Always On My Mind." His clear voice came over the loudspeakers, echoing in Carol's heart. How she loved him as her mind remembered last year at her first powwow. He had always been on her mind and in her heart. His voice spoke to her heart again to remind her she was his eternal love and always would be. He moved into "I Will Always Love You." After the song, the audience shouted and whistled. When the crowd quieted down, Big Bear asked Carol to come up and sing with him. Carol handed Molly to Walking Elk, then made her way up on the stage. The blue of her eyes reflected the love she had for Big Bear. She placed her arm around his shoulder as they sang, "Have I Told You Lately That I Love You?" Carol moved with Big Bear, letting him take the lead. She felt the love in his heart being expressed in his singing. The people listening howled for more, so they sang the second verse over. Afterward, Big Bear said he had an announcement: "We are having a three-day wedding basket ceremony on our ranch on September third, fourth and fifth; early the morning of the sixth, Little Dove and I will be married. Then we will stay on the lake in tepees. Please let Big Eagle and me know if you want to come. We have limited space, so get your name in first. Thank you; we will be back tomorrow night." Big Bear spoke for all the family. He took Brian in his arms and Carol's hand, and they left the stage.

Big Bear and the children took their seats. A woman had followed them to their seats. Mrs. Boles came close enough so they could tell who she was. "I was hoping to see the girls at the powwow. How are they doing? They are looking good; they sure have grown. My son will be up for parole in another year and he wants to take the girls to live with him." She watched their reaction to the news she gave them.

Big Bear rose from his chair, taking the woman by the arm and leading her away from Carol and the children. "Mrs. Boles, I don't appreciate your upsetting the girls and Carol. Mrs. Boles we have had those girls for a year and you have called only twice to find out how they were living. The news you gave me only made me think it's time to see the judge and end this situation. Don't think you can threaten my family, for we will go to court. We love those girls and they love us, and we will not give them up. You better get yourself a lawyer, because you're going to need one."

The old lady said no more to Big Bear. She walked away mumbling something under her breath. He returned to Carol and the children. Molly was hanging on to Carol's neck. Carrie was shaking as she held on to Walking Elk. "Big Bear, what are we going to do?" Carol asked.

"Honey, don't worry; everything is fine. We'll discuss it tonight. Let's enjoy the dancers," he said, assuring her.

That night, when Molly was put to bed with Carol's parents in the trailer, Big Bear had his mother stay with the boys and Carrie, while he and Carol took a walk beside the river. There they talked about the girls. Big Bear told her what Mrs. Boles had said. "Darling, I'm certain the threat was to get money from us. Well, she just pushed me to do what I have to do, making sure what she said never happens."

Carol was weeping softly. Her heart was broken, thinking of possibly losing the girls. Big Bear hugged her to his chest, saying, "Darling, I can't stand the thought of losing Molly and Carrie, either; I just can't." Her sobs wet his shirt. Big Bear smoothed her hair. Their attention was drawn to a light over the water. The light kept coming closer until it stood next to them.

White Eagle stepped out of the light into tangible form, saying, "Little Dove must know girls go nowhere. They chosen for spirit children. The power of love in Little Dove and Big Bear is greater than evil in hearts of others. Big Bear take steps, make girls safe from harm. White Eagle and many more stand with Big Bear and Little Dove; no one take children." Then he was gone in the light.

Carol cried as though her heart would break, but her tears were tears of joy. "Carol, don't cry; everything will be worked out and soon. I'm going to see the judge who handled the adoption of the boys. He can help us. No one is going to take those girls. White Eagle said we had power over evil and I know that. We can't say a word about this around the children; they wouldn't understand. Some day we can tell them they are spirit children. Do you want to go home tomorrow? We will if you want to, my darling."

Carol wiped her eyes on Big Bear's handkerchief. "No, we don't run from anything or anybody. The children would be disappointed to go home early. We won't let Carrie and Molly out of our sight," she said.

They walked slowly back to the camp holding hands. "Monday, we have a date in town to get a marriage license, then I'll call the judge to see if we can make an appointment with him. We will probably have to go to Billings for the hearing. Whatever we have to do, we will do. I love you and will miss sleeping with you tonight."

"I'm okay, honey; White Eagle strengthened me to go through whatever we have to, to keep our family together. I love you and always will." She smiled at him under the moonlight.

The next morning, they all met outside Two Feathers' trailer. The breakfast was served outside, with all sitting around a picnic table. The children were so excited about the rodeo and all the activities of the day. Billy asked, "Big Bear, you riding the wild bronco this year?"

"No, Billy, I'll let someone else have the chance this year," he replied, laughing and showing his beautiful smile.

Mr. and Mrs. Fletcher joined in the family fun, watching the love and joy of the Indian people. They had begun to loosen up and joined in the laughter, but they helped keep their eyes on the children, especially Carrie.

After the rodeo they listened to Big Bear sing his love songs to Carol. She kept looking out for Mrs. Boles, but she didn't appear again. Carol relaxed and enjoyed the rest of the powwow with her family.

After breakfast Sunday morning, everyone pitched in to help get things packed up and ready to go. Carol thought it couldn't be soon enough to get her family back to their mountain home, to safety. She placed Molly in her car seat, and put Carrie in the back with her grandparents. Big Bear had the trailer hooked up and ready to leave. With the boys buckled in, they pulled out first. Carol followed, with Songbird, Big Eagle and Andy bringing up the rear. Walking Elk sat in the back of the van saying nothing, but thinking of the troubles Carol and Big Bear faced with the girls. Walking Elk thought, I will go up the mountain early tomorrow morning without the children to make spirit trip. Walking Elk make big medicine.

Carol had to stop at the store for some supplies before going home, so they planned for all of them to eat in town. Carol's father said he wanted to treat them all for lunch. They stopped at the best restaurant in town to have lunch, the children having their grandparent's permission to order whatever they wanted. The children stuck to their vegetables and fruit. After lunch, Big Bear went one way and Carol and her parents went to the store.

Sunday night was quiet as they settled down at home. Big Bear asked Songbird to take the school class the next morning for him and Carol to go into town for their marriage license. Carol's mother was up early to help with the children and housework, as there was laundry to do from the weekend. Carol dressed Molly to take her with them. Brian wanted to go, but Big Bear told him no, he had to be in class.

Walking Elk had been gone since daylight. Carol wanted her

to return before they left. She wanted to instruct Walking Elk to watch over Carrie, and not to let her out of the wise woman's sight.

She was gathering up her pocketbook when Walking Elk came in the door to Carol's bedroom. "Walking Elk take Carrie and reader to the woods, stay till Little Dove and Big Bear return. Little Dove feel safer," she said.

"Oh would you, Walking Elk? I would feel better if I knew she were with you. Please keep your eye on her, and away from the house. We should be home right after lunch; take some fruit and nuts with you. I love you, Walking Elk." Carol wiped the tears from her eyes.

"Little Dove don't worry; Walking Elk give life for Carrie," she said, hugging Carol.

Big Bear was waiting in the van. Carol buckled Molly into her seat and they headed out of the yard, as Carol watched Walking Elk and Carrie going up the mountain trail behind the house. Big Bear looked at Carol without saying a word.

The trip to the courthouse was a quick one and they easily obtained the marriage license. Afterward, Big Bear called Judge Smith, asking his secretary if it was possible to see him today. She put Big Bear on hold. In a few minutes she was back on the line: "Yes, Mr. Nelson, come on over; he is waiting."

Big Bear hung up the phone, smiling at Carol: "He will see us as soon as we can get to his office in the courthouse," he said.

They walked around the corner with Big Bear carrying Molly. They entered the courthouse, going up to the judge's office. "Go right on in, Mr. Nelson; he's expecting you. You want me to keep the little girl?"

Carol quickly took Molly, saying, "No, thank you; she's no trouble."

The judge opened the door for them, saying, "Have a seat, Mr. Nelson and Carol. How can I help you?"

Big Bear explained the situation with the girls' grandmother wanting to take them back, thinking she should have them, although they had been with Big Bear and Carol a year. The judge asked what right did they have in keeping the girls. Big Bear said, Only temporary custody through the judge in Billings. "Judge Rider, I know him well," he said picking up the phone, making a call. "Hi, Bill, how are you? Fine, fine. We'll have to have lunch soon. I have a couple in my office with a problem with some girls you gave them temporary custody of from a Mrs. Boles. You remember the case? Yes, they are having trouble with Mrs. Boles. You have a few minutes to see them? I appreciate it, Bill," he said, hanging up the phone. "He will see you at two this afternoon; is that okay with you? If not, I'll have my secretary call him back."

"That's fine with us; we will go right over to Billings and have some lunch, then to his office. Thank you for your time and help," Big Bear said, standing and shaking the judge's hand.

"Honey, I think we should call home before going to Billings," Carol said, as they came out of the courthouse.

"We can call from here. You take Molly to the van and I will make the call. Big Bear took out his calling card, placing a call home, "Hello, Songbird, this is Big Bear, I'm calling to let you know we will be later coming in than we thought. We have to go to Billings to see Judge Rider. How are things there? What do you mean she came out there, threatening to take the girls away from us? Where is Carrie? You take her to your house when Walking Elk comes back and keep her there until we return. I don't want Carol to know about this, so tell her parents to say nothing about it. Okay, Songbird, I know everything is in good hands, bye." Big Bear hung up the phone, wanting to get back home as soon as possible.

He opened the van door, smiling at Carol: "Everything is fine, quit worrying; Walking Elk and Songbird can handle things there.

They arrived in Billings in time to have some lunch, then went to the judge's office in the courthouse. "Go in, Mr. Nelson; he is waiting for you," the judge's secretary said.

They sat before the judge, telling him the same story over. He listened patiently to Big Bear before saying a word. "This is a problem with a temporary custody order; but, in this case, I will allow the order to stand until there is an investigation from a social worker from Billings. The court will contact the parents in prison and let them know the situation. In the meantime, I will order a restraining order on the Boles so they can't come around the children because of their threats, until I set the hearing. Mr. Nelson, you will be hearing from a social worker soon. I thank you for coming by, but I would recommend your getting a lawyer." He stood and shook Big Bear's hand.

"Thank you. I have an attorney, and I will call him tonight after I get home. We appreciate your seeing us," Big Bear said.

They left the courthouse with mixed feelings, not sure where they stood legally; but, for now, they had the girls. All at once Carol knew in her spirit the girls were theirs and nobody would take them. "Big Bear, I know the girls will never leave our home. Molly slept in the van all the way back to the mountain home. The moon was coming up as they drove in the driveway.

Songbird lay asleep on the couch next to the fireplace. She opened her eyes, looking up at Carol.

"Songbird, where is Carrie?"

Carol stood holding Molly, who was still sleeping in her arms. Big Bear had gone into the library to call the attorney. "Where are Carrie and Walking Elk?" Carol asked, with fear in her voice.

"Songbird lie here waiting for them to come home. They no come; Songbird don't know," she said with concern.

Carol carried Molly into her room, removing her clothes and replacing them with her night clothes. She tenderly covered Molly in her bed. Big Bear came in the room. "Where is Carrie? Is she upstairs with Mom?" he asked.

"No; they haven't come home, what are we going to do?" Carol spoke, knowing Big Bear would handle the crisis.

"Honey, if she is with Walking Elk she is in good hands, and there is no reason to be concerned. I think I know where they are, up at the lake. I'll go up in the morning and bring them down," he said with a smile of relief.

Carol didn't show that much relief, saying, "I don't know; why can't we go tonight?"

Big Bear answered her. "Darling, you don't understand Indian ways, you put Carrie in Walking Elk's trust, now you have to trust her; anything less would hurt her pride, or she would lose face with you. That would hurt your relationship. We don't have to do that; they will be back in the morning."

Songbird stood in the door listening to the conversation: "Big Bear is right, Walking Elk strong spirit woman. She be back in daylight. Songbird go home now."

"Thank you, Songbird, for staying over. I'll see you in the morning. Have a good night." Carol hugged Songbird in appreciation.

Big Bear and Carol went into the kitchen, sitting at the breakfast table. When Carol's parents came into the room, her mother asked, "Have you heard anything form Carrie?"

"She is with Walking Elk; she is okay," Carol answered, trying to be brave.

Carol's mother made some coffee and hot tea. They sat and talked about the day and what they planned to do. Big Bear told them, "The attorney said he would get right on the case and notify the court of our petition to adopt. He also said he would do this with no charge." This news brought a smile to Carol's face. Big Bear continued to talk. "But even with a restraining order, I don't trust these people. We won't let the girls out of our sight. I will keep Carrie with me a lot, even when we go up to the wedding ceremony."

Carol's mother spoke up. "We'll be there to help with the children. We pray everything will work out so you and Carol can adopt the girls, our granddaughters. You better set up one of those tepees for John and me."

Big Bear looked at Carol and cracked up laughing. They looked at Big Bear as if to say, What is so funny? Then they all started laughing. Carol tried to visualize her mother in an Indian dress and moccasins cooking over an open fire. She began laughing real hard. "Mom, I can see you living in a tepee, cooking over an open fire, beating a drum." They all laughed harder as Carol continued to painting this picture of her mother. "I think it is best Big Bear pulls the trailer up for you and Dad to stay in."

Carol could see the relief come over her mother's and father's faces when they realized they didn't have to stay in a tepee. They finished up their coffee, saying their good nights.

Carol checked on Molly, then she settled down with Big Bear for a peaceful night, trusting Walking Elk with Carrie.

Carol was up at first morning light. Big Bear tugged at Carol to come back to bed. She heard someone in the kitchen, and she was eager to find out if it was Walking Elk and Carrie. She dressed hurriedly in her jeans and shirt, stepping into her bedroom slippers. She peeked in on Molly and went on through the living area of the enormous house into the lighted area of the kitchen. There stood her mother over the stove making coffee. Her father sat at the table reading a ranching magazine.

Carol's face was filled with disappointment. "I thought the noise in here could be Walking Elk and Carrie."

As the words came out of her mouth, Walking Elk opened the door into the kitchen. "Did Walking Elk hear name?" Carrie walked in next, full of stories.

"Mom, Walking Elk taught me how to fish with a string and a pen. We roasted fish over the fire last night. We had the most fun time; wait until I tell Scottie. I'm going up and see if he is awake."

"No; wait a minute, Carrie. You go first to see your father. Let him know how much you love him." Carol spoke with tears in her eyes as she hugged the small girl.

Carrie took off toward the master bedroom shared by Big Bear and Carol. Carol embraced Walking Elk, thanking her for caring for Carrie. Then she told the old woman what had happened with the Boles coming looking for Carrie. The wise woman listened to the whole story before speaking: "Spirits told Walking Elk to take child to safe place and not return until morning light comes again. Walking Elk done what spirits say, knowing Little Dove trusted Walking Elk. Feet tired—go take good bath."

When she left Carol wiped the tears from her eyes and thought, I will never question your wisdom again, Walking Elk; I love you.

Big Bear was up now. He insisted that Carrie take a bath and go to bed for an hour. Then she could tell of her adventures in the classroom. The rest of the children were up and Songbird went to work making breakfast. The family came together at the table, full of talk and excitement for the day.

Big Bear gathered up his students in the classroom, except for Carrie, who was fast asleep in her bed. Carol was busy planning the week ahead and the time to go up to the lake. Meals had to be planned, and food packed, clothes taken for the children—thank goodness Big Bear agreed to take the trailer. She could store the children's clothes in the trailer. Big Bear and Big Eagle had three more tepees to put up, prepare dug-outs for cooking outdoors and wood to cut, portable toilets to be placed by a company in Bozeman. There was so much to be done in the next week, but with Big Eagle's and Andy's help they would be able to manage.

Carol was thinking of all these things when the phone rang. "Hello. Yes, he is here. Just a minute; I'll call him to the phone." Carol laid the phone down and hurried to the classroom, announcing, "Big Bear, you are wanted over the phone."

Big Bear picked up the phone. "Yes, this is Jim Nelson. That will be fine, any time; we will be here. Thank you for rushing the request." He placed the phone down. He looked at Carol, who anxiously waited the news. "The social worker from Bozeman will be out tomorrow at two for an interview with us and the girls. The judge has put an order in for the proceedings to be a priority of the department. They have contacted my attorney and are working with him through the court. Everything is working out; before long, Carrie and Molly will be our girls and nobody will be able to take them." Big Bear reassured Carol with a kiss on the lips. Just as he started back to the classroom, the phone rang again. Big Bear picked up the phone. "Hello, yes; I just heard from the social worker, Miss Langford. She will be here tomorrow for an interview with Carol, me and the children. I'm glad the order has been served; she's not even supposed to call the house. That is good, for I don't want her upsetting Carol. I think it would be a surprising move for you to request going to the prisons to see the parents with the social worker. Yes, I agree. Okay, thank you." Big Bear seemed pleased as he looked at Carol. "Somebody, maybe White Eagle, is working for us; the judge has put a rush order on our case. The attorney has had the restraining order served, and they can't even call us. I better get back to class. Those kids will run your mother wild." He left grinning.

Carol took Molly out of school, into the yard with her to the herb garden. She wanted to gather some herbs for drying and an extra supply for the time to be spent on the lake.

The next day Miss Langford arrived promptly at two o'clock. "Mr. Nelson, I have reviewed your application for the adoption of the two boys—pretty impressive. Has anything changed since then? Have you married?"

"No, but if you give us a few more days we would have; September sixth is the day. Things are the same as last time." Big Bear thought the report was complete.

"Carol, being a mother to four children, especially young children, is a full-time job. Are you willing to take on this job with love and care for these children?" She looked straight at Carol.

Carol knew she had to answer for herself. "I asked for this 'job,' as you call it. I call it life and a good life. These girls are my responsibility because I wanted them to be, and I love every minute of it. We have had the girls for a year and they are a part of us. I have plenty of help with the work and that gives me more time with the children. We are thankful to have the resources to care for the children." Carol spoke from her heart.

"Mr. Nelson, where are the girls? I would like to see them," she said.

"This way; they are in the schoolroom doing some extra work, making up for the days they will be off next week." Big Bear led the way, with the social worker and Carol behind him.

Big Bear opened the door and they walked in on the children, one of whom was reading aloud to Carol's mother. They stopped and the children stared at the stranger. "Carrie, please stand up and read aloud for the lady," Big Bear told her. Carrie proudly stood, reading perfectly from a fourth-grade reader. Molly took her turn, reading from a beginner reader. Carol and Big Bear beamed with pride.

Miss Langford took Carrie aside and asked her if she liked school. She said, yes, but she liked the horses best, and Daddy had promised she could have her own next year. Molly shied away from the woman; she went straight to Carol's arms. The social worker exited through the school door, followed by Big Bear. He thanked her and returned to the classroom, hugging each one of the children. Scottie asked, "Daddy, who was that woman?"

Big Bear looked at Carol. Before he could answer, Carrie spoke up. "The woman for court; she came to see if Mom and Daddy want to adopt me and Molly. Is that right, Daddy?"

Carol hugged her close to her. Before she could speak, Big Bear answered, "Yes, Carrie. Remember when we went to court for the judge to give us Brian and Scottie? Well, this is what is happening with you and Molly. We will go to court and the judge will give you to us so no one can ever take you from us. Now school is out; go play."

Carol stood holding Molly's hand, for it was time for her nap. Carrie and the boys ran out toward the barn with Big Bear.

The days passed without hearing a word from the lawyer about the adoption. Two days before leaving for the mountain wedding ceremony, Big Bear received a phone call from attorney, who said the court date was set for September tenth at two p.m. The Boles have waived their right to be present; the son and daughter-in-law had decided not to contest the adoption, realizing it was in the best interests of the children. Big Bear almost dropped the phone; when he did replace the receiver, he grabbed Carol, dancing around the room without telling her the news.

"What is it, Big Bear? What is it? Tell me." She wanted to know what had made him so happy.

"They signed the adoption papers; Carrie and Molly are ours. Little Dove, they are ours," he kept saying. "They are ours."

Carol yelled so loudly everybody came running, Walking Elk with the girls and the boys upstairs with their grandparents, Songbird out of the laundry room. "What wrong with Little Dove? Scare Songbird to death."

"Songbird, they are ours; the girls are Big Bear's and my children," Carol explained, gathering the girls up in her arms. With tears in her eyes, she told the girls, "You are our little girls."

"Did Little Dove ever doubt spirit? Spirit speak truth. Come on, Carrie, we finish work," Walking Elk spoke truth for all to hear. "Spirit always speak truth," Songbird repeated the words. "We have big celebration up mountain tomorrow. Songbird one day get her girl, happy for Big Bear and Little Dove." She returned to the laundry.

Carol realized how selfish she had been in thinking of herself. She would join in the spirit chant for the spirit to bring a girl for Songbird and Big Eagle. Andy would be leaving for college and their home would be empty.

The morning of September 3, the air was cool and the leaves of the maple were turning deep red. The colors were painting a change in life's cycle; sunrays caught the gold as aspens and cottonwoods turned. Carol and her crew made their way up the mountain road in the van. Big Bear and the boys had left earlier with the trailer. They were meeting Two Feathers and his family early. Nancy Johnson and her family were staying in one of the tepees. All their friends were gathering for this occasion of Big Bear and Little Dove's wedding. Carol was thankful her mom and dad were there, wishing Tony could have been a part of her wedding celebration. They left Running Deer to watch the place while they were away.

By noon, the place was teeming with people moving into the twenty tepees that had been set up. It seemed that everyone had a canoe and the older children were already in the water. Carol thought this was like a huge family picnic. They started the fires, and soon there was coffee boiling in large coffee pots, potatoes baking, corn roasting, and chickens cooking in foil. Everybody was doing their part, and having fun doing it. Most of the men were dressed in their Native American clothes, buckskin and moccasins. The children were playing stick games the older Indians had taught them. The night descended on the lake. There was a large campfire burning for warmth. Indians were singing in their native language. Carol thought, What a wonderful life this was, particularly the beautiful people that she was a part of. The campfire was kept going all night because of bears; the men took turn watching the camp. Carol felt safe with Molly in the tepee with her.

The next day about midmorning, Carol saw Running Deer coming through the woods with someone with him. Carol was down at the lake washing Molly's face and hands. Then she noticed the other person with Running Deer was Tony. Carol grabbed Molly up in her arms, running to Tony. "Tony, you did make it. Mom, Dad, Tony is here."

Carol's parents came out of the trailer, hugging Tony. They had a family reunion. Big Bear came over to see what all the noise was about. "Tony, this is my husband to be."

"Pleased to meet you. Carol was hoping you could be here. Welcome to the Indian life." Big Bear spoke for the group. Then he turned his attention to Running Deer. "How is everything at the house?"

"Have phone call from woman in Bozeman, want you to call when have time."

Big Bear thought, Who could be calling? Well, it had to wait; he had a wedding to attend. Now all the family was there.

Monday morning dawned brightly as Little Dove and Big Bear took their vows, with Two Feathers taking charge of the services. The whole encampment gazed at the beauty of Little Dove's hair glistening in the sunlight like cornsilk and her blue eyes sparkling like sapphires. She stood with her hands in Big Bear's hands and they gazed into each other's eyes. The children stood close by as Big Bear spoke: "Now the spirits of Little Dove and Big Bear have completed their circle of life. They have found peace in the hearts of Jim Nelson and Carol Fletcher, never having to roam, searching for dry land again. Our life is forever in the spirit." He placed a ring on Little Dove's finger.

Carol could see White Eagle standing by the lake with a host of Indian spirits, smiling upon Little Dove in her moment of completeness. "I have always loved you and always will; you are my life, and we are one," she spoke, with tears streaming down her beautiful face radiant with love.

The simple ceremony for them was over. Then Walking Elk brought out a wedding basket that was breathtaking. Wild flowers were skillfully woven into the basket. Wearing her native clothes, Walking Elk had Big Bear and Little Dove hold the basket as each person walked up to them, putting money in the basket for their children's fund. The celebration of the wedding basket started, with all taking part in the colorful dances, wedding feast, drumming and chanting. Later, as an approving moon appeared over the mountain, Big Bear took his bride into the tepee. Closing the flap, they closed the world out and clung to one another. Tonight they would have the mountain to themselves to make love under the stars, from whence they came. By the time the clear sky darkened, the people had descended from the mountain, leaving Big Bear, Little Dove and the spirit of White Eagle for a three-day spiritual quest.

Little Dove spoke these words into Big Bear's spirit: "We will study war no more; our life together will be peace and love for evermore.